PEACE COMPANY

CALIBER
B O O K S

Also from ROLAND J. GREEN

WANDOR Series
Wandor's Ride
Wandor's Journey
Wandor's Voyage
Wandor's Flight

PEACE COMPANY Series
Peace Company
These Green Foreign Hills
The Mountain Walks

STARCRUISER SHENANDOAH Series
Squadron Alert
Division of the Spoils
The Sum of Things
Vain Command
The Painful Field
Warriors for the Working Day

ACKNOWLEDGMENTS

The Peacekeepers series wouldn't have come into existence without the contributions of a great many people besides the author.

Susan Allison, of Ace Books, who had faith that I could do military sf and the even greater faith that I could design the series myself. The many delays that she endured with admirable patience were a very poor return for that faith.

The authors of all the books that have fed my knowledge of war for the past thirty years. Among these, the man to whom this book is dedicated, the late Lieutenant-Colonel John Masters, Indian Army (Retired), holds a distinguished place.

All the people whose personal anecdotes of their military service have helped provide an additional dimension to my knowledge. These include Robert Asprin, Rodgers Bradley, William Bryan, Curt Clemmer, Gordon R. Dickson, Alan Frank, David Gelushia, my father, the late James Green, Joe Haldeman, Daniel Houton, Clyde Jones, Gail Matthews-Bailey, Jerry Pournelle, Eric Webb, and no doubt a good many others over the years to whom I can only apologize for letting their names slip my memory.

Frieda, as always my lady and love.

Midge Gutierrez, "third grandmother" to our daughter, Violette, and her daughter, Sharon, for making Nana's Day Care virtually a second home for Violette while Group Fourteen took over ours.

The late Stan Rogers, folksinger, poet, composer; musician, raconteur, for the inspiration of his song, *"The Mary Ellen Carter."* One day I may be able to find the right words to say how much I owe him for his songs.

Roland Green
Chicago, Illinois
April 1985

A GLOSSARY OF INITIALS
(not guaranteed to be regulation)

A.I.	- Artificial Intelligence
C.D.Z.	- Center, Drop Zone
C.I.C.	- Combat Information Center
C.O.	- Commanding Officer
C.G.P.O.	- Conseil Général Politique de l'Ouest
D.A.	- Defended Area
D.F.F.	- Death from Flying Fruit (casualties caused by air-dropped supplies
D.Z.	- Drop Zone
E.E.	- Electronic Emissions
E.I.	- Electronic Interception
E.V.A.	- Extra-Vehicular Activity
F.A.E.	- Fuel-Air Explosive
G.C.&O.	- Ground Control and Observation
I.F.F.	- Identification, Friend/Foe
I.G.O.C.	- Initial Ground Operations Capability
IR	- Infrared
L.Z.	- Landing Zone
N.C.O.	- Noncommissioned Officer
O.D.	- Officer of the Day
O.P.	- Observation Post
P.B.I.	- Poor Bloody Infantry
QM	- Quartermaster
R.P.	- Reflective Powder
R.T.F.	- Reinforced Titanium Fiber
Three-C	- Command, Control, Communications
T.O.&E.	- Table of Organization and Equipment
X.O.	- Executive Officer

PROLOGUE

Helmsman Paul Rebenc adjusted the throat microphone, checked the displays on the autopilot, and began recording his log entry.

2715. Steaming as before. Ground speed 11.7 knots. Course 340 true. Les Fourchettes bearing 72, 8 km. Steward has just delivered coffee and sandwiches for the manual helm watch.

He cut off the microphone and watched the log display register the voiceprint pattern that marked the entry as his. Another look at the autopilot displays was interrupted by a grisly snore from the comer of the wheelhouse.

Rebenc looked over his shoulder. He'd been tempted to record the fact that First Mate Laszlo Fuchs was still in the wheelhouse, still drunk, but now sound asleep. Very tempted, since God willing he would never have to serve under Fuchs or Captain Warren again, and what they thought of him might make little difference. It would also serve them right, for coming aboard the *Celestine Auphan* as they had done, them and their passage crew, taking her away from those who'd served in her for ten years like Rebenc or fifteen like Katie Halloran.

But as they had come, so they would go away again. It would be *les copains*, the chums, who took the *Celestine* out to her new life as a floating fish factory and taught the fishermen of the Storm Coast how to treat her as a ship instead of just a place to cut up and freeze down grillback and orange runner. When Fuchs died raving, he would have long forgotten the *Celestine Auphan*.

No part of his or Warren's grubby little souls would have entered into hers.

Also, some of the rest of the passage crew seemed to be loyal to Warren and Fuchs. This did not say much for their taste in officers, but even a man with poor taste in officers could meet you in a dark alley in Havre des Dames and make the meeting one you would not forget even after your bones knitted.

In any case, another eight or nine hours, perhaps ten or eleven if the rains upcountry made the outflow from the Gros Chaudron worse than usual, and the *Celestine Auphan* would be anchored safe in Havre des Dames.

Rebenc started for the warmer at the starboard end of the console. The manual steering watch would never miss one cup of coffee, although nobody but a fool would try stealing sandwiches or anything else edible from Nils Bergstrom. Rebenc would make do with warmed-over beef and beans in the galley after he got off watch.

He'd taken two steps when the cord of his throat microphone-headset combination jerked him to a halt.

"*Merde!*"

The cord seemed possessed of a perverse animation, always looping itself around an arm of the helmsman's chair the moment he took his eyes off it! Rebenc sighed and bent over, mentally damming the dim red light inside the wheelhouse, which saved his night vision but made it rather hard to undo subtle tangles in a thin black cord...

"Torpedo afloat, Team Leader."

"Very good."

The Team Leader set his boots against one side of the rock chimney and his back against the other, then worked his way up five meters to the top of the bluff. It was an unnecessary piece of rock climbing, since there were several easier ways up from the beach. The Team Leader hoped his men would dismiss it as a display of his well-known gymnastic skills and not guess that it was really an attempt to relieve taut nerves by physical activity.

On top of the bluff the Team Leader joined the security and communications squads to watch the torpedo squad wading out the frigid waters. They moved silently across the shingle beach, paying out the glass-fiber control line of the torpedo as they went. Even from less than fifty meters away they were barely formless dark shapes, showing only vagrant gleams of moonlight on wetsuits. From the bridge of a ship six kilometers out they would be as invisible as if they'd been on a training exercise on Terra's Sunda Straits, fifty-five light-years away.

A mule stamped and said something guttural to a friend. One of the security squad started toward the tethered mules, but the two mule drivers were already quieting the beast. The Team Leader would have vastly preferred an all-wheel-drive truck to the string of mules he'd had to use to carry the torpedo, its controls, and the electronic-intercept equipment.

Preferences didn't conjure all-wheel vehicles out of the back roads of this dismal planet, and a hovertruck would have been out of the question. Too much noise, too vulnerable to weather, and too big a heat signature just in case anybody was using IR scanners in the wrong place at the wrong time.

At least the Game Master would most likely approve. He'd always said that the Teams would have to spend years or even decades relying heavily on local resources, regardless of the technological level, with the absolute minimum of imported components. He'd even said that most of the locals would be too greedy or apolitical to care about what they were hired for, while those who might make trouble could always be terminated to some purpose, if their deaths could be laid at the door of local Union supporters.

The Team Leader hoped that the final tactic would cover the Teams' tracks as effectively as the Game Master thought. He couldn't do more than hope—and, of course, hide the fact that he doubted one of the Game Master's tactical principles. A mere Team Leader was not so indispensable to the Game Master that he could afford the luxury of being known to ask questions not required by his tactical duties.

The Team Leader raised his night glasses and looked out into the bay. The microcomputer in his helmet translated the IR emissions of the approaching ship into a more conventional image.

It was the *Celestine Auphan*, without a doubt. Four thousand tons, steel hull, multi-fuel compression-ignition engine driving a single controllable-pitch propeller. He recognized the superstructure and bridge aft, the single funnel, and the tripod mast perched with one leg on the wheelhouse and two braced against the funnel. The tripod looked oddly bare compared to the photographs they'd used for recognition training; the satellite communications gear must have been removed before the *Celestine* set out on her final voyage as a seagoing ship. A stupid economy by her owners, when that final voyage was as dangerous as any she'd ever made, but a piece of luck for the Team Leader. With only short-range radio communications, the *Celestine* might not even be able to get off a distress signal.

"What are you picking up?" he asked the EI technician. The man silently made a thumbs-up signal, for "Nothing unusual."

"Good."

The *Celestine*'s silhouette was foreshortening a trifle now as she came about to pass clear of the extreme southern end of Les Fourchettes. Another kilometer and she'd be in a position where the torpedo explosion might be confused with running on an uncharted rock—which Kali had strewn in great abundance at the end of Les Fourchettes, if the sailors' tales weren't all spun of wind and beer.

Four minutes to go.

Four. Three. Two. One. The Team Leader activated the chronometer-display in his glasses.

Thirty seconds. Twenty. Ten.

"Launch torpedo."

"*Hai!*" *Remind Hiko to use Standard.*

"Torpedo running true and normal, Team Leader," said Hiko, catching himself.

"Very good."

Three meters below the surface the rocket-propelled torpedo was racing toward the *Celestine Auphan* at nearly eighty knots. Hiko was guiding it through the glass-fiber wire it trailed behind it, steering it toward the acoustic signature of the ship its own sensors were picking up. If Hiko lost control, the torpedo would slow down and actively home in on that signature, but wire-guidance gave better results, particularly with Hiko on the controls. He could put a torpedo through a ring three centimeters wider than its diameter at forty knots, a skill (and it was only one of many) that made his occasional linguistic lapses forgivable.

"Range to target one thousand meters, Team Leader. Six hundred. Three hundred. Two hundred."

Paul Rebenc had just straightened up after untangling the cord when the deck heaved under him. A fierce roaring came not only through the air but through the ship's structure itself. It was as if the *Celestine Auphan* herself was in rage or pain.

The plex of the wheelhouse windows shivered in the corroded frames, shattered, and sprayed the deck both inside and out. Rebenc clapped his hands over his face and saved his eyes, but the backs of his hands and one ear felt stung by angry wasps. Without a hand to hold on to anything, he fell heavily to the deck, mentally cursing himself for forgetting the adage "One hand for yourself and one for the ship."

When he opened his eyes he saw that he could have used a third hand for a shipmate, even as disreputable a one as First Mate Laszlo Fuchs. Fuchs must have just been rising to his unsteady feet when the deck under them became still un-steadier. Falling forward, he'd rammed his head into the corner of the warmer. The plastic was harder than Fuchs's head. Rebenc wouldn't have sworn that the First Mate's head contained any brains without evidence; he now had that evidence conspicuously visible on the deck. Coffee from the warmer dripped into the mess and made the deck treacherously slippery.

The self-contained emergency power supply for the wheelhouse had cut in automatically; the lights and the consoles still functioned. The feel of the deck underfoot was less reassuring. Rebenc no longer felt the steady pulse of the engine, but erratic bursts of vibration, as if weights were shifting far below—weights massive enough to twist and strain the ship's structure until its protests reached the soles of Rebenc's boots.

A look at the instruments told Rebenc that the ship was losing way and had an eight-degree list to starboard. She was also five degrees down by the stem.

At least the helm was still answering. Rebenc threw it hard over to port, to bring the *Celestine*'s head around toward Les

Fourchettes. There were clear patches of shallow water in among the fangs of rock. If the ship had enough way on her she might be lucky enough to find one of those patches before she sank. The sharp turn increased both the list and the vibration from below. Rebenc was holding on to the helm console to keep from slipping when the portside wheelhouse door flew open. Juliana Geesink, the lookout, staggered in, followed by Boatswain Nils Bergstrom.

Bergstrom took one look at Fuchs and spat, another at the helm setting and nodded. "I saw Katie going below to man the engine room. If she can tinker us up some power we may just make it."

"If we don't hit another rock," said Rebenc.

Bergstrom frowned. "You thought it was a rock? Did anything show on the fathometer?"

"No, but—"

"I know, I know. Uncharted pinnacles and all that. But to me it felt more like an explosion." For the first time Rebenc noticed that Bergstrom was wearing his pistol and had two magazines of solids and two of flechettes hooked over his belt.

A sudden uproar from the main deck forward kept Rebenc from asking silly questions like "Why are you carrying that gun?" Several people were cursing, an emergency raft was inflating itself with a screaming hiss, then someone switched on an emergency light. It showed Captain Warren, two of his men supporting him, and four more of the passage crew all standing around the fast-inflating raft. Roman Talgas, one of *les copains*, was standing on a cargo winch and cursing the raft party.

Rebenc was inclined to agree with what Talgas was saying about men who abandoned a ship without finding out if she was sinking, but not about the wisdom of saying it here and now. He stuck his head through the broken window. "Hola, Roman! Don't waste your breath—!"

"Down!"

Bergstrom's left hand plucked Rebenc back through the window while his right thrust the pistol out of it. He'd seen Warren's radio operator raising the riot gun even faster than Rebenc. Bergstrom's slug wasn't an explosive round, so it didn't smash the tough emergency lamp, merely sent it skittering across the deck and

12

over the side. Talgas jumped down from the winch as darkness swallowed the deck and the radio operator let fly.

Two billyrounds *splatted* against the winch, then Bergstrom let fly with another slug, apparently aimed over everybody's heads. The riot gun *whomped* again, sending a billyround God knew where, then Rebenc heard the scrabbling of many feet and the sound of a raft being pushed across a steel deck. After that came the hisses of life jackets being inflated, a large splash as the raft hit the sea, and smaller splashes as Warren and his passage crew followed it over the side. When Rebenc's night vision returned, he could see Talgas crouching behind the winch, apparently unhurt but definitely the only man on the main deck.

"Why didn't you aim for the raft?" he asked Bergstrom.

"I might have hit one of those sons of seaweed scavengers. Even if I'd hit the raft, there are others. We're best off rid of them. Now—is the emergency transmitter on?"

Rebenc pointed at the console. "It went on automatically with the emergency power." He tried not to grin; it was rare that the imperturbable Bergstrom grew excited enough to forget anything.

"Good. Now let's find Tom and—"

Bergstrom broke off and all three forgot about the other radio operator to stare at the deck underfoot. Rebenc almost crossed himself, then leaped for the helm.

The engine had started again. No, not quite, Rebenc corrected himself. The instruments and the feel of the helm told him it was more likely the generator coupled to the shaft. Damage enough to destroy the main engine should have wrecked the generator as well, but perhaps not beyond Katie Halloran's ability to improvise repairs. It did not take a miracle, unless, perhaps, engineers like Halloran were miracles themselves.

Miracle or not, they now had a real chance to bring the *Celestine Auphan* into water shallow enough for salvaging or even beach her outright. Rebenc watched the speed indicator hold at three knots, then with desperate slowness start creeping up again.

Bergstrom looked at it, too, and grunted with satisfaction. "Paul, carry on. Ju, take the lookout again but keep your back to a bulkhead all the time. I'm going to look for Tom, then down to the engine room."

"Do you think—?" Rebenc began, then decided that Bergstrom probably did think it and he was probably right. They might not be able to do much against their enemies except prevent any more surprises, but at least they could do that.

Also, *Celestine* somehow felt cleaner with Warren and his gang of wharf-rats and snake-rapers off her deck. Maybe this would give her the strength she needed to fight for her life.

"Still nothing but the standard distress call?"

"Nothing, Team Leader." The E.I. man shook his head. "I'm surprised the people who abandoned aren't transmitting as well, but I've done a full-frequency scan without picking up anything."

The Team Leader shrugged. That might indicate trouble from the raftload when they reached shore. More likely it indicated that they didn't want their hasty abandonment to be known until they'd reached shore, worked out a cover story, and learned if any of the people left aboard had survived to call them liars. Without wishing such cowards well, the Team Leader intended to take a hand in the last matter.

He looked over the bluff. The torpedo team was coming out of the water again, leaving the back-up torpedo ready to go. Two of them stripped off their wetsuits, picked up their webbing gear and weapons, and joined the second security squad by its inflatable boat.

The Team Leader thanked Kali that inflatable boats were "local technology" within the Game Master's definition. Otherwise he'd have no easy way of sending six men across the channel to deal with anyone left aboard the *Celestine Auphan*. At least not before help arrived—and the distress signal would summon it even without satellite assistance.

No distress signal, however, would provide the details of what had happened to the ship that the remaining crew members would no longer be able to supply. And there was still one chance of finishing this the easy way—

"Launch torpedo."

"Torpedo running, Team Leader," said Hiko.

It was a gamble, sending a torpedo in among the rocks of Les

Fourchettes even with Hiko at the controls. However, it was always prudent to take some risks to increase the mystery associated with the Game Master's work. This was a proven rule from two generations' experience on Earth, so the Team Leader saw no reason to quarrel with its application on the first out-system mission.

Celestine shuddered and seemed to flex like a fishing rod throughout her length. The deck under Rebenc heaved so that he would have fallen again except for his grip on the helm.

At the same time the fire alarm shrilled, the remaining plex fell out of the wheelhouse windows, and a blast of spray-laden air swept through the wheelhouse from aft. Rebenc turned and saw a column of water a hundred meters high towering five hundred meters astern. Wraithlike in the darkness, it loomed over the *Celestine* like a monster about to carry her off, then collapsed into a broad patch of froth and foam. More spray blew in through the broken ports.

Bergstrom muttered something eloquent in Scandic, then said, "I think I was right. That first time was an explosion. This was the second time."

"Will there be a third?" said Rebenc. He was back at the helm, but didn't like the new feel of it. Five hundred meters was much too close for a powerful explosion and a wounded ship.

"Maybe," said Bergstrom. He cut off the fire alarm and punched the intercom for the engine room. "Bridge, Bergstrom here. Report on the fire!"

A breathless reply came:

"Vasi, it's Vasi. No fire but Halloran's burned. She's burned all over. It was the wiring. No fire. No fire."

"Was it a short circuit?"

"N-yes."

"Can Halloran walk?"

"She—no."

"Can you carry her?"

"Tell him not to bother," came a voice that had to be Katie Halloran's. It was diabolical that a voice could hold so much pain and still be coherent.

"I'm coming down," said Bergstrom. "Joseph, give her first aid and—"

"Nils, don't waste your time. The engine's room flooding too fast. That second whatever-it-was must have popped a few more seams—ahhhhhhh!"

"Sorry, ma'am, but you're on the sick list. You can't give me any orders."

"Nils, let me come with you," said Geesink. "That hatch is treacherous. Two might not be—"

"Two's enough to do it. Besides, if the flooding's gaining on us, she might go fast. If we're trapped below, Paul will need some help to get Tom off."

The look Geesink threw at the unconscious Thomas Delcaze said clearly that the radio operator was dead anyway. Since his chest had been caved in by a billyround fired at point-blank range, Rebenc was inclined to agree. It was a miracle that he'd even lived until Geesink found him, lying in the passageway where Warren and company had left him.

"Don't argue, Ju," said Rebenc. "Better you should get down on the main deck and inflate a raft. I can carry him that far if we have to leave in a hurry."

Bergstrom was already gone. Rebenc held on to the helm as if the sheer force of his grip would keep the *Celestine Auphan* afloat. The shudderings going through the ship wanted to make him cry out, as if his own joints and bones were tearing apart. He recognized shell plating and frames tearing under the weight of the flooding, and bulkheads rupturing as the flooding raised the air pressure against them. The *Celestine* was dying under his feet.

Dying, but not dead. Paul Rebenc swore that the *Celestine Auphan* would not be dead until she'd not only sunk but crumbled into rust—and maybe she could be salvaged before she did that.

He looked at the fathometer. Thirty meters of water under the keel, and far enough inside Les Fourchettes that a salvage crew might be sheltered from the worst of the weather. She was listing only eighteen degrees now. If the damned fish factory gear on her deck didn't make her capsize and she went down on an even keel...

Geesink climbed back into the wheelhouse and knelt beside

16

Delcaze. "He's dead. I inflated two rafts. Talgas is standing by them. One of Warren's gang left a pistol and a riot gun behind. I've got the pistol." She wrapped her arms around herself. "I may ignore Bergstrom's orders and go below to help. The factory gear's going to start breaking loose any minute." For all of them, bringing the *Celestine* up again would lose most of its joy if Katie Halloran wasn't around to share it.

An emergency lamp lit up the main deck, showing one factory container straining at its lashings and four people gathered around one of the rafts on the starboard side. Even from the wheelhouse Rebenc could see enough of Halloran's face to be glad he wasn't closer.

"Ahoy, Paul, Ju. Secure the wheelhouse and come on down!" shouted Bergstrom. "Time to abandon ship."

"Aye, aye," replied Geesink. Rebenc pulled the main throttle back to Full Stop and punched the manual release for the bridge log's memory. It slid out on to the deck with a clatter.

As Rebenc picked it up, the ship gave a long, shuddering groan. Rebenc told himself that it was only a particularly massive shifting of weights below decks. He also gripped the helm for one last moment while Geesink stood in the doorway, her back turned.

"Don't worry," whispered Rebenc. "We'll be back." Then he set the helm amidships and followed Geesink down the ladder to the main deck.

Dawn reached the bluffs, to find the water bare of both ship and survivors, and an irritable Team Leader contemplating the spectacle.

The mere fact that his mission had begun in such a partial and untidy victory would not have been enough to irritate him. Such victories were a test sent by Kali, to learn if her sworn servants had the wits to turn them into complete victories.

However, the particular *form* of the untidiness was another matter. All of Hiko's skill hadn't kept the second torpedo from exploding among the rocks of Les Fourchettes, giving unambiguous evidence of what had happened to *Celestine Auphan* for anyone who had eyes and ears. Both the men who'd abandoned ship at once and the party who'd tried to save her qualified there. The first party might be silenced with money or more direct methods; the second party would be a more difficult proposition.

At least they would be now. If the security squad had caught them among the reefs or on the beach, it would have been a different matter. Unfortunately, an Air-Sea Rescue plane appeared when the security squad was in mid-channel. They had to go over the side, to give a minimal radar profile and the appearance of an abandoned raft to any visual or IR scan. By the time ASR had picked up the first party, the second was on shore and radioing their location. They could not disappear quietly now; their disappearance would in fact simply make things noisier. The security squad could only come back.

Or rather, they could try to come back. They found the tide and current too strong for their motor, even aided by paddles, and ended up on the far side of the channel. At least they hadn't been swept out to sea, and their gear and survival training should keep them from being too uncomfortable. But they couldn't re-cross the channel until after nightfall, which meant the Team had to remain here for an extra half day beyond what the Leader had planned. The squad couldn't even provide more than the one signal reporting their safe arrival, since mysterious radio signals added to the torpedo explosion would certainly raise eyebrows at Air-Sea Rescue. And since the Union always made a point of placing moles in Air-Sea Rescue...

At least the security squad could make an on-the-ground reconnaissance of the shore where the *Celestine Auphan* went down. The Team Leader had both satellite and aerial photographs but trusted neither without a report from human eyes.

Also, this shore was neither Rancher nor Fisherman country, but it was twenty kilometers closer to the nearest ranches than to Havre des Dames. That opened real possibilities, if the Ranchers were prepared to commit men and weapons to be trained and organized for preventing the *Celestine*'s salvage.

The Team Leader decided to explore those possibilities, even if he had to divide his Team and even if he was able to cripple the second party of survivors before they could organize a salvage effort. The Ranchers would have to be prepared to stand up and fight to keep the Fishermen off their coast if they were to be worth supporting. An ally who expected you to do all the work while he raked in all the profits was not an ally worth having.

Besides, in this area the Ranchers were divided, with some outspokenly hostile to the anti-Fisherman policies of the Rancher Party, the Conseil Général Politique de l'Ouest. Training the "loyal" Ranchers could encourage them to move against those they considered traitors, and even attract weapons and financial support from extreme elements of the C.G.P.O. There would be a price to be paid in C.G.P.O. interference, but it might be offset by a much larger victory.

The Team Leader stretched and began to exercise chill-stiffened muscles. As warmth flowed through his limbs he felt more content with the night's limping victory. It must indeed have been one of Kali's tests. Granted the strength of his men and his own unimpaired skill and wits, he would pass that test so that neither Game Master nor goddess would find him wanting.

CHAPTER 1

"Fort Crerar. Station stop, Fort Crerar."

Sergeant Major John B. Parkes unfolded from his seat, hooked his boarding bag out from under the seat ahead, and stepped into the aisle. His six stripes and torch cleared a path through his fellow passengers, mostly other Peace Forcers or Base Command people. He was second out of the car, on the heels of a Navy lieutenant-commander who looked as if she had a bad hangover.

Parkes stood with his back to the station as the train whined away toward its last two stops. Discarded snack packs and bits of paper rose in a flurry from either side of the magnetic rails, settled back to the ground, then rose again as the field-green hoverbus slid to a stop.

A quick scan of the fifty-odd service people showed no N.C.O.'s senior to Parkes. He signaled to the bus driver, who nodded and pulled down the rearward-facing jump seat available for the senior N.C.O. of a busload.

A longer scan of the load as they dropped their baggage in the rear and filed to their seats showed Parkes four PFers with Group Fourteen shoulder patches. A big brunette valkyrie type, a nuggety little man who looked part Afroam or Abo, two unmemorable redheads who looked as if they might be brothers, and nothing in any of them to tell Parkes anything he didn't already know about Company Group Fourteen, Seventh (New Frontier) Brigade, Peace Force.

A pity about that. Parkes wasn't inclined to look gift horses in the mouth, and Field Squadron Sergeant-Major was a pretty fine horse.

Still, he would have liked to know something about Group Fourteen besides its being a newly raised group with Lieutenant-Colonel David MacLean as C.O.

MacLean was an ex-N.C.O., easygoing by reputation but in fact pretty much unscarable by either armed enemies or senior officers. He'd probably be a really good man at keeping peace between the Field and Support Squadrons, particularly if the Support C.O. made martyred noises every time the Field C.O. wouldn't lend him extra bodies for some civil-action job.

MacLean would also be someone the bad actors would try to take advantage of, and *any* newly organized unit would have more than its share of those. Parkes called it the garbage dump syndrome. That would make the job of the two Squadron Sergeant Majors really hairy for a while, unless the Company C.O.'s were really iron-butted types, and since Parkes didn't know who they were...

Hindsight was always 20-20. Parkes now saw clearly that he should have stayed in Fort Montgomery's Visiting N.C.O. Quarters until he could punch up a preliminary T.O.&E. for Group Fourteen that at least told him how many known losers he'd face among the officers and other senior N.C.O.'s.

Unfortunately, if he'd taken that extra ten days the word would surely have reached his home that he was close enough to drop by for a visit. Then he'd have had to do it. Without Louise at home on leave, that would have been about as much fun as a glacier-survival course with inadequate equipment and an incompetent instructor.

He could have thumbed his nose at his stepmother, of course, but then he'd be facing an even worse time on his next visit. Unless he decided to cut completely loose from his family, but he knew what that would do to his father, and the old familiar stomach-twisting guilt about what he'd already done.

"Sergeant Major?"

The bus driver was as close to telling him to get his ass in gear as a lance-corporal dared with a Sergeant Major.

"Coming."

The clerk's console let out a series of rude noises, hummed

quietly to itself, then gave a single *squeeep* and disgorged Parkes's ID deck. The clerk picked it up and handed it to Parkes. "There you are, Sergeant Major. You're now legal, moral, and nonfattening all over Fort Crerar."

"When's the next bus to Templeton Barracks?"

"Half an hour. But if you're in a hurry—"

"Supposing I was?"

"Then there's a hovertruck from Fourteen's Transportation right outside the door. The driver'll be ready to give you a lift as soon as she finishes her coffee."

"Fine." Parkes smiled. "Now, if she didn't drink all the coffee—"

The Receiving Clerk couldn't have moved faster without breaking an ankle. Parkes was on his third cup of coffee and second bowl of grapefruit when the driver came out, still wiping bacon grease off her face.

"Sergeant Tyndall?"

"Sarge—oh, excuse me, Sergeant Major! Welcome back. I heard you were coming to Fourteen. Field First?"

"Yes. You still with Dozer?"

"And how. She's Support First."

"Oh-ho."

Parkes's boarding bag seemed five kilos lighter as he handed it to Pat Tyndall to carry out to the truck. Dozer di Leone was an old friend and one of the two or three best Support Sergeant Majors in the Peace Force. The headache quotient of Parkes's job had just shrunk to manageable size, no matter how many foul-balls and fart-arounds were plugged into the T.O. elsewhere.

"Who's Support C.O.?" Parkes asked as the truck pulled off the Personnel ramp onto Duncton Road.

"Kuzik."

"Who?"

"Somebody named George Kuzik."

"Never heard of him."

"Welcome to the club. Nobody's met him either, except Dozer. He's on leave now. Word is, he's a direct commission two years ago. Used to be a flood control engineer in Morgan City."

22

That didn't say anything really bad about the mysterious Major Kuzik, since direct commissions *usually* weren't handed out to total turkeys. It didn't say anything positively good either about one of the most important officers in Group Fourteen. And a direct-commission officer with only two years on the Force as cadre for a new Group—?

That said something, but Parkes decided he wasn't going to waste time speculating about what. He jacked his seat back and relaxed as Tyndall fed more power to the fans and the familiar scenery along Duncton Road began to unroll.

LeMay Base, with a shuttle being towed toward the launcher.

Pearl Creek, with a few kids stopping off to wade in the chilly water on their way to school.

The manicured, frost-whitened grass around Dump Seven, and the innocent-looking concrete blast deflectors around the F.A.E. tanks. A fatigue party was working on Seven, mostly spray-patching the deflectors but a couple of controlling robots who were giving the grass a totally unnecessary mowing.

"Kilpatrick still running Maintenance?"

"Who else would be having the lawn mowed this late in the year?"

"Yeah. Some things never change."

Tyndall looked sideways at Parkes. He realized that he must have said more with his tone than with his words. Well, it was good to know that some things didn't change in the Peace Force world he'd made his own for twenty-two years.

A curve, and then Collishaw Field, with a vertiplane sliding down past the perimeter lights, transitioning to vertical flight and floating to a touchdown beyond the fringe of hammernut trees. Parkes remembered a pleasant company picnic in the shade of those trees five years ago, when he'd been no more than first sergeant of Second Company in the Field Squadron of Group Nine. There'd been Hugo Delapore to back him up if anything went wrong and a nice, almost-lovers friendship with Minnie Farren of 3 Platoon...

And now five years later Delapore was dead on Bifrost, Minnie Farren was a civilian with a daughter, and he was on his way to being the man who would have a baker's dozen of sergeants looking to him to back *them* up.

Well, there wasn't anything in the Peace Force Regulations that said they issued you immunity to new-tour jitters along with that torch. It would have been nice, but neither MedCorp nor Ordnance nor QM had any in stock and that was that.

"Want me to drop you off at the Barracks before I head over to support HQ?" said Tyndall.

Parkes saw that they were less than a kilometer from the Templeton Barracks complex. It would be nice to sit down with Dozer for a second, decent breakfast, but knowing her she was probably on the move already. Besides, while MacLean probably wouldn't care when his Field First showed up, the unknown Field C.O. might be a real iron-butt.

"Do that. And thanks for the lift, Pat."

"Any time, Sergeant Major."

CHAPTER 2

Parkes had stayed in Templeton Barracks several times when they were the Visiting N.C.O.s' quarters. Now they were being converted with what seemed indecent haste into quarters for a new Company Group. Parkes had to brush construction dust off his uniform three times before he found someone who knew his quarters assignment and could take his boarding bag there. He had to dust his boots once more on the way to Group HQ, as well as dodging a robot pallet with a load of wallplex and cans of bonder/sealer. Finally he had to pass two electricians performing what looked like rites of exorcism with welding lasers over some exposed wiring, then recover from the coughing fit the acrid smoke gave him.

For the moment Templeton Barracks had an improvised and chaotic appearance that Parkes hoped they would lose before Fourteen was called on to deal with any large drafts of new people. New Groups always got more than their fair share of new recruits. Quarters where you didn't know what would come out of the faucet when you turned it on never helped start an enlistment off right.

There was nothing improvised or chaotic about the Navy lieutenant Parkes found at the Duty desk in HQ. The name on the display was Katherine Forbes-Brandon and the appearance matched the name—nearly as tall as Parkes, blond hair with not a strand out of place, a complexion that glowed, teeth bright enough to reflect lasers, and large blue eyes at the moment regarding Parkes as if not sure about his species, let alone his rank.

Even without the unpromising look in her eyes, Lieutenant Forbes-Brandon would have struck Parkes as a prime specimen of one of his least favorite forms of military life. She looked like a typical child of one of the rich English-descended families (no other way to explain the double-barreled name) with enough political connections to wangle a commission in the more glamorous Navy instead of the Army. How she'd managed to wind up on Peace Force duty was still another question, to which many of the possible answers meant another headache for the Field First.

Parkes ran all this through his mind in the time it took him to come to attention and salute.

"Sergeant Major John B. Parkes, ma'am. Reporting as Field Squadron Sergeant Major. I'm looking for the Officer of the Day."

The nostrils of a shapely but undeniably oversized nose flared. The look in the blue eyes made Parkes wish he was wearing thermal underwear.

"Lieutenant Katherine Forbes-Brandon, Naval Liaison Officer to Company Group Fourteen. I am the Officer of the Day. Your file code, Sergeant Major?" as she lifted the pickup on her desk terminal toward him.

"N5-23876445—11B."

The terminal screen lit up, scrolling Parkes's Personal Data File past eyes that were at least now turned away from him. He took advantage of that to study Forbes-Brandon's desk, which was as impeccable as her hair and uniform, and the orderly at her console in a far corner of the room. The console was newly installed and the orderly looked as if she was thinking seriously about crawling inside it.

"You joined the Peace Force after the minimum period in the New Frontier Army, I see," the lieutenant said. "May I ask why?"

"I wanted to get off-planet and see some combat."

"I see that you've been recommended for a commission twice. Why didn't you take it?"

"I thought I had more aptitude as an N.C.O. Also, I prefer duty with troops."

"And officers spend too much time behind desks?"

It went against Parkes's experience to lie to an officer when nobody else was involved, even when the officer was a hardcore

Lieutenant Rich-Bitch.

"Yes, ma'am."

"Maybe," was Forbes-Brandon's only reply. She looked at the orderly. Parkes wondered if she was going to dismiss the orderly to be free to really dress him down. He hoped she at least had the sense not to do it in front of the orderly. If she was that dumb, things were going to hit the fan early and often in Group Fourteen.

Instead, the orderly rose and opened a cupboard. A teapot stood there, baptizing several covered dishes with steam.

"Would you care for some tea, Sergeant Major?"

"Thank you, ma'am, but I've already had breakfast."

The blue eyes turned chilly again, then veiled. "Finished with file," she said, and the screen went dark. "I'll make an appointment for you with Colonel MacLean for 1400 and one with Major Vela for 1500. They're both out on a field exercise with the First Company."

"Yes, ma'am."

"Very good, Sergeant Major. Dismissed."

As Parkes went out, Forbes-Brandon remained standing, to take a cup of tea and a plate of scones from the orderly. From that angle he saw that the body inside the expensively tailored uniform had an agreeably mammalian configuration, that her jaw was nearly as oversized as her nose, and that crows' feet in the corners of those expressive eyes suggested a few more years than he'd been willing to allow her.

Parkes decided that nothing he knew about Katherine Forbes-Brandon right now really added up. He'd have to remedy that situation, and fast, because the Naval Liaison was one of the officers he had to deal with almost every day. It was her regular job to arrange the supply drops from the Group's ship or orbital depot. It was her combat duty to arrange for heavy-fire support from orbit. Finally, in the last resort she had to help organize the Group's withdrawal, whether orderly or *sauve qui peut*—and if it was the second kind, she was one of the officers who damned near had a duty not to survive.

Definitely it didn't add up. Naval Liaison wasn't a job for good-looking little girls who wanted to increase their marriage value or get away from home. And taking O.D. duty as well—Parkes couldn't recall any regulation against it, but he'd never seen it done except once after Bifrost, when Group Nine had to get back to something like peacetime routine before it replaced its forty-percent casualties (seventy percent among the officers).

Was Group Fourteen that short of officers now? Like the mess in the barracks, Parkes devoutly hoped that such a situation would be corrected before they had to start seriously knocking the Group into shape, let alone taking it out to shoot at anybody.

Meanwhile, he decided to keep his mouth shut, his ears and eyes open, and all of his anatomy out of Forbes-Brandon's path until something about her *did* add up.

Outside the HQ Parkes found a place upwind of all the construction work and took deep breaths of the autumn-morning air. He would have given a good deal to have reported last night and be out on the exercise. It was going to be one of those perfect autumn days you always thought were just right for battles when you were a boy. After you were a soldier who'd been in a battle or two, you realized they were much too good to waste on killing or being killed. Battles, Parkes had decided some fifteen years ago, should always be fought in weather too wretched for anything else.

His stomach made an irritable noise, reminding him that it wanted more of a breakfast than coffee and grapefruit. It still wouldn't be smart to head over to the Mess Hall or the N.C.O.s' club, not after lying to Forbes-Brandon. If the tea had been a peace offering and the lieutenant found out that he'd turned it down with a lie—well, the only question would be which of fifty ways to retaliate she would choose.

Parkes decided to draw some running clothes and hit the track for a quick six kilometers. Then he'd have plenty of time for a leisurely lunch at the N.C.O.s' club, where there was bound to be somebody worth listening to even if they didn't know it themselves.

Parkes munched the last piece of an apple and stared across the bar at the holograph behind it. The cube was an exceptionally good reproduction of Csilgas's *The Sharp End*, one of the Peace Force's private jokes.

It showed two soldiers, a man and a woman, standing in a somber landscape full of tortured trees, rock formations, and the bones of fantastic animals, under a flame-shot sky. They wore only breechclouts, and their only weapons were the man's bow and the

28

woman's sling. Advancing toward them was a long column of tanks, bristling with lasers, guns, rocket launchers, and smoke mortars.

Across the sky was calligraphed, "Having for so long done so much with so little, the Peace Force will soon be qualified to do anything with nothing."

Parkes picked up a third apple and reflected that he wasn't quite as badly off as those two. He had somewhat more than nothing to work with, and he could at least hope that before he had to do anything he'd have even more.

Also, he was only the Field First. There were a baker's dozen of officers whose necks would be measured before his for any nooses that Peace Force Command was issuing.

Was that why he'd never accepted a commission? He'd asked himself the same question twenty times since the last time he turned one down, and always came up with the same definite "maybe." Maybe he hadn't quite grown up to the point where he could really accept responsibility as a part of the price of authority.

Parkes was just about to extract a neat cylindrical core from his apple, when someone slapped him on the shoulder.

"Hey, fruit merchant. Welcome to Freaky Fourteen."

Recognizing Dozer di Leone's voice made it easier for Parkes not to throw the apple core at the hand's owner. He still turned and made a gesture of rubbing it into di Leone's gray-streaked black hair.

There was more gray than the last time he'd seen her, Parkes noticed. Otherwise Sergeant Major Maria Camilla di Leone didn't seem to have changed; she still looked as if she could walk through a brick wall without breaking stride.

"Where's your *esprit de corpse?*" Parkes replied.

"Maybe I should tell you, but not here," said di Leone. She waved a large right hand with a fresh scar across the first knuckle of all four fingers toward a table in an alcove at the far end of the room from the bar.

"Can do."

Two fresh beers and another bowl of fruit were waiting for them when they reached di Leone's table. She waved aside Parkes's offer to pay and handed him a ripe horsehead. He was twisting off the stem when she looked at him sideways and said, "I hear you've had a problem with the Amazon."

"A little orderly bird told you, of course."

"Would I betray my sources?"

"Not to me, but then, I couldn't meet your price."

"Go bugger a goat." She sipped her beer. "Or wouldn't you call it a problem?"

Parkes made an A-frame of his hands on the table. "It might become a problem. We certainly got off on the wrong foot with each other, but we don't have to stay that way. Not unless she goes on taking herself too seriously—"

"Or you go taking her for what she looks like instead of for what she is."

"Was I doing that—I mean, so that she noticed?"

"It stuck out even farther than your nose. Or hers. I'd really like to see the two of you try to kiss someday. Those noses would hang you up—"

"Dozer, do you want to drink this beer or shampoo your hair with it?"

"Okay. The Amazon does know her job. At least all the book parts, and the rest she's learning pretty fast. Not as fast as she would if she was willing to listen, but fast enough so that I wouldn't lose any sleep over D.F.F. if I were you."

"All right. So she's not in the Navy or assigned to Peace Force for fun. Anything else?"

"Yes. Even if she fouls up, walk easy around her the first couple of times. She's a pet of Admiral Newton."

"Newton? The Vice-Chief of the Naval Staff?"

"I think his son's commanding *Bellerophon*, so it would have to be—sorry. I will be serious. He took an interest in her when he was a captain, and he's eased her way into any job he thinks she can do ever since."

Parkes sucked on his lower lip. It was a gesture that he'd substituted for raising his eyebrows when he discovered that only called attention to their scantiness. Di Leone shook her head.

"Not that kind of pet, I'd bet."

"What made you think I was thinking that?"

"You sleep with women, not men. Also, I saw you staring at

that blonde in the breechclout in *The Sharp End*."

"I guess there is sort of a resemblance, at least from the neck up." He suspected that the resemblance didn't stop there, but he'd be damned if he'd say so. Di Leone was bad enough even without any encouragement.

Parkes finished his beer, contemplated ordering another, and decided in favor of coffee. "Dozer, I haven't had time to check out the T.O. Can you give me a rundown of the N.C.O.'s as far as you know them, including any people I don't know who might be on the Network?"

The Network was the highly informal organization of the senior N.C.O.'s of any Group or other unit, who kept things moving in an efficient if not always regulation fashion by a judicious exchange of information and favors. Wise officers let the Network go its own way as long as it didn't do anything too flagrant. Unwise officers frequently got themselves into serious trouble trying to go against the Network, although a few Network careers usually became casualties in the process.

Katherine Forbes-Brandon—"the Amazon"—looked as if she might be an unwise officer, at least where the care and feeding of N.C.O.'s was concerned. It wouldn't help either that the Group C.O. was the veteran of as many Networks as battles, and likely to be a much more formidable enemy than the average C.O. if he was forced to be one.

To keep that from happening Parkes had to take control of his part of the Group Fourteen Network last week at the latest, divide the people into assets and liabilities, and if the Wise One and the C.O. smiled, ship out the liabilities before Group Fourteen had to shoot at anybody.

"You could have checked it out after you left the Amazon."

"Yeah, I suppose I could have. But she got under my skin. I won't do it again, so please tell me who our Network is so that if I trip over any of them on the way out I can apologize properly."

"All right, all right. Group Sergeant Major's Hatcher, the Gray Eminence. He's tight with the C.O., and only about two years from retirement. He'll be more afraid of losing his retirement fund than making enemies in the Network."

"Fine. We'll be nice to him without telling him anything. You I know. What about your Company Sergeants?"

Di Leone was running down the senior N.C.O.'s of the Engineering, Medical, Transportation, and Supply Companies when Parkes saw Sergeant Tyndall talking to the bartender. Then she turned and started toward them.

"Heads up, Dozer!"

"Sergeant Majors Parkes and Di Leone?" Tyndall didn't quite salute. "There's a General Command Briefing for Group Fourteen at 1600 in Group HQ."

"Is there now?" said Di Leone.

"Don't shoot the messenger," said Tyndall unrepentantly. She lowered her voice, "Also, the C.O. hauled in both the Amazon and the Squadron C.O.'s for a pre-briefing. He dragged Vela out of the shower and the Amazon off the track."

"That doesn't sound like he wants to discuss excessive tea consumption," said Di Leone. "All right. You've brought your message. Now, remove yourself."

When Tyndall had done so, Parkes found that his breath was coming faster and his pulse had speeded up. A General Command Briefing now stood a very good chance of giving them hard data on Group Fourteen's first mission. If so, he might have to put off meeting the Group Network, or even meet them one or two at a time.

That could leave him with dangerous holes in his knowledge. On the other hand, knowing what the next mission was would be a big help in sizing up people. Anybody who had too much belly to be comfortable in an environment suit, for example, wasn't going to be out in front if they had to work on an asteroid with a lot of E.V.A. as part of the job description. Also, knowing that a mission was coming up tended to make people work harder, so that those who didn't stood out further and could be dealt with sooner and more quietly.

"Pass the word to your company sergeants that I'd like to see them as soon as possible, either individually or together. You can chaperon them if any of them think a Field First might be dangerous to their virtue. Now, let's go and watch the officers pretend they know what's going on."

"Fruit Merchant?"

"Yeah, Dozer?"

"I'm going to propose a bet."

"I suppose I should have been cured of betting with you on Hephaestion, but I'm not very bright. What's the bet?"

"Two parts. One is that you'll be offered a commission before you've been Field First two years."

"No bet, Dozer. I'd have to be court-martialed to avoid it."

"Maybe, maybe not. I'll drop that if you'll take on the second one. Word of honor?"

"May the Wise One forsake my tongue, my eyes, and my ears if I do not take your second bet."

"Okay. You'll take that commission."

Parkes wasn't quite sure that his jaw actually hit the table. He was fairly sure that di Leone was nearly out the door of the club before he got his mouth closed again.

CHAPTER 3

"Attention!" shouted Major Vela.

The twelve officers, three Sergeant Majors, and one civilian seated around the long briefing table rose to their feet as Lieutenant-Colonel David Maclean entered. He returned their salutes with as broad a smile as his long face could hold.

"Be seated, ladies and gentlemen." As chairs scraped he pressed a plate on his console and the main cube lit up with a display of an Earth-type planet.

"This briefing has an Ultra-Secret Classification. Have you all read and understood the penalties for the revelation of any of its contents to unauthorized personnel?"

The mumbled chorus of "yeses" was as ritualistic as the question. The only people who sounded fully awake were Vela and Forbes-Brandon.

Hatcher said nothing at all. Parkes noticed that he was staring at the cube as if he expected evil spirits to pour out of it any moment, and his prominent Adam's apple was bobbing up and down.

Maclean nodded. "First, this Company Group has been declared Grade Two Deployable and is now on Grade Three Alert." That meant fit to be deployed on any Earth-environment planet and ready to move out, personnel and gear, after thirty New Frontier days.

MacLean clasped his hands behind his back. "Now, if anyone has any serious objections to our being Alerted, I'd like to hear them. I'm as concerned as you are that Group Fourteen deploy on command

and succeed in its first mission. I don't need to tell you that will do a lot for our reputation, morale, and future effectiveness.

"However, I also don't want anyone to carry their concern for the Group's future reputation to the point of not being concerned for their people now. Does anyone feel that their unit or any of its members would not be effective in a deployment?"

Captain Hansen, C.O. of First Company, cleared his throat. "I've got thirty-five people with less than one year's Peace Force service. Six of them have enough Army time to know their way around, but I'd like to reassign about half of the others to Second and Third Companies, if their C.O.'s don't mind."

Captain Klin of Second Company nodded, but Lieutenant Simmel gave Hansen a dirty look. She pulled her face straight hastily as MacLean also nodded.

"I see no objections to spreading the newlies around even a trifle more. Major Vela, Sergeant Majors Hatcher and Parkes, and the company C.O.'s—work out a scheme that satisfies you and I'll approve it."

Parkes, Hatcher, Hansen, and Klin all nodded at once. Simmel nodded more slowly, and Vela last of all. Parkes wondered if the small red-haired lieutenant was a pet of Vela's, and had been spared her fair share of the inexperienced people because of that. He'd know better after the reassignment conference, and if there was a Vela-Simmel alliance it would need watching.

Meanwhile, MacLean was turning the briefing to Fourteen's impending mission. The planet in the cube was Bayard, a daughter colony of Clovis settled in 2096. Like most such daughters settled in the wake of the Collapse War of 2088, it had gone through a period of near-primitive civilization and was now very much a technological mixed bag. One thing it lacked was cheap protein synthesis, and that lack had given rise to the problem Group Fourteen was intended to solve.

"Here's the western half of the Grand Continent, or Nouvelle Bretagne," he continued as a map replaced a view of the planet. Parkes noted an island-studded coast and a long, mountainous tail trailing off to the south from the main land mass.

"The inland area is held by a semi-feudal society of ranching barons. Using adapted Terran livestock and two native ungulates, they supply most of the planet's animal protein and the largest part of its export income as well. Through their political arm, the Conseil Général Politique de l'Ouest, they also exercise a near-veto on any policies of the government that affect their interests. They control no more than ten percent of the population, but it's the best-armed percent, and the toughest next to the fishermen of the west or Storm Coast.

"The fishing off the Storm Coast is extraordinarily rich. Properly managed, with enough capital invested, it could replace the ranchers as the main source of animal protein for Bayard. Needless to say, the Ranchers and the Fishermen aren't on the best of terms. So far the Ranchers have prevented the Nouvelle Bretagne government from providing large-scale financing for the Fishermen. They've been able to raise private loans for at least one fish-processing ship, but they need much more.

"The other or Petit Continent of Bayard is occupied by a collection of small countries and glorified city-states mostly irrelevant to our mission, and one—let's call it a dictatorship and not bother being polite—that goes by the name of the Fourth Empire.

"The Empire has offered direct or indirect military assistance to the Fishermen, but so far they have refused. However, if the Ranchers take any overt action against them or their ships, they might see the Fourth Empire as their only possible friends. Then there would be war between the two continents on Bayard, giving the Ranchers a perfect excuse to occupy the Storm Coast in self-defense and incidentally erasing the Fishermen. Their National Militia units already have a high priority for modern weapons with the Ministry of Defense because of fear of the Fourth Empire.

"By now most of you will have guessed what our mission on Bayard will be. We are to deploy on the Storm Coast, based around the capital city of Havre des Dames. We are to prevent any military action by irregular Rancher forces against the Fishermen. They can't use their National Militia units now without rebelling against the government, and according to Intelligence they don't appear to be ready for that."

The last phrase came out with a wry tone that told Parkes that MacLean agreed with the old saying: "There are four kinds of intelligence—human, animal, artificial, and military."

"With the support of our ship, we are also to prevent any small-scale military intervention by the Fourth Empire against anybody in Nouvelle Bretagne. In the event of large-scale military intervention, contingency plans exist to reinforce us to a two-Group Task Force or even a full Peace Brigade with appropriate supporting ships.

"One Standard Supply Load is being prepositioned in the Bayard system now, in addition to the standard sixty-day resupply. We are going to be quite well off for supplies as long as nobody shoots off five units of fire to work up an appetite for breakfast!"

There spoke a man who'd captained the Peace Force rifle team and been an instructor in marksmanship. Unspoken because unneeded was the summary that Parkes mentally filled in.

"People, this is the usual Peace Force mission. Trying to keep two factions away from each other's throats with minimal strength and few or no friends among the locals. We can hope that while we're freezing in the hills outside Havre des Dames, the diplomats in nice warm suites will use the time we've brought them to hammer out a permanent solution. Even if they don't, we have to do our duty."

Not to mention that undoubtedly any solution hammered out by the diplomats would make the Planetary Union somewhat richer. The official motto of the Peace Force was: "If you seek peace, prepare for war." The unofficial one was: "Make peace so much more profitable than war that nobody can afford to fight."

Parkes doubted that the human animal was made to respond that way to profit-and-loss evaluations, but any effort to keep the peace was better than none. Humanity among the stars had lived in the shadow of the Collapse War of 2088, which killed two-thirds of Earth's five billion people, and the Century of Chaos that followed. It was engraved on their souls that war and rumors of war were not something to take casually.

The map vanished from the cube, to be replaced by the picture of an *Enterprise*-class Peace Cruiser. "Our Group ship for this mission will be Peace Cruiser *Ark Royal*, Captain Daniel Cooper commanding."

Forbes-Brandon smiled at this news, a smile that lit up her whole face and made it even more striking than usual. Parkes wondered what she knew that he didn't, but also felt like smiling. The

Ark Royal had the reputation of being a good ship; she'd been in commission two years since her last refit, and Cooper was a common-sense type who wouldn't try to command the embarked Group from the ship's C.I.C.

None of this would hurt Group Fourteen once they grounded on Bayard. A Group's ship provided not only transportation but 3-C, limited reinforcements, and heavy fire support. A badly run ship, a new ship, or a captain who tried to mind the Group's business could lead to a failed mission, or at least a lot of unnecessarily dead Peace Forcers.

The briefing continued into the physical characteristics of the Bayard planetary environment. Parkes listened with only half an ear; all of this would be hypnotically memorized over the next few days. Once he'd discovered that the Bayard planetary environment would require mostly precautions against cold and damp and nothing else extraordinary, he concentrated on covertly studying the other people around the briefing table.

Apart from the Amazon and MacLean, four people stood out. Hatcher no longer looked surprised or expectant. He barely seemed to be listening at all, as if his mind had already crossed the light-years to Bayard.

The Mediator, Arthur Goff, was a tall, thin, indeterminately middle-aged Afroam gentleman dressed in a subdued green suit and polished civilian boots which still looked rugged enough for field work. He seemed to be taking everything in with great attention but with equally great care that nobody noticed him doing so.

Parkes doubted that Goff was trying to be mysterious. A Mediator had to be the world's best listener to get total and frequently hostile strangers to confide in him. Even if he did turn out to be a bit of a mystery man, it wouldn't do any harm. A Mediator could do his job quite well without any personality that would put its stamp on the job.

Next to Goff sat Captain Sondra Dallin, a minor legend in the Peace Force for her thirteen rejected applications to be reassigned for fighter duty. Her long thin nose seemed thinner and her auburn hair had a few more strands of gray. Parkes wondered if there'd been a fourteenth rejection since he last saw her.

Personally, he felt that Dallin might not be the best person for the job she held, legend or not. As Transportation Officer she had charge of things that ran on wheels and fans as well as things that flew. If she spent as much time as usual playing hot pilot on hairy missions, she might leave a rifle company short of ammunition at a time when that would also shorten their life expectancy.

Parkes made a mental note to get together with the Supply Company first sergeant and set up a few compensators for Captain Dallin. He knew better than to try with any of her Transportation crew chiefs; Dallin had their loyalty to just this side of idolatry.

Sitting beside Colonel MacLean was a not so minor legend, Major Jesus Desiderio Vela. The Velas were one of the oldest military families on New Frontier, and Vela himself was one of only four Peace Force field officers who'd started his career an officer of Hrothmi *Jagruns*. He'd commanded both a battalion of the raccoon-like Hrothmi in the service of the Trade Council and a company of Domiciled Humans in the Akkwasi War before transferring to the Peace Force. With that and other smaller wars as well as what passed for "peacekeeping" on Hrothma, he'd seen more fighting than any other three people in the room put together.

Parkes wondered if he should give Vela the benefit of the doubt. Certainly the man wouldn't have reached field grade in the Peace Force if several somebodies over the last ten years hadn't decided he knew something about facing modern weapons and handling human soldiers. He'd still acquired his first military experience in bloody, all-out wars, commanding non-humans who were much more resilient in the face of casualties than any Peace Force unit would be, and against weapons that would have been at home on the battlefields of the First Terran War. The first battles an officer fought and the first soldiers he commanded always left their mark on him, for better or worse.

Not to mention that Vela's uniform was the only one more elegant than the Amazon's. That suggested a personal weakness for spit and polish.

There were worse combinations than Major Vela, Parkes decided. There were also better ones for the job—much better, when the job was that of Parkes's own direct C.O.

Parkes's thoughts had taken him that far when he realized that somewhere in the middle of Maclean's description of the military resources of the various governments and factions on Bayard, the words *Terran intervention* had popped up. He turned his full attention back to Maclean.

"—known only as the Game Master. This seems to be a name he's accepted for himself. It certainly matches his attitude, which is that warfare is the greatest game of all."

Vela said something in Hispanic about the Game Master's ancestry. Maclean frowned. "I would agree, and I would have expected the Terran governments to deal with such an individual and his men fairly quickly. Intelligence has only guesses as to why they didn't. It appears that he mostly operated in the parts of Asia, Africa, and South America not part of any major sphere of influence.

"Now he's acquired a body of highly trained and experienced men. It appears that one or more Terran governments are willing to finance his sending some of them out-system to destabilize planets under Union influence. The idea apparently is to tie up Peace Force strength and possibly provoke conflicts among the Union planets that would prevent concerted action against Terran interests."

Forbes-Brandon made a disgusted noise, "Excuse me, sir, but what concerted action, and what interests? Is there some germ left over from the Collapse War that's making all the Terran politicians paranoid? If they were going to subsidize a free-lance mercenary, I would think they'd be sending him against the asteroids or at least Mars, if he didn't have people trained for E-suit combat."

Maclean frowned. "Your germ theory makes as much sense to me as anything Intelligence has offered. They believe that the Martians have strengthened their orbital defenses so that the Game Master's standard operational methods would not be particularly effective. Also, the Martian ground forces have always been more effective than most of the out-system ones." The Game Master's methods indeed seemed to depend on the local ground forces being either scattered, ineffective, or preferably both. This still left him a large choice of planets—too large for the sleep of any Peace Forcer.

The method was simple, given trained men who could be relied on to analyze a situation and act independently on that analysis. Land cadre Team carrying disguised or broken-down personal weapons and 3-C gear. Covertly land heavier equipment, either disguised as freight or else left in orbit and then brought down on command once the Team was established on the ground.

After that the way was open to either direct action by the Team or its remaining a cadre for training and leading local people, equipped out of local resources. What direction they were led in apparently didn't matter much to the Game Master. His reported base was in the Hindu Kush Mountains, but that didn't prove anything about either his ideology or origins.

Parkes hoped the Teams had no qualms about being expendable. If they were sufficiently tough-minded to handle that fact, the rest of the Game Master's strategy had a simplicity that Parkes had to call "elegant." It also had a good chance of being quite effective against anything short of large commitments of ground forces or planetary blockades—and the Union *would* start cracking at the seams if it had to make a habit of either.

The deadliest and most easily concealed weapon in the universe was a well-trained human mind. Wasn't there some Old Terran military theorist who'd said, "There are no dangerous weapons. There are only dangerous men." Parkes wondered if he should look up that theorist; his work might give a few more clues to what Group Fourteen would be facing on Bayard.

At least they could be facing a Game Team on Bayard if Intelligence's estimate of the planet as the likely first out-system target was correct. Also, if the Team was on Bayard before *Ark Royal* burned into orbit and launched her orbital surveillance system. After that anything in orbit large enough to hold a useful amount of weapons or equipment would show up like a priest in a whorehouse; and anything that showed up could be destroyed.

Bayard, Parkes decided, wasn't the place he would have chosen for the first mission of a newly organized Group. He suspected that Colonel MacLean wouldn't have chosen it either.

However, neither of them was at the level where the decision was whether to dig or even where. Both of them in their own ways just picked up shovels and started digging.

The briefing wound down in a flurry of questions about minor administrative matters and the whine of the printer running off printouts of the full Mission Data File. Computer memories were fine for guided hypnotic memorization, but not for sitting down with a drink just before lights-out.

Parkes was leaving the briefing room with his printout under his arm when a MedCorp captain hurried up. She was on the lower edge of middle age, with a round, perspiring face and a uniform that looked like a poorly fitting costume. She hurried into the briefing room and nearly collided with Lieutenant Forbes-Brandon.

"Oh, I'm sorry"—she looked at the Amazon's insignia—"Captain. I didn't know that I was supposed to be at the briefing."

"You are Captain—?"

"Marian Laughton," said the doctor. "I'm the Group Surgeon. Oh, well, I suppose it doesn't matter whether I know where my casualties are coming from, as long as I can treat them."

Parkes suppressed the urge to cringe. Forbes-Brandon didn't. She also started turning red. Like her smile, the blush made her face even more striking than usual.

Parkes decided to speed his departure. As a Navy lieutenant and a line officer, the Amazon ranked the Surgeon, and was entitled to give her a right royal dressing-down. If she had to suppress the impulse, she might have a stroke—and she would have to suppress it as long as Parkes was in hearing.

Parkes turned and hurried down the corridor after Dozer di Leone. He'll have to ask her permission before approaching the Supply sergeant, and she might also have a few ideas of her own about making sure that Fourteen's wheels as well as its wings were fit for duty.

He was safely on his way before Forbes-Brandon got any further than "Captain, I don't know when they commissioned you or why, but—" As he reached the outer door it occurred to him that one good thing was sure to come from the Group's now being on Alert.

Forbes-Brandon would be too busy to make any trouble for him—if she knew her job, and if she didn't she would soon be in no position to make trouble for anyone. MacLean and Vela weren't going to take a new Group into combat carrying avoidable dead weight, no matter how well-connected or interestingly packaged it might be...

CHAPTER 4

Paul Rebenc pulled up his coat collar as he stepped out from behind the warehouse. The wind off D'Entrecasteaux Channel was blowing hard, and the dampness made the chill seem to eat into his bones.

A ferro-cement self-unloading barge lay at the pier, pitching uneasily as the waves rolled in under it and broke. Mooring wires thrummed and scraped as the strain came on them, then eased again. An unpainted wooden gangplank with two gaps bounced up and down with the motion of the barge.

Rebenc felt even colder. "Is *that* the best you could do?"

Bergstrom snarled something fortunately untranslatable. "It was the only thing I could find. And if you think I could have done better here, look around you."

The request was rhetorical, but Rebenc looked around anyway. The waterfront of Port Tourville at just past dawn was about as dismal a sight as he'd ever seen. Three piers, two quays, four warehouses, and a small slipway were the total. At one quay three elderly fishing boats were nested, and smoke rising from a shed by the slipway told of at least a watchman on duty.

Out in the channel a coastal steamer was heading north, butting recklessly into the seas as if she couldn't wait to leave Port Tourville. Rebenc sympathized with such an attitude. Once the town had been a major lumber shipping port, but then the Ranchers opened up stands of better timber more accessible to the eastern markets. That was the end of Port Tourville as everything except a stopover port and the Prefecture for a district of small farmers and recluses. If it had a thousand people Rebenc would be surprised.

At least anything that could be bought there at all could be bought cheaply. Somehow Bergstrom had learned that there was an old lumber barge available at a price *les copains* might be able to afford. Rebenc walked out onto the pier and inspected the barge more closely.

It might do. In fact, it probably would. Bergstrom was drinking a lot these days even when he should have been sober, but he hadn't lost his eye for a ship. The anti-fouling bonder looked sound except for the normal marine growth, what machinery was visible seemed to have been properly weatherproofed, and the cabin looked rundown but repairable.

"We'll need a survey, of course," said Rebenc.

"No, we won't," said Bergstrom, grinning for the first time in days. He pulled out a print certificate, which the wind nearly snatched from his hands. "Look at the date and the authentication code. The owners must have wanted to unload her in a hurry."

"Let's hope the surveyor was honest," said Rebenc. He had to admit that the survey certificate and his eyes agreed.

"We have to trust somebody," put in Juliana Geesink. "Otherwise we might as well all cut our throats right now."

"That's too chilly a thought for here and now," said Bergstrom. "Let's go warm up and talk about what to do next."

As they walked back up the hill from the waterfront Rebenc realized that they certainly would have to talk about what came next. When they'd been collecting patches and torches, bonder/sealer and diving gear, pumps and laser cartridges, all they'd thought about was getting together enough equipment. When they'd been in search of a diving platform, all they'd thought of was finding one large enough to support the equipment and ride safely over *Celestine*'s temporary grave.

Now they had their barge, but she was in Port Tourville, twelve hundred kilometers from Havre des Dames and their equipment, more than a thousand from *Celestine*. How to get it from here to there?

They met Roman Taigas and Joseph Vasi outside the grandly

44

named Auberge Henri Quatre and ended up in a minuscule bistro nearly on the edge of town, the only inhabited building on a street of abandoned ones. The only other customer was clearly the town's last surviving prostitute, trying to kill a hangover, and the landlord would clearly have served not merely strangers but Hrothmi, robots, or Galactic Overseers with equally bad coffee.

Rebenc added some bad absinthe to his coffee. At least they neutralized the worst of each other's flavors. When he'd finished his second cup, he said, "All right, do we take this barge? And if we do, how do we get her to Havre des Dames? And from there to Les Fourchettes?"

"Tow," said Bergstrom succinctly.

"What with?" said Vasi. "I don't see any tugs here. Haven't seen one since we came, in fact."

"There are always fishermen on their way north," said Bergstrom. "We can ask a couple of them to tow us."

Vasi frowned. "The passage won't be too bad at this time of year, but still, it's their boats or at least their gear they'll be risking. They may love us for what we're trying to do, but will love be enough? Particularly if the Ranchers decide it's worth money to keep *Celestine* on the bottom after putting her there."

"What's the matter, Joseph?" said Bergstrom. "Has fear of the Ranchers got to you? Or maybe the Ranchers themselves?"

Rebenc tapped Geesink on the knee and they both pushed their chairs back, ready for action. Vasi looked about ready to draw a knife or even vault the table and tackle Bergstrom barehanded.

"Nils, put some more coffee in your absinthe and apologize to Joseph," said Talgas wearily. "Joseph's righter than he knows, I think. When we were looking for our diving platform in Havre des Dames, I dropped in at the local office of Rougier et Filles, the towing people."

Bergstrom turned even redder and opened his mouth, then closed it again as Geesink kicked him under the table and managed to say with deceptive mildness, "That was taking a big risk, wasn't it?"

Talgas shrugged. "Not as big for me as for one of you. I used to be winchman on the *Therese Rougier*, and the machine shop foreman is an old friend. I talked to him and only to him."

"So what did you learn?" said Bergstrom.

"Rougier won't take any towing jobs connected with the *Celestine Auphan*. Anybody who does will never work for Rougier. Since they're bigger than the other four towing firms on the coast put together..." He shrugged again.

"Didn't Warren and Fuchs used to work for Rougier?" said Geesink. "Maybe they believed what Warren said, about our being mutineers and shooting at his men?"

"Ju, you've got too much faith in human nature, believing anybody would turn down a contract out of loyalty to those (long and complex Scandic obscenity). If the world ran the way you think it does, all the Fishermen would be rallying around us. They'd be carrying the damned barge to Havre des Dames on their—shoulders, for God's sake!"

The prostitute was staring at Bergstrom, and now the landlord came out of the bathroom and thrust a hand under the counter. Rebenc made a placating gesture to him and put a hand on Bergstrom's shoulder. The boatswain shook it off angrily.

"All right, all right. It's just that I'm so sick and tired of anybody hoping for help. If *Celestine* comes up again, it's going to be us five and Katie Halloran's prayers that do it!"

The mention of Katie Halloran lowered a curtain of silence on the table. After a moment the landlord grunted and pulled his hand out from under the counter, and the prostitute turned back to her drink.

Rebenc sighed. God help them, Bergstrom was right. And it didn't help to know that the money they were spending might have already bought Halloran surgery to erase her scars, rebuild her shoulder and neck, and restore her sight. She'd refused to accept more than enough to keep her in the nursing ward at the hospital in Havre des Dames, and refused in a way that made it impossible to deceive her.

They salved their consciences with the knowledge that if they could salvage *Celestine*, there'd be francs enough floating around to buy Katie one blue eye and one brown eye if she wanted them. Even if they didn't salvage the ship and had some equipment left over, they could sell that for enough to make Katie able to support herself again.

But what Roman had learned made it sound very likely that the ranchers themselves were keeping an eye on *Celestine* and the six people who were still loyal to her. What if *les copains* lost everything except their lives? What if—

"A couple of practical suggestions," said Geesink. "I'm a licensed crane operator, and I think Paul's done some crane-swinging too." Rebenc nodded. "Then we can always trade some cheap lifting for a tow. There's always plenty of crane work to be done around Havre des Dames or somewhere in the Gros Chaudron. I know that will take time that we might not have, but if we have to save money, we have to be ready to spend time.

"Also, I suggest that we find *one* fishing boat big enough to handle the tow herself. We'll need two people aboard the towing vessel to keep an eye on the crew and each other's backs. Otherwise the barge crew might suddenly find themselves on a short cruise to nowhere."

Bergstrom forced a smile. "I take back what I said about you being too nice, Ju. You're getting almost as cynical as you ought to be."

"It's the company I keep," said Geesink.

Rebenc relaxed, but the coffee and absinthe had warmed his stomach without warming his thoughts. If this venture ended with *les copains* out of money and the Ranchers looking for them, he and the other men could at least ship out to the Petit Continent and enlist in the Fourth Empire's bad joke of a navy, or as mercenaries in one of the city-states.

Before they did that, though, he and the others would take what money they had and buy Juliana as well as Katie a passage back to the east and civilization. The Petite Continent was so barbaric that it did not let women fight, and for her to be left behind in such a land while the men went off to fight could end only one way. It would mean breaking up *les copains*, but if this venture failed, it was long odds against their all even being alive in five years. If all else failed, he could always tell Ju that Katie Halloran would need someone to take care of her who was more reliable than the Sisters of Charity.

For now he would buy himself a gun and stay very sober. He did not want to become the leader of *les copains*, but what he wanted might matter very little if Nils kept on drinking. If he did become leader of *les copains*, there was sure to be at least one moment in the process when it would be very useful to have a gun and to be in condition to use it.

* * *

"Aiyyyy! No, no, no! Do not bunch up! As you are, one rocket could kill you all!"

The two dozen ranch hands stopped their headlong run toward the tree line and looked at the Team Leader in confusion. He would have liked to think it was his accented Francone that confused them, but knew that would be a delusion. These people did not understand infantry tactics fit for use against modern weapons. Perhaps they would make good soldiers against one of the Hrothmi countries where they still used muzzle-loading black powder rifles, but they would not be fight Hrothmi here on Bayard.

They gathered around the Team Leader and his two sergeants. At least no one pulled out a cigarette. The Team Leader decided to reward them for having at least that much discipline, which was more than they'd had three weeks ago.

"You may smoke."

The men lit up. Some of them started counting their ammunition. A few even inspected their rifles; the Team Leader recorded these names on his belt comp for possible promotion. He would need squad and even platoon leaders before long. His Team could not be the whole cadre for more than a hundred men and still be free to take more direct action.

"You may think you're not going to face any weapons dangerous to you even if you do bunch up. That is not thinking at all. Even a thrown charge of blasting explosive could have disabled half of you from the concussion alone. If it had been wrapped in as little as a sheet of aluminum, fragments would have taken most of the other half."

"When are we going to have body armor?" said one of the men. He was one of the potential leaders and a nonsmoker, so the Team Leader answered him politely.

"When you will be more dangerous to the enemy than to yourselves in the kind of fight where armor will help you."

"When will that be?"

"Not before the next cycle of the Universe, if you must learn what children in my homeland know as soon as they can run." *Or at least children who grew up in the rat-infested ruins of Calcutta and lived into manhood only by learning skills that brought them to the attention of the thugs.*

No one asked what his homeland was. They had learned that question was imprudent, since the night when two men who had asked it disappeared. It was said that they'd deserted, and to support this tale the Team Leader led his whole Team and the best of the trainees on a search for them. He wondered how many believed it, but as long as no one was prepared to act on any other belief, it hardly mattered. The Team Leader had little fear for his back from these people.

"All right. Let's do it again, and try to do better."

This time the Team Leader and one of his sergeants ran with the trainees. They did not do so badly; only about half of them clustered dangerously together.

Halfway across the open ground the other sergeant opened fire with a magazine of blanks. Some of the trainees ran around like headless lizards. Others threw themselves flat, some of them even looking for cover before they did so. Two of these opened fire in the direction of the attack.

Four of the trainees found cover in a line of squat pig's-foot bushes. The Team Leader ceased firing long enough to roll on his side and remote-fire the smoke bomb wired into one of the bushes. Three of the four trainees promptly jumped up again, coughing and sneezing, their faces the color of a baboon's backside. The other one simply rolled to the far end of the line of bushes without appearing in the open again, then thrust his rifle through the gap between two bushes and opened fire.

"All right," said the Team Leader. "Gather round again. You, you, and you"—he pointed at the three who'd stayed under cover and opened fire—"you may smoke. The rest listen to me."

He lectured, demonstrated, threatened, swore, and cajoled until he'd satisfied himself that he'd put across as many points as these men were equipped to understand at this stage of their training. He did not tell them the truth, which was that at least some of them were beginning to put lectures and exercises together in a way that made them at least passable imitations of soldiers. That would encourage them to relax. Better that they sweat now in fear of the Team Leader's

49

tongue than bleed and die a month from now because they knew less than they thought they did.

After the lecture the Team Leader and one of the sergeants held weapons inspection. The Team's money would not buy talent for its trainees, but it would at least buy enough hunting rifles to arm all of them alike. Not only did this simplify ammunition supply, always one of the headaches of irregular forces, but it gave the men a weapon with a familiar feel to it. Most people in the back country of Bayard hunted, and the Team Leader had found better marksmanship and less trigger-freeze than in any other group of recruits he'd ever met. If they could learn at least as much about being shot at as they already knew about shooting, much might be done with them.

Halfway through the inspection the Team Leader became aware that lunch and the ammunition supply had arrived on two mules and an elderly white man. It wasn't until after the inspection that he learned there was also a coded message for him. He let one sergeant issue the ammunition while the other led half a dozen trainees on an inspection of the ground for any traces of the exercise, sat down with his back against a tree, flipped up the screen on his belt comp, and inserted the message disk.

Decoded, the message ran:

CHANDRAGAN TO TEAM LEADER.
REPORTING FOUR FLIGHTS PLANNED WITH HIGHLY PROBABLE CAMP SITE, FIRE BASE, AND OBSERVATION POST SURVEY PROFILE IN NW AND W HAVRE DES DAMES QUADRANTS. EMPLOYEES OF GRETTON ET CIE. SEEN AT SERVICES DU CIEL OFFICES. IN THE SERVICE OF THE MASTER.

The Team Leader smiled. The commander of whatever Union military unit—probably a Peace Force Company Group—was not going to be among the warmest admirers of the local Union mole. Not that the man had much choice if he wanted to do any advance surveying of the Group's operational area. Air-Sea Rescue was not infiltrated by the Union to the point where one of its planes could be used for the flights, and Services du Ciel was the best-equipped air service on the Storm Coast.

What the Union man should have been able to do, and had not done, was balance the minor advantage of doing in advance a survey that the Group's own aircraft could easily carry out with better equipment, against the major disadvantages of employing a civilian firm that might have been penetrated by enemies of whose existence the Union man could hardly be unaware. Otherwise why would off-planet forces be coming in?

Unless the action was not Union-inspired, in which case the men coming in might be from the Fourth Empire? The Team Leader assessed the probabilities both mentally and with the computer and decided that anything but off-planet forces was only an object for contingency planning. Gretton et Cie was *the* Union front in Havre des Dames; his sources of intelligence in the C.G.P.O. had established that beyond serious doubt. Also, Fourth Empire troops were more likely to be a problem than a solution.

The Team Leader shut off his computer and folded himself into the lotus position. He was not as limber as he once was; it was not entirely comfortable with field boots on. However, he wished to give only the appearance of meditating.

Three things had to be done at once. The Team's contacts in Havre des Dames had to be made capable of action or else changed. Changing them might involve a few terminations. While no police force ever objected to a sudden epidemic of unexplained deaths among street criminals, even the Mobile Guards might ask impertinent questions to find out why they'd died.

The real action would probably be outside the city. That meant seeing that Chandragan flew as many of the survey flights as possible and learned of the results of the rest. This would not be hard, and indeed could be left to Chandragan once he'd been given his orders. The man was as skilled in the cockpit of light or medium aircraft as Hiko was at the controls of a torpedo. Although the junior of Services du Ciel's five pilots, he was already the one most often called on for difficult missions.

The sergeant in charge of the clean-up party approached and saluted. "That's it, Leader." He held out a bag containing a few cigarette butts, a lighter cartridge, a couple of strips of velcro, and the scraps of the smoke bomb.

"Very good." The Team Leader rose and looked over the exercise area. With all the debris policed up, there was nothing but footprints to show even a trained observer what had been going on here. The footprints themselves wouldn't outlast the next rain, and it rained every other day here.

He looked back to the trainees. They would need better weapons then hunting rifles if they were going to face the Peace Force. Evasion, concealment, dispersal, and surprise would all help, but they would have to be able to fight as well. Hunting rifles would not be enough to face the Peace Forcers or even give the trainees confidence in their ability to do so. Soldiers had to have that confidence even before their first battle, along with rations, clothing, and ammunition.

The best source of weapons on the Storm Coast would be the National Militia units of the Ranchers farther inland. It was a source that could be tapped only with the aid of the C.G.P.O. man who called himself Nestor, but one that should provide adequate light-infantry equipment. Against the heavier weapons and the ship-support of the Group, the best defense would be the political barriers to the Group's using them at all, the next best the use of hostages.

The stakes were about to increase. So was the danger—of failure, of death, even of the destruction of the Team. He still couldn't help being more aware of the challenge of facing a Peace Force Group than of the danger. That challenge made him feel more alive than he'd felt since landing on Bayard.

He sprang to his feet. "Come along, men! Let's try a five-kilometer run and see who's made of what!"

CHAPTER 5

"At ease."

Parkes clasped his hands behind his back and stood beside Major Vela, facing the test of Field Squadron HQ. A chilly wind blew across the apron at the end of the LeMay field launching complex, carrying the smell of hot metal, ozone, and oil.

From closer to hand it also brought the thin wail of a bagpipe. The base piper was playing for somebody aboard the passenger shuttle, probably Colonel MacLean. At least the C.O. didn't have his own personal piper on the strength of Group Fourteen, to lend his noisemaking abilities to ceremonial occasions. Parkes thanked the Wise One for that. He agreed with an Old Terran composer that the pipes were "an ill wind that nobody blows good," and would not have been at all surprised if a C.O. who'd begun his career in the Selkirk Rifles had insisted on having the pipes about him all the time.

A thunderclap hammered at Parkes's ears, followed by a long, dying rumble of tortured air as a cargo pod was laser-boosted from the launcher. The rumble died away into silence; the piper must have finished his tune.

A hoverbus whined toward the HQ ranks, followed by a field-condemned weapons carrier. Everyone except Vela and Parkes climbed into the bus. Vela sat down beside the carrier driver, leaving Parkes with the choice of the back seat or the cupola. He chose the cupola, a better place to get his last breath of unrecycled air for a month.

From the cupola he could see the launcher swinging down into position for the loading of another cargo pod, ready for its ten-G takeoff. Two more pods, and then the manned shuttle with its much larger booster stage that gave it a comparatively sedate three G's at liftoff. Parkes himself had taken ten G's twice, once on a centrifuge, once in a combat maneuver when air defenses that weren't supposed to exist at all suddenly went into action. He could manage perfectly well without going through it again.

The last of the busload was boarding—Fallon, a lance-corporal computer tech who'd transferred from two years in the New Frontier Coast Guard. Not very imaginative, but thoroughly reliable for everything he knew and honest enough to admit it when he didn't know.

The month since Group Fourteen went on Alert had been one eighteen-hour day after another. Parkes hadn't had time to sit down with the Network N.C.O.'s and learn all that he needed to know about them, or let them form a clear impression of him. He'd barely had time to sit down at all, as one job after another dragged him back and forth in a continuous furious effort to fill up Fourteen's T.O.&E.

His job was made no easier by the fact that Group First Hatcher had taken as much time off as he could wangle from MacLean, which was enough to force Parkes more often than not to solve problems by private arrangements with Dozer di Leone. Fortunately Hatcher had approval-coded these arrangements every time, otherwise Parkes's job would have become impossible enough to require an appeal to MacLean. As it was, he wrote Hatcher off as a particularly bad case of the last-tour blahs and got on with the work.

He had managed to size up most of the Field Squadron HQ people, from Major Vela on down, and that at least meant he had no unknown enemies right at his back. He'd be eating, sleeping, fighting, and if necessary dying with these people. He had to be able to trust them or at least know which ones not to trust.

So far he hadn't found any real bad actors a Sergeant Major needed to worry about. Vela himself had been a pleasant surprise. He'd learned the difference between Hrothmi and humans, and while he did insist on sandwiching his tactical problems between two ten-kilometer hikes or five-kilometer runs, the tactical problems themselves showed a first-class mind at work. Vela did tend to be rather formal, and his undeniable liking for spit-and-polish had already put Parkes to the expense of two pairs of boots and a new field jacket, but worse could be forgiven in an obviously effective combat leader.

The three rifle companies seemed to have no really dangerous soft spots either, although Parkes had only penciled in some of his conclusions about them. Certainly Vela favored Lieutenant Simmel, but not enough that Simmel felt inclined to try getting rid of some of her recruits. Parkes's sixth sense for that sort of thing also told him that they weren't lovers.

At platoon level Parkes already knew about half the sergeants, including the two who were commanding their platoons in the absence of lieutenants, and didn't anticipate any trouble from that quarter. No trouble that came from poor-quality leadership anyway; the platoons averaged four people short even now on the day of shipping out. In a prolonged peacekeeping operation there were always accidents and illnesses, and you often had to rotate people simply to keep them alert and halfway happy. A shortage of thirty-odd people was something Parkes couldn't ignore, but it was also something he'd refused to lose sleep over once he knew there was no helping it.

Another thing he'd refused to lose sleep over was Lieutenant Forbes-Brandon's reputation for holding snap inspections for "unauthorized or illegal equipment." Since the Field Squadron's "underground T.O.&E." included at least one still, four cookers, and enough tentage and furnishings for a small resort, the outcome of such an inspection would be hairy. Parkes recalled Corporal Brezek, the manager of the still, asking him flat out if they should walk soft where the Amazon was concerned and leave the good stuff behind.

Parkes shook his head. "No. We don't know what they have on Bayard or if we're going to be where we could get it if they had it. Use your head about hiding the stuff carefully, and I'll see about laying down a smoke screen and a few diversions."

"Can do, Sergeant Major."

Parkes wondered afterward if he'd said that just because he'd be damned if he'd let the Amazon intimidate him or let anyone else suspect that she'd done so. Certainly he was sticking his neck out far enough so that she'd have an easy chop at it if she wanted one, and to oblige people half of whom he didn't know. One of them could easily have some reason to want to hang him.

But if you started playing the percentages with loyalty, you might just as well hang yourself. That was one unwritten rule that Parkes had learned in twenty-two years was sheathed in R.T.F. armor.

The shuttle on its launcher was looming ahead now, with an elevator car already on its way down from the entry hatch to meet the hoverbus. Parkes slid out of the cupola and had his boarding bag in hand by the time the weapons carrier slid to a stop beside the bus.

The blast shutters over the cockpit of the booster were already closed, but the intakes to the ramjets in the wing roots were changing shape as the pilots finished testing them. The shrouds were gone from both the booster's cavernous firing chamber and the orbiter's three comparatively dainty nozzles, although a bluesuit was still peering up one of the nozzles as if she expected to find the Azteca Expedition in it.

Parkes stepped out of the carrier into a wind that plastered his field jacket and trousers against his limbs and blew dust into his eyes. Squinting upward, he saw that the wind was also tearing holes in the cloud cover. Something flashed across one of the patches of blue sky — a drone cargo pod returning from orbit, probably after delivering its load to the *Ark Royal*. He shouldered his bag and walked toward the elevator.

How many times had he walked toward elevators that would be the first stage of a journey into space? Parkes realized that he'd actually lost count. Not less than thirty times and probably not more than thirty-five was as close as he could come.

Maybe he should start keeping a diary, like that creative-writing teacher he'd met on Zauberberg. He didn't take seriously her notion that such a diary might be material for a novel, even if she had said, "You have a way of describing people that suggest you might have a real talent for characterization." He'd never told Denise that, of course; they'd been having too much non-literary fun to risk spoiling what they both knew would be a brief time together with quarrels over trivialities.

Still, a diary might be the basis for a few articles in *Peace Forcer*, particularly the Leadership column. It would also help on those cold nights by a warm fire in his old age, when he'd otherwise have nothing but fading memories to tell him of what he'd been proud to do and whom he'd been proud to serve with.

Of course diaries were also sufficiently close to the borders of regulations that you needed to take a few security precautions against your own superiors as well as against outright enemies, social, political, or military. For some of those precautions you also needed help, and Parkes had a hunch that he'd just about used up all the favors anybody owed him to do his share of getting Group Fourteen mission-ready. He filed the question of a diary under his mental Priority Twelve and stepped into the elevator.

As he stepped out of it on to the bridge to the orbiter's main batch, the cargo pod slipped out of the clouds almost directly overhead. He watched it bank to the left as Ground Control adjusted the shrouds of the Rogallo-wing parachute to bring it on to a more precise course for the runway. The landing skids were deploying as Parkes ducked through the hatch.

Inside, most of the thirty-six seats were already filled. Parkes took one toward the rear, passing Forbes-Brandon on the way. The Amazon gave him a polite smile and returned her gaze to the handbook in her lap. If she was planning anything by way of snap inspections or other officer-type troublemaking, she was a good enough actress not to give Parkes any clues. Or maybe she'd had some planned, discovered Parkes's own precautions, and retreated to regroup and advance along a different axis?

Parkes shoved his bag into the netting under the seat in front and started pulling his harness into place. He'd just finished when the cabin speaker flashed its telltale, then came alive.

"Your attention please, ladies and gentlemen. This is your pilot, Lieutenant Tham. Please fasten your safety harnesses and place all loose items in the holdnets. We will be receiving launch clearance as soon as the pod some of you may have seen coming in is clear of the runway.

"We will reach a maximum acceleration of three point two gravities during our launch. After burnout we will be under zero-G conditions for approximately one hour and fifty minutes. Our estimated time of rendezvous with *Ark Royal* will be 1240. Docking and debarkation will take not more than thirty additional minutes."

Parkes relaxed. He wondered not quite idly if Forbes-Brandon was going to be spacesick. He'd seen her at the Departure Orbit Grille, getting outside of a colossal breakfast that he wouldn't have tackled unless he'd fasted for a day beforehand. He found himself hoping that she wouldn't be.

He didn't expect that he would ever like the Amazon particularly well, but he didn't need to do so. He did need to respect her, which he had begun to do. It would be easier to go on doing so if she didn't turn out to have a grounder's stomach.

Besides, as the senior N.C.O. aboard, he was at the head of the line for boss of the cleanup party if anybody made one necessary.

The telltale beeped again.

"Attention, please. We have been cleared for launching."

The deck began tilting upward as the launcher swung the shuttle toward the vertical. The gimbaled seats swung, too, until Parkes was lying on his back, spine and buttocks sunk deep into the padding, ready for the acceleration.

Crunnnnggggg! They'd unlocked from the launcher tower. It would now be rolling away, leaving them poised vertically over the blast pit.

"Attention, please. We are entering the final countdown. Thirty seconds to ignition. Twenty. Ten, nine, eight, seven, six, five, four— lasers activated—one—"

Zero.

The mirror-focused beams of twelve lasers tore upward into the hydrogen pouring down into the main combustion chamber of the booster. The hydrogen boiled, then turned incandescent, just short of plasma—and on its thrust the shuttle rose.

Parkes didn't need Tham's announcement, "We have liftoff," to know that he was on his way back into space.

CHAPTER 6

"Your attention, please. All hangar personnel to your launching stations. All unauthorized personnel, please clear the hangar area."

The petty officer repeated the announcement twice, then shut off the loudspeaker console and floated up to where Parkes hung with one leg hooked around a stanchion. "That includes you, Sergeant Major. Sorry. And you too, Lieutenant."

Parkes looked around to see who was the object of the second request and saw the Amazon clipped to another stanchion by her belt, to have all four limbs free. She was nearly at a 180-degree angle to Parkes, and bobbing slightly in the air currents inside the hangar. At fifty meters long and thirty in diameter, it was one of the few compartments in the *Ark Royal* large enough to generate respectable ones without help from the ventilation system.

Parkes unhooked his leg and Forbes-Brandon her belt. Together they pushed off toward the light-coded entrance to the Axial Passage. Parkes pushed off cautiously, but Forbes-Brandon kicked off like a high jumper. Parkes wondered if he'd just seen her finally make another recruit's mistake; at that speed she'd be lucky not to sprain something stopping herself.

Halfway down the hangar Forbes-Brandon curled herself neatly into a ball, like a cat on a cold day. Then she uncoiled from the ball like the same cat leaping, coming out feet first. She still seemed on a collision course with a container of spares lashed to the deck. Parkes was just about to shout a warning when she curled herself into a ball again. She sailed past the container with a good twenty centimeters to spare.

She reached the far end of the hangar feet first, legs slightly bent. Parkes wasn't surprised to see her bounce back, then flip and bounce off two more surfaces in rapid succession, killing her velocity until she could touch down by the hatch again as lightly as a snowflake. He was pleasantly surprised to note that when he reached the hatch she was trying to hide a triumphant smile.

Parkes appreciated the courtesy. He also appreciated that he'd just seen a display of near-professional zero-g gymnastics. Did the lieutenant ever visit the Zero-G Gymnasium at the O'Neil Homes? The thought was idle, and so was Parkes's fleeting vision of Forbes-Brandon in the usual clothing for zero-g gymnastics, which was either very little or nothing at all. Now it was his turn to hide a smile as he floated into the Axial Passage and placed feet and hands into a set of stirrups on the personnel hoist.

Sixty meters aft along the passage, Forbes-Brandon vanished to one side, toward wardroom country. Another thirty meters, and Parkes passed a working party of two Navy hands and a Support Squadron lance corporal, fiddling with the screen that divided the personnel hoist from the cargo hoist. Parkes couldn't see anything wrong with the screen himself, but was willing to give the Navy the benefit of the doubt—at least when they were running a tight ship like *Ark Royal*.

Twenty meters farther on came the side passage marked EMBARKED PEACE FORCE N.C.O.'S. Parkes swung himself into it and pulled himself hand over hand up the ladder until he had a clear jump to his designated cabin.

Parkes found himself with a two-bunk cabin to himself, after expecting to be cabin mates with Group First Hatcher. This didn't exactly break his heart. You could always learn a lot about your cabin mates in the thirty or forty days a Peace Cruiser took to reach the average mission planet, if there was anything to learn. With Hatcher, being two years from retirement had apparently turned his soul as well as his hair gray. A month cheek-by-jowl with him would have tried the serenity of a Zen master.

Parkes's boarding bag, footlocker, and issue gear were already stowed. He unpacked what he would need aboard ship and restowed it in the ready-use locker, then inspected the cabin. Even after several centuries of space travel, bunks and fixtures designed to function equally well under zero-g, acceleration, or spin, inevitably had a lot of moving parts, and moving parts were the Achilles heel of machinery.

Not that Parkes expected to find anything wrong. The cabin had the indescribable but unmistakable quality that came with being aboard a well-run, well-maintained ship, and so had everything else Parkes saw from the moment he floated out of the shuttle hatch into the hangar. It still did no harm to remind the Navy that some of the Peace Forcers had enough ship time to be able to detect faulty maintenance or equipment. Just as it probably didn't hurt Group Fourteen to know that the Amazon could not only stand a bridge watch aboard the *Ark Royal* but keep up with the ground-pounders on a field exercise with a full pack and personal weapons and armor.

The second bunk was fully deployed, but inside its frame was lashed a net full of miscellaneous small stores. Somebody was following Supply Officer's Rule No. 2: "There is always more stowage than you thought there was."

Parkes checked to see if that someone also knew how to choose and lash a net. To be sure, it was aboard a light cruiser accelerating at five g's that the net came loose and the can of figs cracked Nate Rehnquist's skull, but still...

It was only after he'd finished the inspection that Parkes noticed the non-regulation box stowed inside the net, wrapped in silver paper with a handwritten note pasted to one end. He undid the nearer end of the net, fished out the box, and read the note.

Dear Parkes,
Have a few on me, and sure, let's get together on the way to Bayard. Do you play chess?
Rufus Garron, Chief Warrant Machinist

Inside the silver paper was a bottle of Armagnac, complete with a squeeze bulb for zero-g drinking. Parkes stowed the bottle in his ready-use locker. He preferred to drink brandy under acceleration or spin, when you could use a conventional glass and enjoy the bouquet.

Still, it was pleasant to see that at least one slice of the bread he'd cast on the waters had floated back. If the currents were right, it might not be the last one.

Warrant Officer Garron was the Chief of the Ship aboard *Ark Royal*, officially the senior enlisted man, unofficially the spokesman for the enlisted men in any situation where spokesmen rather than channels or regulations were called for, or at least were needed to supplement them. He could be a good friend or a dangerous enemy to an embarked P.F. Group, particularly its senior N.C.O.'s.

Even less officially but possibly almost as important, Garron had been Forbes-Brandon's division petty officer during her first cruise as a sub-lieutenant. He'd known her at a particularly important point for judging what kind of an officer she'd make, and apparently they'd struck the right note. Parkes now understood Forbes-Brandon's smile when she'd learned Group Fourteen would be aboard *Ark Royal*. It would be a meeting of old shipmates or even friends, and Parkes suspected that she didn't have all that many.

Garron might be able to confirm that and a lot of other suspicions if he wanted to. If he didn't, Parkes wasn't going to push. The bread he'd cast on the waters had taken the form of extra allowances and guest privileges for Garron and *Ark Royal*'s own Network, out of the Group's resources. That should at least have given him Garron's ear in case Forbes-Brandon decided to be sticky over inspections or anything else that needed Garron's cooperation. He didn't really need any more to do his job. Knowing a little more about the Amazon might help a bit, but not enough to make it worth trying to squeeze a probably un-squeezable man.

Besides, Forbes-Brandon deserved her privacy, unless she turned out to be one of those commissioned turkeys a Sergeant Major had to treat as natural enemies. Anyone in her position—young, gifted, and widely suspected of being ambitious for at least two stars—was already living in a sensor-saturated observation tank. Her being a memorably attractive woman wouldn't help either. Parkes wasn't going to join the battalion of gawkers around the observation tank unless he absolutely had to.

That thought struck him as sufficiently interesting to deserve a brandy, and never mind the bouquet. Only one, because he was still technically on duty until Captain Cooper called all hands to departure stations, and he might actually be needed to round up a few PFers the Navy couldn't or wouldn't handle. However, nobody was ever unfit for duty after one brandy, and that might be enough to help him understand where this unexpectedly strong desire to guard the Amazon's privacy came from...

One brandy didn't tell Parkes anything he didn't know already: that he'd had only three hours of sleep last night; that forty-one-years old wasn't nineteen when it came to going short of sleep; that he shouldn't make a habit of that even if he only wanted to avoid a thumbs-down Efficiency Report, never mind plumb the depths—erase and correct, puzzle out the motivations—of blond female naval officers.

He put the brandy away, cut the cabin video off the master circuit, and slipped in a tape of the history of Bayard. The hypno material had included the basics, but Parkes had known a number of people who got themselves killed because they violated some local custom or taboo not covered in the basics.

He'd just reached a long-winded explanation of why the planet's leading dictatorship called itself the Fourth Empire instead of the Third, when the override light came on above the screen. The thin, dark face of a Navy commander followed on the screen.

"Your attention, please. We will be calling all hands to stations for departure in approximately ten minutes.

"For our embarked Peace Forces comrades, I am Commander Marie Dubignon, the Executive Officer. On behalf of Captain Cooper and our crew I say welcome aboard, and look forward to a long and agreeable association. All Peace Force personnel who are not in their quarters should return there now. Dinner will be served at 0200 ship time, 1630 New Frontier time."

The announcement was repeated three times as a recording, then the screen went blank. The loudspeaker stayed live, counting off the minutes and occasionally paging some member of the ship's crew. Parkes hooked his emergency gear to the head of his bunk but otherwise stayed ready to move.

When the count had reached one minute he strapped himself down on the bunk and unlocked it so that it would swing freely under acceleration. Either everybody in the Group had been too well-behaved to need a big stick, or else the N.C.O.'s on the spot had gambled that they were big enough and won their gamble. Parkes was inclined to both suspect and hope it was the second. There was always somebody too new to space not to let curiosity and wonder carry them into unauthorized spaces, but good platoon sergeants and squad leaders should be able to handle them without invoking the lawful majesty of the Field First, let alone an officer.

The announcement, "All hands to stations for departure," came without any calls for Parkes. He finished strapping himself in and slowed his breathing. The screen showed a brief view of the bridge, with the key people—captain, navigator, talker, sensor monitor, helmsman—already in their cocoon-equipped seats. The rest of the bridge crew, who could afford to leave their seats to get emergency gear, were hurrying to their posts. On a bridge screen Parkes saw a light tug docking with a cluster of empty pods.

The bridge vanished, and in its place was a view transmitted from Depot Two—a starscape, with *Ark Royal* herself poised against it. Parkes noted that *Ark Royal*'s silver-gray hide showed more patches and shadings than her hatches and ports could account for, but that didn't worry him. *Ark* was an old lady, the second oldest of her class still in first-line service. She'd been commissioned in the year Parkes's father graduated from high school. That didn't matter in the vacuum of space, where a ship could last a century or more as long as her vital systems were repaired or replaced as necessary.

Ark had the basic shape of all three major classes of Peace Cruisers, a fat spindle with a flattened equator and cut-off poles. At the equator she was a hundred and fifty meters in diameter, at either end more than fifty, and just under two hundred and fifty meters from bow to stem. Apart from the hangar at the bow and the rockets at the stem, it took a very experienced eye to tell where anything was, particularly since most of the antennae and all the launchers, lasers, and beam projectors had been retracted.

It made matters even worse that the outside of the hangar was covered with cocooned and containerized aircraft for the Group's Transportation Company and nearly the whole aft end of the ship had vanished under two heavy tugs that would boost her out of New Frontier orbit. The tugs were simply collections of fuel tanks attached to docking gear and rocket motors. They could be manned, but for boosting the *Ark* they were probably being remotely controlled from her bridge.

Like every ship of water, air, or space since Neanderthal man discovered that a fallen log would float him across a river, the *Ark Royal* was a compromise. Being designed to act as a troop transport, orbital battle station, base for light spacecraft, and in a pinch space-to-space warship, she and her sisters were more of a compromise than most. One of the places where the compromising pinched was on fuel.

Ark Royal could have made the round trip to Bayard on internal fuel plus a couple of disposable strap-ons. She would have been very short of reserves to change orbit, fight battles, or even rendezvous with her own pre-positioned supplies.

That situation had a distinctly negative index of desirability. It would force *Ark Royal* to either remain in a fixed orbit, by space-war standards a sitting target, or else improvise a new fuel load from some satellite of a gas giant. That made it a toss-up as to whose next of kin would first receive the "We regret to inform you—" message from Peace Force Command, *Ark Royal*'s crew after she was blown out of space or Group Fourteen's people after they were overrun due to lack of mobility and fire support while Ark Royal was six hundred million kilometers away refueling.

The tugs radically improved the whole equation. They would boost *Ark Royal* up to a velocity that would have her ready for her Yariv Jump in twelve days, without using a ton of her own fuel supply.

A faint vibration told Parkes that the tugs had started their fuel pumps. A moment later the traditional getting under way tune "Anchors Aweigh" drowned out any ship's noises and the getting under way lights came on, blue, green, red, and yellow, dancing in their complex pattern all over *Ark Royal*'s hull. Ships of space couldn't fly flags, but they'd worked out satisfactory substitutes with computer-controlled external lighting. Parkes recalled that the various appropriations committees were always grumping about the extra cost of those lights, just as they always grumped about dress uniforms. So far the grumping had stopped there. Please the Wise One it would never go any further, because Parkes had read enough about the usual fate of armed forces that weren't allowed *esprit de corps* and whatever they needed to support it to know how fast he'd hand in his ID deck if the Peace Force ever joined that company of losers.

A blue glow showed aft, around the tugs' engines. It turned into steadily brightening blue flames. Before the flames turned white, Parkes felt the building thrust pressing him into his swinging bunk.

The screen filters had gone on, to protect watching eyes from the glare of hydrogen being heated hotter than the surface of most stars. There were no flames visible anymore, only raw light to match the raw power that was beginning to move a hundred and fifty thousand tons of metal, flesh, and fuel.

Maybe space flight had helped bring about the Collapse War of 2088, as the Populists claimed. Certainly it had given the human species immortality by spreading it first off one planet, then across the stars, to find seventy-five homes instead of one, not to mention proving that humanity wasn't the only Intelligent species in the galaxy. Parkes wasn't prepared to write off the four billion people who died in the Collapse War and the Century of Chaos as a necessary price for the stars, but they could have also died from a solar flare, a crashing asteroid, an Ice Age, or the Wise One knew what, if space hadn't been there.

Also, the War had taught a long-overdue lesson about taking "crisis management" seriously. The Peace Force was the Planetary Union's main weapon in making sure that the lesson stayed learned, and that the people who would destroy half the world in order to rule over the rest were stopped while they were still small enough to stop easily. That there were still people like the Game Master was enough to give Parkes an easy conscience about drawing his salary.

That thought deserved another brandy, but not now. When the acceleration reached one g, he would unstrap, make the rounds of the troop quarters, and deal with the inevitable minor problems. By the time he'd finished handling those or reporting to the relevant officers the ones he couldn't handle, the mess would be open for dinner. Then he'd have the brandy, and after that a little sleep he'd missed last night.

CHAPTER 7

Mission Date/Time: 17.4.22.

Chief Warrant Machinist Rufus Garron looked at the magnetic chess board.

"Mate in four, I think."

Parkes looked at where Garron had placed the knight. He had to look twice, as usual, when Garron played black. Black pieces were almost perfectly camouflaged against his hand.

"So do I, but let's play it out just to see what happens."

What happened confirmed Parkes's suspicions that Garron was a very good but thoroughly orthodox player. Parkes decided to try an unorthodox or even berserker approach a few games down the road. It could work in unarmed combat, as four broken ribs had once taught him, and chess had just enough in common with unarmed combat to make the experiment worthwhile.

The bottle of Armagnac lasted them through two more games. Parkes managed a draw in the second by a headlong offensive that followed no pattern and seemed careless of losses. He decided that a draw against a former runner-up for Fleet Champion was enough laurels to rest on.

"Satisfied that I do play chess?"

"Sure," said Garron without taking his eyes off the screen where he was playing back the last game. He finished the playback, then cocked his head to one side as he looked at Parkes.

"Nobody's caught on to my weak spot that fast since the

Amazon."

"When was that?"

Garron gave Parkes a don't-pretend-you're-not-fishing look, then shrugged. "When I was her division P.O. aboard the *Bellerophon*. Surprised the hell out of me, too, her playing that well. I wonder if that helped with Newton."

"Newton? The Vice-Chief. He gave her one of the Superintendent's Discretionary Appointments when he was top at the War Academy."

Parkes sucked in his lower lip. Garron frowned. "You're thinking pretty loud, First."

"Was I? Then maybe you could tell me what I was thinking?"

"The same thing everybody's thought after meeting the Cat the last five years. Not that I blame them. I'd have thought it myself, meeting her two years after she left Old Billy, if I hadn't known her before. Newton likes plenty to get hold of, and the Cat wasn't hardly there at all when she was a sub. Oh, she was tall enough, but she damned near had to stand sideways to cast a shadow. That's why we called her the Cat—she looked like she'd just come in off the street. Ready to claw anybody who tried to pet her, too."

Apparently Forbes-Brandon had not always been so admirably mammalian. As to the insight into Vice-Admiral Newton's preferences in bed partners, Parkes was about to file it under Unproven and Irrelevant until he remembered that Newton had risen from the ranks and was a near-contemporary of Garron. Was one of Garron's unofficial assignments keeping an eye on Forbes-Brandon for Newton?

Since Parkes had no designs on the Amazon that anybody could legitimately object to, he mildly resented Garron's oblique warning. Violating Article Forty-six was always a hairy proposition, even with seniority, discretion, no damage, and no neglect of duty or mission to wave in the face of official snooping. On an actual mission with a new Group, only a bigger fool than Parkes hoped he was capable of being over any woman wouldn't keep his pants on.

Or maybe, Garron suspected the Amazon of—call them impulses? That seemed even less likely, although a Sergeant Major with twenty-two years in might actually have less trouble from a Forty-six investigation than a junior officer who'd been in pigtails when the

Sergeant Major signed on. (Somehow pigtails were part of his image of Forbes-Brandon as a girl. The rest of her looks might be a recent acquisition, but that mane of heavy blond hair had to go back a long way.)

"That's one quality I don't think she's lost," said Parkes. "Not that it bothers me much. She knows her business and as long as she keeps her nose out of mine—"

"You're in a hell of a position to talk about noses," said Garron.

"It grew on me. Besides, it has one advantage. I can always use my handkerchief for a poncho."

Garron looked at the bottle and seemed to take it as a personal insult that it was empty. "If you want another game, I can see about wangling another one of these."

Parkes shook his head. "I have to see a woman about a doghouse. Specifically, the one she'll be in if she hangs up our data on Bayard's civilian vehicles any longer."

"I won't promise to build a fire under Gabreski," said Garron slowly. "But I'll see about lighting a match. Also, I'll see if there's anybody with ground-vehicle experience we can spare for the ground party."

"Fair enough. Although don't send anybody until I can square it with Dozer and Guslenko."

"Dozer won't kick. She was First to a heavy construction outfit on Timur when I was ground party chief. Guslenko I don't know."

"Let's just say that he's an artist with a temperament to match. Don't imply that he needs help unless you want the people you send around used up a trifle."

"So that's why he's only a buck sergeant?"

"Yeah." It was also why the Vehicle Maintenance Depot at Fort Crerar had been so willing to transfer Guslenko to Group Fourteen. By and large, Parkes didn't mind. He'd promised Dozer and Shapely of Transportation Company an extra N.C.O. for ground-vehicle maintenance in return for their help in hiding non-regulation Field Squadron equipment. Thanks to Guslenko, he'd been able to keep that promise fairly cheaply. As for the man's temperament, that would be Dozer's headache. If she couldn't keep Guslenko on a

69

straight course, nobody could.

Parkes also knew that Garron himself had once been in charge of a ground-vehicle maintenance depot at Nimitz Base on Alliance Two. Maybe he'd like to come groundside and take a hand with Fourteen's wheels and fans? He probably would, but he wouldn't be free to go unless *Ark* was in no danger of having to space out. It would be at least a week before they were in radio contact with Bayard, and they wouldn't know either the starside on the groundside situation for a while after that.

Parkes decided that promising something he couldn't guarantee to deliver would look too much like an outright bribe. That would spoil what had so far been a fair and pleasant swapping of information and favors. It also might get Garron suspecting Parkes of something—maybe not of wanting to play Don't Get Caught with the Amazon, but of wanting his goodwill a little too badly. Garron was about the last man aboard the *Ark Royal* Parkes could afford to have suspecting him of that.

Mission Date/Time: 17.5.30.

Garron must have landed on the Intelligence chief both fast and hard. The complete dossier on Bayard's ground-vehicle resources was ready for printing when Parkes arrived.

"Not much that's really up-to-date, I'm afraid. Bayard isn't one of those planets that likes to make our job easy." The chief ran a fingernail down between two of her lower front teeth. "My guess is that on the west coast of Nouvelle Bretagne it's going to be all local stuff and most of it old."

Parkes refrained from reminding the chief that he knew some economics, too, probably more than anybody whose major contact with non-Union planets was probably their spaceport bars. He also refrained from bolting with the printout to Dozer's cabin and sat down to skim it in the Intelligence office.

A wide-awake hangover came on before he'd finished it, but the brandy had been worth it, to sit down and talk with Garron, and learn (among other useful things) that the Chief could not only promise but produce.

* * *

Mission Date/Time 20.6.12.

First radio contact with Bayard. *Ark Royal*'s ETA in parking orbit 30.17.20.

Mission Date/Time: 24.18.30.

Summary court-martial on two crew chiefs in Transportation Company. Charge: "That they did assault another person in Peace Force service, to the bodily harm of that person and the prejudice of the good order and discipline of the Force."

Dozer was challenged as the N.C.O. member of the Court, so Parkes wound up with the job, for the single morning the dreary affair lasted. It had a familiar ring to anyone who knew the fanatical loyalty Captain Dallin drew from her aviation people.

The victim was a communications specialist who'd been watching Dallin burrowing into the engine pod of one of her vertis. He'd muttered something to the effect that "too bad those things didn't have dildoes, or she could marry one." He'd muttered loud enough for the two crew chiefs to overhear.

They'd promptly broken his nose and loosened two of his teeth before they were reduced to order.

Since the crew chiefs hadn't resisted arrest and even the Navy embers of the Court admitted considerable provocation, the sentences were limited to three months' restriction and one month's loss of pay plus an E.R. downcheck for the quarter. The Court further recommended that the communications specialist be charged with incitement to riot and abusive language to the prejudice of good order and discipline, and he was so charged.

"Thank the Wise One and anybody else who's listening that I won't have to sit on that one," said Parkes afterward in Dozer's cabin. Court-martials always left a bad taste in his mouth that even Dozer's private-stock *grappa* couldn't wash out.

"If you're praying, add a prayer that Air Corps gives Dallin a medical waiver and a transfer to a combat squadron," said Dozer.

"She's got a medical downcheck? I thought she'd rubbed

somebody the wrong way in A.C. HQ and they were erasing her applications as fast as they came in."

"Her eyesight is just under the limit. Nothing I'd worry about, considering that she'd be worth three of those keen-eyed little boys and girls they're putting in cockpits these days. Besides, even if she wrecked up a couple of planes, it'd be cheaper than the court-martials and medical bills."

"Her crew chiefs would make just as much trouble if she was flying combat."

"Yeah, but it wouldn't be where we had to deal with it."

Mission Date/Time: 28.5.45.

Rendezvous with pre-positioned Standard Supply Load One, aboard P.F.T. *Ivanhoe*.

Parkes listened to the rendezvous as it came over the intercom in the Petty Officer's Mess, where he was having a large and early breakfast after being up late the night before. Dr. Laughton's unloading tables for the Medical Company had been so full of errors that Parkes and Dozer had to sit up with the Chief Nurse and covertly produce a corrected set. As far as Parkes was concerned, Laughton didn't have too many more bites of that sort before she was in serious trouble, however good a doctor she might be.

"*Ivanhoe*, we have a visual on your burn. Looks nominal."

"*Ark Royal*, that's what our instruments say. Welcome to the Bayard system."

A momentary burst of static, probably artificial to drown out a reprimand on radio discipline. It was one of Cooper's fetishes, Parkes knew, and only two days from Bayard they could be picked up by ground-based receivers possibly in unfriendly hands.

He still had more than a little sympathy with the woman at the *Ivanhoe*'s radio. She and her thirty shipmates must have had a long, dreary time of it, waiting in radio silence at the rendezvous for over a month, with Bayard showing a disk to the naked eye but as unapproachable as if it had been in another galaxy.

If Bayard had been a planet with an established Peace Force garrison, *Ark Royal* would have either come alone or escorted her own supplies. If Bayard had been an un-garrisoned but "Secure" system, with at least one Peace Force ship already there, *Ivanhoe* wouldn't have come this far. She'd have come out of Yariv Drive, sent her cargo pods into orbit around Bayard under automatic pilot, and gone home again.

As it was, *Ivanhoe* had to be in the Bayard system before the *Ark Royal* arrived because her cargo might be needed immediately. She had to be close enough to the planet for easy rendezvous. She also had to be out far enough to be neither detected nor attacked without the kind of space weaponry Intelligence said the "enemy" here couldn't have.

So *Ivanhoe* and her people must have spent more than a month of prime-grade tedium, hoping that Intelligence was right or if they were wrong that *Ark Royal* would show up before the attack came in. It was no wonder that the radio operator sounded almost hysterically grateful to have someone to talk to.

After a few more official exchanges the screen came on, showing *Ivanhoe* magnified until she filled the whole starscape. The transport looked rather as if a smaller version of *Ark Royal* had been sliced in two like a bagel and the two slices separated by two hundred meters of skeletal framework. Most of the framework was invisible behind the cargo pods, and the stem was almost completely hidden by fuel tanks to just forward of the rocket nozzles. *Ivanhoe* was even less likely to be called beautiful than *Ark Royal*, but she was just as functional for her designed purpose, hauling three months' supplies for a Peace Force Company Group to any human-inhabited planet,

Ivanhoe was moving slightly on the screen. More blue flame flared aft, a two-second burn for a minor adjustment in relative velocity, then she was motionless relative to *Ark Royal*. The fact that both ships were plunging through space at rather more than sixty kilometers a second was irrelevant; they would arrive together at the same destination,, the point for their orbital Insertion Burn around Bayard.

Parkes sucked in the last mouthful of egg and raised his bulb of coffee at the screen in silent greeting. Considering how little Group Fourteen could have done without *Ivanhoe*'s cargo, it wasn't only her crew who had reason to be relieved at the successful rendezvous.

However, Parkes would be damned if he'd admit that to any Navy people.

Mission Date/Time: 30.15.00.

"All hands to stations for Bayard Orbital Insertion."

Parkes was already at as much of a station as he had for the maneuver, the On-Board Field Squadron HQ. Nothing and nobody was giving him headaches like the court martial or Dr. Laughton, but the usual half-dozen minor emergencies had surfaced at the last minute, demanding attention if they weren't going to turn into major ones. Not to mention that Hatcher had suddenly come to life and was riding Parkes's tail, to get all personnel records in order before anyone climbed aboard a shuttle for the ride down to Bayard.

It would be unjust to Hatcher to say that he didn't care who got killed as long as their records were in order, but additional aggravation at a time like this had been known to overcome Parkes's normally well-developed sense of justice.

So he and the Field Squadron clerk worked through thirty-nine personnel-record discrepancies while *Ark Royal* launched three communications and satellites into synchronous orbits, flipped end for end, and gently pushed her people into their seats with a half-g braking burn.

The clerk brought coffee and sandwiches, and they ate as the intercom announced the launching of *Ark Royal*'s fighters. The four two-man lifting bodies would not be accelerating to their positions ahead of the ship and clear of her own weapons' fields of fire. Their wings would still be retracted but their missiles would be armed, ready to ride beams or home themselves against targets that everybody devoutly hoped wouldn't show up. Their radars would also act as *Ark Royal*'s eyes while her engines were firing and their plasma was wiping out her own sensors.

Opposition in space now would mean that the Game Master—or somebody—took Bayard much more seriously than Intelligence had believed. Peace Force Command would respond appropriately, of course, but such a response would most likely be too late for *Ark Royal*, *Ivanhoe*, and Group Fourteen.

Parkes reflected that one of the occupational hazards of the infantryman's life was dying to prove that Intelligence had lived down to its reputation.

Parkes drank a second bulb of coffee as the air scrubbers cleaned out the odd crumb and the odor of pressed turkey and the fighters tested their engines. For a strictly space-to-space mission, they would be carrying strap-on fuel tanks. Parkes remembered his sister Louise telling of a mission that had started out strictly space-to-space but suddenly turned out to require a landing after the Bifrost Confederacy staged their suicidal attack on Peace Cruiser *Suffren*.

"We were all set up for reentry and Lieutenant Kube punched the jettison switch. No jettison. Again. Same non-result. At this point, guess who had the job of EVAing with a cutting torch and trying to cut the tank loose, flush with our hull, before we reentered and tumbled or burned through?

"At least I knew there was enough fuel in the tank that I might set it off with the torch. Then I'd be dead so fast I wouldn't have time to know it, instead of burning up slow and nasty."

Louise cut the tank loose and got back inside the fighter in time to ride it down to a safe landing. The matter of Kube's error in judgment was settled when the landing turned out to be far enough outside Peace Force lines to leave Kube and his systems operator facing a twenty-kilometer hike. Louise Parkes still wore on her belt a fragment of a Confederate mortar shell dug out of her thigh. The same shell had also removed a fatally large portion of Kube's anatomy.

How long had it been since he'd heard from Louise? If he'd gone home while he was on post-school leave—but no point in going over that again. Also, if Louise had written, his step- mother might not have let him know what she'd said, let alone shown him the letter. He'd gone through two fights like that already, and given a choice he'd seriously consider going through the whole Bifrost campaign again.

One by one, every object picked up by *Ark Royal*'s or the fighters' radars was scanned and interrogated. Every one of them must have passed their interrogation, because Parkes never heard the "Prepare to launch missiles," let alone the "Launch!"

Most of what was being picked up must be orbiting junk or Bayard's own rudimentary satellite network. Parkes would be happiest with a nice, dull approach to Bayard, free of dangers that an infantryman had to just sit and swallow because there was no cover or concealment in space. He remembered one of the few survivors of *Suffren*'s Embarked Group describing the final order from the bridge— to salvo all remaining missiles in active-homing mode, so that *Suffren* could at least take some of her killers with her. She had, too, but there still were eight hundred new Peace Force names written up on the Memorial Way after the fight was done.

Finally Parkes heard the reading off of the identified ships in orbit around Bayard. There were four freighters, a ship with a long classification Parkes didn't catch but which sounded like something to do with asteroid mining, and an immigrant transport listed as from Akbar.

Parkes wondered if the transport was bringing people in or taking them out. From what he'd heard of Akbar, it was as hot and dry as Bayard was cold and wet, and the air was thin and full of garbage, On the other hand, it wasn't divided among several governments, one of them on the edge of civil war and another run by a dismal band of tyrannical clowns. Akbar's government was amiably corrupt, but it ruled the whole planet with a light hand.

Then a final bum, three minutes at something like two-thirds of one-g, and—

"Bayard Orbital Insertion completed."

Parkes looked at the screen. It showed what looked like an endless expanse of gray-blue ocean with the end of a chain of islands peeping out from under a storm front. That would put them somewhere over Golfe du Sud and heading northwest over their intended area of operations.

Parkes waited until the gentle swiveling of his chair and a new sensation of weight told him that Captain Cooper had put spin on the ship. *Ark Royal* had now converted herself from a starship into a space station, and would maintain a half-g for her crew and the few PFers left on board until either the mission was completed or she had to maneuver to provide fire support to the people on the ground.

Parkes stood up. His job now consisted mostly of helping break up Field Squadron into working parties to help Support Squadron and *Ark*'s crew disembark the Group, as well as handling the inevitable minor crises that cropped up during the disembarkation. He could easily spare an hour to check his field gear, weapons, and dress uniform, although he probably wouldn't be needing the greens.

Or would he? If the mission lasted long enough that the PFers would be making leave in Havre des Dames, something besides field kits might be needed. Not to mention that it would at least keep them from being mistaken for Navy people or the local Mobile Guards.

As he left, Parkes took another look at the screen. The storm front seemed to extend all the way over Fourteen's mission area, so for a while they'd be seeing even less than you usually could from four hundred kilometers up. He also made a mental note to raise the question of leave policy with both Vela and MacLean. A dull mission on a dull planet in rancid weather with no leave policy would produce everything from self-induced trench foot to general court-martials inside of two months.

Mission Time/Date: 31:20.50.

A shuttle launch from Havre des Dames, reported destination *Ark Royal*. Outside work to continue.

Mission Time/Date: 32.1.03.

The shuttle matched orbits with *Ark Royal* and *Ivanhoe*, then started pussyfooting her way toward *Ark*, through the miniature globular cluster of pods, containers, and components surrounding both ships. Over the intercom a pleasantly tired Parkes heard Dallin and Dozer cajoling and cursing their E.V.A. crews.

"Don't look at the flare. And don't turn the back on the shuttle either, you (something impolite in Sicilian dialect)!"

"Tupper, Shihano, get on that container! It's drifting too close to the shuttle's path."

The last thing Parkes remembered before he turned out the lights and pulled the blanket up over his head was what sounded like "Prepare for shuttle docking."

CHAPTER 8

Sometime in the middle of the night.

"Sergeant Major. Sergeant Major! Hey, Fruit Merchant!"

"Hunnnhhh..."

"Wake up, Sergeant Major, damn your hide, sir!"

"I'm a-awake."

"And I'm the Force Commander."

"No, you—you're Sergeant Tyndall."

"Right. Dozer sent me to wake you. It's hit the fan."

"It's—" Something in Tyndall's voice told Parkes that this wasn't a practical joke. Dozer was fond of them, but she seldom involved other people in them where they might get caught in the fallout.

Parkes willed blood and breath into his body and clear sight into his eyes. Dozer must have not only sent Tyndall but sent her on such short notice that she'd had no time to dress. She looked like a living invitation to an Article Forty-six and Parkes had a moment of pleasurable temptation.

He let the moment pass, swung his feet to the deck, and put his head between his legs. Tyndall massaged his neck and shoulders until some of the stiffness was out of them. Then he stood up and patted her on the cheek.

"Thanks, Sergeant. If I ever need my neck set, I'll call on you."

"You'll need more than me to cure what they'll do to your

78

neck if you aren't in HQ in ten minutes," said Tyndall. "C.O.'s called a Command Group meeting."

Parkes now badly wished he could believe Tyndall was joking, because a Command Group meeting in the middle of the night always meant something hairy. Or at least something that somebody with enough rank to call the meeting thought was hairy, Parkes corrected himself.

He decided that the return of his cynicism about officers was a sign of being awake enough to attend the meeting. "Did Dozer give you any clues as to what 'it' is?"

"Something about a security leak was all she said."

That told Parkes just enough to let him know that the C.O. wasn't pushing the panic button without reason. Security leaks could be hairy indeed, not only in the direct damage they caused but in what they might imply. MacLean must have decided that a half-asleep Command Group now would be more useful to the mission than a wide-awake one tomorrow morning.

"Okay, Sergeant. Report back to Dozer, 'Mission accomplished.'"

Tyndall saluted, a salute that the low gravity and the incomplete uniform caused to involve parts of her anatomy not regulation for the purpose of saluting.

"Yes, sir."

Major Vela had barely been able to contain himself while MacLean told of the Union agent's breach of security by conducting air reconnaissance of possible Group Areas of Operation. Now he burst out indignantly.

"That son of more fathers than he could count without taking off his shoes betrayed us! A newly promoted *engba* would have known better!"

"As far as I recall, *betrayal* implies intent to aid our enemies or at least do us injury," said MacLean mildly. "We have no evidence of such intent, and I'd rather not make the accusation without evidence."

Vela sighed. "Very well. But you must admit that it was an incredibly stupid thing to do. If our agent had even been *advised* by someone with the slightest military background—"

"He might have ignored the advice and gone right ahead," said Captain Dallin. "Why such a believer in advisers all of a sudden—sir?"

That was closer to insubordination than even the tart-tongued Dallin usually came. It was also treading on thorny ground. Vela had made no bones of his belief that those Hrothtmi nations that allowed only human advisers for their armed forces were wasting their money, and usually wound up wasting their soldiers when the human-commanded forces of their enemies smashed them.

Parkes began to wonder if maybe the meeting was quite such a good idea after all. Dallin looked five years older and her eyes were the same color as her hair. He waited for the thunderbolt from Vela.

Instead, the major shrugged. "That is true enough. But at least there would be some knowledge to hand that he could tap if he had the wits to know that he needed it, if you understand my meaning. As long as the Union agents on backwater planets like this have to be civilians—"

"That will be a lot longer than our mission here on Bayard," said MacLean briskly. "Also, it's not our job to debate Council policy even if we could change it. We're soldiers with another job to do. Dr. Lewis has made that job more difficult. He hasn't made it impossible. Let's see how our plans have to be changed."

Vela appeared to be muttering under his breath something about the Union Council performing unnatural acts with hegoats and corkscrews, but MacLean let it pass. Instead, he rose and turned on the display. From the slithering sound his feet made, he was wearing carpet slippers, and Parkes realized for the first time that he, the Amazon, and Major Vela were the only people in complete regulation uniform. Not only that, but the Amazon didn't seem to have a hair out of place.

It would be a pity if MacLean had forgotten the need to keep up uniform standards, particularly on a mission where the appearance of the troops could make a difference. The troops always took their cue from the Command Group, and if the Command Group got sloppy...

Come on, John, he told himself. *You're just as tired as the rest, except that with you it's showing up in jumping to conclusions instead of not dressing properly. Relax and let MacLean get on with the briefing.*

The display showed a two-hundred-kilometer square around Havre des Dames, with the whole north and northeast quadrants lighted in yellow. "Those are the areas where Lewis had the aerial reconnaissance done. Logical enough, considering that those areas are also closest to organized Rancher-controlled militia units.

"Now, from what Intelligence said, the Ranchers aren't likely to be committing their organized units without the tacit consent of the Nouvelle Bretagne government. That consent isn't going to be forthcoming, as I think our Mediator can confirm."

Goff nodded. "I wouldn't absolutely rule it out, but I would certainly say the possibility was negligible."

"Negligible enough to risk my people against Rancher ambushes before they're organized and deployed?" said Vela. He fixed MacLean and Goff with an over-my-dead-body look.

Goff smiled. "Unlike Dr. Lewis, I won't claim military knowledge I don't possess. All I can say is, from the Ranchers in that area I'd expect arms and supplies to somebody else's recruits. Maybe some vehicles, certainly a blind eye turned to at least a few 'desertions.' How dangerous that could be to us, I leave to the combat leaders to judge. I don't want to get *anybody* killed unnecessarily."

An excellent philosophy, Parkes thought, provided that one had the knowledge to judge when getting people killed might be necessary. Without that knowledge the excellent philosophy became one of those good intentions that could be more dangerous than outright evil.

Forbes-Brandon was turning slightly pink, and her nostrils were flaring elegantly. Parkes decided that the lieutenant still had to learn one of the basic rules for junior officers making suggestions: don't let your seniors know that it annoys you to be ignored.

"I wasn't going to propose that we move into the reconnoitered areas at all," she said in a tone nearly matching the flaring nostrils. Vela's eyebrows rose and she hastily looked down at the display.

"Then propose something else, by all means, but do it quickly," said MacLean, swallowing a yawn. "I don't want to ignore anyone's opinions or suggestions. I also want us to have a course of action chosen before we go back to bed."

The Amazon nodded. "I'm suggesting that we ignore the two compromised quadrants entirely, at least until the Group is fully grounded. We can put our main base to the southeast of Havre des Dames, and make our initial area of operations here in the southern quadrant. I know we haven't scouted the area, but we can drop a pathfinder team somewhere between here and here"—one long finger tapped the display twice— "and the aerial reconnaissance can be done under cover of providing them with air support."

The eagerness in her voice as she said "drop a pathfinder team" left Parkes in no doubt that she intended to lead the team herself. On the whole, Parkes had to admit that he'd heard worse ideas.

"Even if we don't find anything, there are a lot of isolated Rancher communities down there. We'll be demonstrating how quickly we can put down people and firepower. That may cool some hotheads and save us ammunition later."

"What force were you thinking of putting down?" said MacLean.

"Two squads of the HQ security platoon, a Navy G.C.&O. team, and a sensor squad from Communications. Standard pathfinder loads all around."

MacLean looked at the display. "I wouldn't quarrel with that for the demonstration force. But I want to have a full platoon ready to board a shuttle and drop as reinforcements. I also want to have the *Ark* deploy the battle stations, so that you can have full fire support if you need it. Demonstrations are all very well, provided that you're ready to handle them turning into something more on short notice."

MacLean turned to Dallin. "How long will it take you to have three of your vertis loaded as part of our I.G.O.C.? How long after they land will they be ready to retrieve the demonstration team?"

"Twenty-two hours to launch, time from orbit to ground, plus six hours to set up. That's pushing everybody without much sleep..."

MacLean frowned, and Parkes could practically see the mental calculations displayed on his forehead. Treat the demonstration as a combat operation where speed was vital and push everybody without regard to sleep? Or assume that it would be unopposed and just as effective if everybody saved their strength for later, when they might really need it? That was one of those command decisions that MacLean couldn't delegate or even discuss.

"Don't push this time," said MacLean finally. "We can launch the I.G.O.C. pods and the demonstration shuttle at the same time. They should be safe enough with the battle stations and the ready platoon for backup for at least a day."

That was going to mean sending quite a few loads through the battle stations' sensor nets at once. Parkes hoped their on-board computers were properly programmed, otherwise there might be some expensive mistakes. The shuttle would have good I.F.F., plus maneuverability and the ability to drop chaff. The pods would be more vulnerable, and although they'd be unmanned, their loss couldn't be ignored. Parkes had lost friends among the thirteen PFers who'd died on Golgotha because the supplies that might have saved them had been zapped on the way down by one of Avenger's mis-programmed battle stations. Then Parkes noted that Goff was shaking his head. "Yes, Mediator?" said the C.O.

"There's a political factor that should be considered. The proposed area of the demonstration is the most divided of the Rancher areas. It contains many of the real anti-fisherman fanatics, who'd be most likely to have secret paramilitary forces. It's also where any Game Master forces would most likely be operating.

"On the other hand, it's also the home of a Rancher faction that wants to throw in its lot with the Fishermen to promote the prosperity of the Storm Coast. They feel that the C.G.P.O. is dominated by the big Ranchers in the north, beyond the Massif DeGaulle, and isn't responsive to their needs.

"If the fanatics do ambush the demonstration team, they have a chance of winning a victory that could boost their morale and discourage their opponents. On the other hand, if the demonstration comes off all right, it could make them cautious and give their opponents time to organize."

"That wasn't in the Intelligence file," said Maclean dubiously.

"The two factions were," said Goff. "The rest is my own extrapolation from the data."

Another command decision for Maclean: Did Goff know what he was talking about so that his extrapolation was a sound basis for risking the lives of fifteen or twenty PFers? And if he decided that Goff was going beyond a reasonable extrapolation, could the Group carry out its mission if the Mediator got a fit of the sulks?

"Major Vela, Lieutenant Forbes-Brandon. Start planning on the basis of a drop tomorrow afternoon. Unless they're actually waiting within range of your D.Z., the worst they can do is force an undignified retreat to a point where you can ambush them. Mediator, I appreciate your concern, but it seems to me that not behaving as if we're afraid of what the local hotheads might have cooked up will have the best results politically."

Parkes raised a hand. "Sir, with the major's and the lieutenant's permission, I'd like to accompany the drop. I can command the security squads and familiarize myself with field conditions on Bayard at the same time."

Vela's eyebrows twitched but didn't rise. The Amazon's grin disintegrated into a look of polite surprise. Parkes grinned back at her as he saw Maclean nodding. He could hardly admit his real reasons for making the drop: to fight boredom and see how Lieutenant Katherine Forbes-Brandon would shape up as a field leader.

CHAPTER 9

"We're about to turn on to our course for the D.Z., people. If you haven't made your final equipment check, make it now."

Pfc. Hagood made a rude gesture at the overhead speaker but started checking his gear anyway. Parkes looked around the shuttle cabin to make sure everyone was doing the same, then started his own check.

From the skin out, it was socks and underwear, field pants and shirt, boots, protective battledress and helmet (with built-in gas mask, face plate, two-way radio, and heads-up display for targeting, communications, and chute status).

Field jacket over the battledress, with webbing equipment over that and on the back of the webbing a pack with spare socks, survival rations, collapsible canteen with purification and patching kits, medkit, and poncho. On the chest rifle with multi-sensor scope and grenade launcher, four extra magazines (total ammo load, 150 caseless 6.5mm rounds) and six grenades. On the belt, personal minicomp, fighting knife, and the collapsible stove for the demo team HQ. Over everything else, parachute harness with main and reserve chutes.

Total weight, 31kg. Not quite the optimum one-third of Parkes's body weight of 80kg, but not bad compared to what some infantrymen had jumped or slogged in. He remembered his first jump instructor describing twentieth-century paratroopers jumping sometimes in nearly their own weight of gear.

"What happened if they landed in water?" Parkes had been

young enough to ask.

"They usually drowned," was the reply he'd never forgot. Anyway, five kg of the weight was the chutes and the harness he'd be discarding, and another five was the battle dress. The team could have jumped without it, but the weight of the dress was a lot less than the weight of a teammate wounded or dead because of some hunting-rifle round that the dress could have stopped.

As for the rest, Peace Force had opted for relying on their ability to resupply their ground parties before they ran short, rather than load them up until they'd be too exhausted to use what they had effectively. It was a gamble, and every so often it was lost and the PFers on the spot paid the price.

The rest of the time the Peace Force Field trooper had the knowledge that he was the most heavily armed and least-overloaded infantryman in history.

"Sound off as you complete your checks," Parkes shouted. He heard Forbes-Brandon echo him for the Navy people and Sergeant Dalmas for the com section. Then the overhead spoke again.

"Coming up on two minutes to the drop. Stand clear of the after hatch. First man into the harness when the hatch is opened."

Corporal Dietsch stood up as the hatch in the after bulkhead of the cabin opened, showing the eight-foot-square tailway, gray insulated sides running back to the still-closed tail hatch. The stirrups and handgrips of the drop harness were hanging in the hatchway; Dietsch put hands and feet in place and twisted a crick out of his neck.

The rest of the team stood up and fell in behind Dietsch. Parkes's place at the tail of the first security section left him just ahead of the Amazon, who was followed by the other security squad, the Navy people, and the com team.

"One minute to the drop. Altitude two thousand meters, air speed four hundred kph. Visibility six km, with scattered low clouds. Ground wind negligible. I'd wish you people luck if I thought you needed it. Go and scare the pee out of the Ranchers!"

Parkes swallowed. This was the second-longest minute of any military operation. The only longer minute was when you were waiting to be pod-dropped from orbit, and a PFer might serve a full twenty years without that happening. Parkes's three orbital drops made him a scarred veteran of that particularly demanding way of getting from space to the ground.

"Thirty seconds. After hatch opened. Harness armed."

Suddenly the tail hatch was splitting into four segments, each retracting out of sight to reveal gray sky and gray-green treetops. Even through Parkes's insulated helmet, the roar of the shuttle's jets tore at his ears.

"Twenty seconds." Then: "Mark-one-*out!*"

"One!" shouted Dietsch as the harness snapped him down the tailway and out into space, then returned to position. "Two!" shouted Hagood. The security squad ahead of Parkes seemed to melt away, until—

"Five!"

—and he was sailing down the tailway and out into the sky of Bayard.

The harness was theoretically supposed to punch a jumper through the shuttle's slipstream in a perfect position for chute deployment once he was clear of it. Rather to Parkes's surprise, it worked. Personally, he would have preferred to rely on training all PFers in jumping until they could go out in the right position without the harness. He wasn't the Force Commander, still less the Union Council who would have to approve the appropriations for more extensive jump training.

Parkes had just finished orienting himself to the sky and the ground and was looking for the shuttle when he heard a high-pitched shout in his earphones.

"Heads below!"

The Amazon came sailing past. Parkes's teeth dug into his lower lip as he saw that her chute was a streamer—trailing out behind her without deploying, so that she was falling almost freely.

He muttered something that was half a prayer to the Wise One for Forbes-Brandon's safety and half a curse on the parachute. After four centuries and with the aid of microchips, harness, training, and everything else, the parachute was still an imperfect method of getting from up to down. Every year it killed a few people who trusted themselves to it.

About the only thing it had going for it was fewer

disadvantages than everything else proposed to replace it, at least for landing an individual soldier in fighting condition with some reasonable precision. Parkes suspected that even if the scientists did turn physics upside down and discover anti-gravity, parachutes would still have their uses.

Meanwhile, the Amazon was rapidly dropping away toward a cloud bank. She had arms and legs properly outspread, but she didn't seem to be making any effort to pop her reserve chute. Parkes wouldn't have free-fallen into a cloud of unknown depth himself; vertigo could strike too easily, making you ignore your altimeter until it was too late for the chute to open. Had the lieutenant frozen?

As he entered the cloud himself, Parkes was devoutly hoping she hadn't, and not just because he didn't want to take command of a badly shaken pathfinder team. An interesting human being might be about to die a messy death. In another few seconds he'd break radio silence and try to crack her out of the freeze over the radio. It had worked before, and—

"Earmuff, this is Acom. Reporting on the ground, one seven five meters from C.D.Z. No sign of hostile activity—or any other kind, for that matter."

The voice was unmistakably Forbes-Brandon's. Parkes looked at his own altimeter and watch, and realized that he wasn't hallucinating. Forbes-Brandon must have free-fallen down to something like two hundred meters before popping her reserve, then gone straight in and landed soft. Had her freeze lasted that long, had her reserve hung up, or—?

A wooded ridge was coming up. Parkes stopped worrying about the Amazon and started worrying about his own landing. He floated over the ridge with about a hundred meters to spare, bobbing a trifle in an updraft that also carried him over a stretch of tall timber. He finally drifted down past the treetops to an easy landing on the wide gravel beach in the bend of a shallow river, without even getting his chute wet.

He'd gathered it up and was heading for cover when he saw someone giving hand recognition signals from the edge of the trees. He returned the signals before he recognized Forbes-Brandon.

She was leaning against a tree, her chute and harness already off and bundled at her feet, her rifle unslung and aimed toward the river.

"Welcome to Bayard, Sergeant Major."

Parkes took a deep breath. The nonchalance of her stance and tone, after the fright she'd given him—

"Lieutenant, I wondered if we were ever going to see you again. At least in one piece."

"Oh, that streamer? It was a bit sticky for a minute or so, because I wasn't sure where I'd land if I popped the reserve. So I just free-fell until I had a reasonably good landing spot picked out, then managed to come down about where I'd hoped to."

Parkes's mouth opened, but no sound came out. As an alternative to standing gaping, he looked up and down the river. Nobody was in sight, let alone within hearing.

"Lieutenant, I wonder if it was too smart to delay opening your reserve—"

"Are you doubting my word, Sergeant Major?"

Parkes had no possible answer to that question that wouldn't mean more trouble than he wanted to handle. There were intelligent and stupid forms of insubordination. Parkes decided to be intelligent.

"Not your word, Lieutenant. Just your judgment. You seem determined to prove that you're the best, even if that means expending yourself in the process. I don't think you're all that expendable, as our Naval Liaison officer. Also, if you do want to get yourself killed, maybe you could do it somewhere when you won't be leaving me to pick up the pieces."

"Sergeant Major, I think this conversation has gone far enough."

"Yes, ma'am."

The tight voice and tighter mouth seemed to demand the formality: A look down the stream also showed Hagood and Dietsch moving toward them along the bank, with another trooper in sight too far away to identify.

Parkes unhooked his chute, unslung his rifle, and chambered a round. Then he looked at his watch. If worse came to worst, he wouldn't be under the Amazon's direct command for very long. The security platoon for Bayard Main Base should be hitting the dirt from their shuttle in another hour. The Main Base perimeter should be secured and the Amazon's X.O. should be guiding in the first pods an hour after that. The vertis should be operational by midnight, and then the pathfinder team could be back with the main Group anytime it seemed they'd be more useful there than here.

This was well ahead of any schedule that Parkes had expected without people being worked to exhaustion, which MacLean had specifically prohibited. However, when he'd led the security squads into the hangar for weapons inspection and testing, he'd seen about two dozen Navy people swarming over the vertis, the pods, and a lot of other gear normally handled by the PFers. They seemed to know what they were doing, and a closer look told Parkes that they probably did, since most of them were rated machinists.

Parkes smelled the Chief Garron-Lieutenant Forbes-Brandon axis at work here, but this also came under the heading of gifts a wise man didn't question. Particularly a Sergeant Major who'd been wanting to see whether Garron would put himself out for the *Ark*'s Group, and now had the right answer.

Have to do something nice for Garron, thought Parkes. This was likely to be the Chief's last cruise, which meant the last chance for any sort of combat award. *Try to get him at least a temporary ground assignment?* Yes, and the Amazon would back Parkes up where Garron was concerned even if she might want to put him on permanent grounds fatigue otherwise.

By now Dietsch and Hagood were in shouting distance, and reporting no contact or signs of recent human activity. Parkes settled down to logging in people, forming a perimeter, and cajoling a couple of clowns from the com team who'd broken radio silence simply to tell the world that they were on the wrong side of the river. He told them that the river could easily be forded and that if they didn't know how to find a ford they should have some brains issued them when they returned to the *Ark* because he didn't know what they were keeping in their heads now...

He stopped twice to look at the Amazon. Once she and one of her people were busy assembling a laser target-indicator, and anyway, that straight back and distant expression didn't encourage hopes of polite conversation.

90

The next time was just after dispatching a three-man patrol to check out a reported fresh trail and try to bring in the two lost sheep. They were the last of the team, barely half an hour after Parkes hit dirt, which made it a good drop by any definition.

He turned to look at Forbes-Brandon, then took a step backward. She was sitting with her back to him again, but one shoulder and her head pressed hard into the shaggy, moss-grown bark of a tree. Both back and shoulders were trembling, and the cheek he could see was so pale it stood out in the shadows under the trees.

"Damn!" said Parkes, fortunately to himself. That was a pretty fair case of the near-accident shakes the Amazon was having, and he'd probably made it worse by tearing that unnecessary and stupid strip off her for taking risks!

It couldn't be nearly as hard for him to live with that kind of pride as it must be for her. She deserved an apology, and if they hadn't been on duty—

The radio made a series of vulgar noises. The operator pressed the Unscramble switch and Parkes heard:

"—unidentified aircraft approaching your D.Z. Civilian E.E. and performance. Services du Ciel frequently ferries aircraft along this route, so that's probably what you have. We are putting a fighter down to 20 km. over the D.Z. just to remind anybody who's watching that we can do it. Forktail out."

"Forktail, this is Acorn. Acknowledge your last message. We'll leave out an O.P. and get everybody else out of sight. Acorn out."

The vulgar noises began again as Forbes-Brandon stood up. For a moment it seemed as if she were waiting for Parkes to say something, then she brushed scraps of moss and bark off her jacket and the moment passed.

"All right, people. We're about to be overflown by somebody who may or may not be one of the Good Guys, so let's not sit around looking pretty for them. Sergeant Major, pick three men for O.P. security."

"Yes, ma'am."

He was calling the lost-sheep patrol to warn them that the main team was shifting position, when he remembered that he should have followed field-service regulations and nodded instead of saluting. Forbes-Brandon might know what kind of officer got salutes in the field and decided that she'd just been insulted again.

Forbes-Brandon, Parkes decided, could do more to unsettle him than any officer he'd dealt with in the last seven years. At least she wasn't his company commander like the last one, who'd finally forced Parkes into requesting a transfer and then given him an ER downcheck that put his promotions on hold until after Bifrost.

Osman was the first to spot the fighter, although the plane was on automatic pilot and Chandragan had both eyes free to look. He remained expressionless as the fighter swept across their course 15,000 meters above them. The Team Leader, however, could tell that the pilot felt he'd been negligent.

"Hold this course and altitude," he told Chandragan. "If they'd thought we were hostile, we'd have been challenged before we even saw the fighter."

"I can't promise that we'll learn much about the P.F. drop on this course."

"No, but the P.F. won't learn that we're interested in them."

The Team Leader didn't add that from the reported position of the drop, the P.F. party would be at least twenty kilometers from any traces of the Team's activities. They would not even cover that distance unless they quite illogically marched off to the south into the belt of forest that lay between their D.Z. and the Team's area of field exercises. They were far more likely to head north, making a demonstration for the Ranchers between the forest belt and Havre des Dames.

Chandragan already knew this, and the rest of the men in the plane were the security squad he was taking to Havre des Dames. They would be in somewhat more danger of capture than the rest of the Team, but what they did not know they could not tell.

The fighter made a second pass at no more than 13,000 meters, still moving so fast that the cargo plane's collision-avoidance radar could barely track it. Then the pilot must have pulled his nose up and is throttles open, because hydrogen flames flared blue-white like a miniature nova as the fighter climbed toward orbit.

The Team Leader saw the flames with his inner eye long after they'd vanished into the clouds. For a moment he envied the Peace Force men, who could command such power and hurl it at their enemies. Even more than before, he would not have to hide and lurk and evade and misdirect and rely on allies, some of whom didn't know what they were.

Kali had set him a very great challenge indeed in the coming of Group Fourteen. Was he altogether unworthy, to wish that it had not been quite so great?

Wishing would not change it, in any case. He would have to spend as little time as possible in Havre des Dames, attempting one operation with the security squad, making a personal reconnaissance of the P.F. Main Base if it were close enough, then returning south. The work in and around Havre des Dames could be done with a minimum amount of radio communication. The same could not be said of the recruiting and training in the south, unless he was there in person.

There was also no alternative to minimizing the Team's radio traffic. The on-board computer of a Peace Cruiser was the next thing to a full-scale A.I.; it could break any of the codes the Team's communications equipment could handle with a very modest number of intercepts to work with. Not to mention that P.F. cryptographers were among the best.

More immediately, he'd best raise the question of speeding the delivery of weapons and equipment from Rancher stocks, at least for the first two hundred men. That would mean weaker Team control as long as he and a squad were in Havre des Dames, and the too-fast promotion of local leaders. It should not mean serious trouble as long as the Team retained leadership at the platoon level and kept the Ranchers from being carried away by their new strength into needlessly provoking the Peace Forcers.

CHAPTER 10

"How is your friend, Monsieur Rebenc?"

"Well enough to be irritable, Sister."

"So I have heard. We are all praying for her, believe me."

"Thank you, Sister."

Sister Jehanne pressed the button under her desk and the door slid open. Rebenc resisted the temptation to run headlong out into the sunlight and the fresh air, at least until he was out of sight from the desk. Then he took the stairs down to the bus stop two at a time.

It wasn't Sister Jehanne's fault that it was easy to mistake her for a robot until she spoke. The hospital's cramped reception area was laid out so that it virtually immobilized the receptionist.

It also wasn't the fault of any of the Sisters of Mercy that their hospital was an open invitation to claustrophobia. When the order came to Bayard a hundred years before, the cheapest suitable accommodations for their hospital was in an old civil defense facility dug half a kilometer into the side of a cliff overlooking the harbor. It needed only a thorough cleaning and the appropriate equipment to be a suitable hospital, although to do the Sisters justice they'd carved out a fifty-meter promenade to give ambulatory patients some sun and air.

Still, Rebenc was a creature of the open, who hated burrowing into the bowels of a granite cliff even in the good cause of visiting Katie Halloran. Katie herself had spent most of her working life in more or less cramped engine rooms, but even she was getting restless as her burns healed.

She would be worse than restless, Rebenc knew, when she learned that there was no way to restore her sight here on the Storm Coast. She'd have to be moved east to one of the big city hospitals.

At least she wouldn't have to learn if *les copains* gave up salvaging *Celestine Auphan* to restore her sight. Rebenc and Geesink had worked out a tale to tell her if it came to that, as well it might. They also had a plan for sitting on Bergstrom so that he wouldn't betray them. All that remained was to pray that the choice wouldn't be necessary, and they'd know that soon enough.

All they needed before they could start for Les Fourchettes was some minor repairs to the crane motor and one of the two big air compressors. Everything else was as ready as it was going to be, and if that wasn't enough for the work that had to be done—well, he could at least ask the Sisters to include the rest of *les copains* in their prayers for Katie.

Halfway down the stairs Rebenc saw a bus pulling away from the stop and a familiar head of blond hair climbing toward him. He hurried toward Geesink, then stopped abruptly when he saw that her eyes were red and stared without seeing him.

"Ju, What's happened? Katie's all right. I just came from—"

"Those bastards! They sold out to the Ranchers! They—God damn them forever and—"

"What bastards? What have they done?"

But she was too angry to hear him. She went off into a torrent of curses that must have been audible all over the hillside but were fortunately in her mother Dutch, so it was unlikely that anyone understood them. Rebenc walked down a few steps to a bench, sat down, and lit a cigarette.

By the time he'd finished the cigarette, Geesink had finished her cursing. She joined him on the bench and for a moment rested her head on his shoulder, the first time she'd ever done that. He was tempted to put an arm around her, but offered her a cigarette instead.

After a few puffs she sighed and stubbed it out. "Those bastards in the Port Prefecture—they've seized our barge! Unpaid mooring fees, safety violations, a whole pile of things like that."

"*Peste!*"

The sunlight suddenly seemed less bright and the wind much

colder. Rebenc felt a moment's urge to run back to the hospital and hide behind its meters of granite.

"We can pay the fees."

"What with? Nils's drinking money?"

"Considering how much he drinks..."

"Even if we paid the fees, we'd have to earn back the money somehow. How could we do that, with no barge?"

"They may let it go once they've finished the inspection—"

"How long do you think that will be? And even if the Prefect hasn't been bought by the Ranchers, do you think that's true of everybody in Havre des Dames? They've towed the barge to the Customs Quay. I went to see it there myself, and the Port Guardians wanted to arrest me just for that! How much do you think it would cost to make them turn their backs while somebody slipped aboard with a laser or even a bomb?"

"Too damned little."

Rebenc wasn't quite ready to curse God and die, like Job in the Bible. This wasn't God's fault. He also didn't intend to make away with himself and give their enemies an easy victory. The people who wanted the *Celestine Auphan* to stay on the bottom of Les Fourchettes would have to kill him, maybe even get blood on their own so-pure hands!

Now that he'd made this fine resolution, what to do about it? The Port Prefect's own little security force seemed to be composed of people who'd failed admission to every other security force in the city, including the guards at the licensed houses on the Quai de la Paix. They probably couldn't keep a saboteur away from the barge if they'd wanted to, and they were so poorly paid that anyone with a pocketful of Francs Bayard could probably make them not want to.

"We'll try killing them with kindness first," Rebenc said. "We'll go down and offer our help in stripping down all the equipment for inspection. We'll even fix it ourselves. That way at least there will be one or two of us around the barge most of the time."

"That should help. We'll still need the fees though. Roman can slip around to a few of the people we worked for and secure loans in return for the promise of more crane work. Or I could go to work in one of the licensed houses—that was a joke, Paul."

"It didn't sound like a joke, Ju."

"Oh, don't be stuffy. I'd never sell myself to sailors. The landlubbers, yes, but never—all right, I won't make any more jokes about it."

Rebenc put an arm around her waist and she not only didn't draw away, she didn't even stiffen. After a moment he added, "We'll have to watch Nils while we're on the barge. The Guardians will be just looking for a chance to arrest us for public disorder. Joseph, too, although he at least stays sober."

It occurred to Rebenc that their enemies had already won a victory of sorts by setting *les copains* against each other this way. Perhaps it would be their last victory, but meanwhile the weight of the gun inside his jacket almost took away his pleasure in having Ju so comfortably snuggled against him.

The thump of a distant explosion made the curtains of Parkes's office dance slowly and sent a stylus rolling off his work table. He let it lie while he picked up his rifle and laid it across the table with the chamber empty and the safety on. For Parkes there was no such thing as ignoring an unexplained explosion, and the same went for all the other veterans of the Bifrost campaign he'd ever met.

Since nothing happened, Parkes went back to work drawing up next week's list of training instructors. He was beginning to hope that something would happen to break the routine of fatigue parties and training exercises and he wasn't too particular with. Not a suicidal assault on the Main Base Camp or a mortaring of the hospital or a verti shot down on its way to South Base Camp, but anything short of those might actually be better than what was more and more obviously make-work. After five weeks the PFers who didn't need to be kept busy to be kept out of trouble were beginning to grumble and even with the bad actors the point of diminishing returns was approaching.

Parkes had just finished writing himself down for three unarmed-combat sessions and two supervisions of the obstacle course, when Sergeant Tyndall stuck her head in the door.

"Hey, Sergeant Major. You heard that explosion a while back? That was Dozer and a demolition crew at the old quarry out beyond

Three Finger Hill. She said she was going to see if we could save having to haul grading stone up from the city."

Parkes nodded. He couldn't remember anything about old quarries, but he had heard Dozer complaining about how slowly the road-building was going and how many trucks they were going to wear out doing a decent job of it. That explained the explosion, then, and also Dozer's absence this morning. She wasn't a qualified demolitions expert, but she took a child's delight in watching explosions go off. The Support Squadron's demolitions people were just going to have to get used to her hanging around.

Meanwhile, the list of instructors was finished, the sun was coming out, and it was time for lunch. Parkes fed the list into the central memory with instructions for a printout to Major Vela, shoved his chair back, and picked up his rifle and beret.

The various messes occupied most of what had been a forest rangers' HQ when this stretch of public land had been intended as a forest preserve in the path of development. That development had ended a good thirty kilometers short of the HQ, so that Group Fourteen now had a large permanent building for cooking and eating their meals.

Sometimes Parkes thought that if he had to plan his career over again, he'd be either a cook, an electronics maintenance technician, or an ordnance specialist. Peace Force rules and customs gave priority to housing electronics, weapons, and cooking gear; everything else could and frequently did take potluck. Parkes didn't quarrel with the notion that a soldier needed a functioning sensor network, a useable weapon, and a hot meal more than anything else but as one of the P.B.I. he'd also been left literally out in the cold often enough.

Not that Group Fourteen was going to be badly housed. The sixty pods that landed its Initial Mission Capability Load had been turned into forty-five Standard Field Buildings and a stockpile of components enough for eight more. With just the pods aboard *Ark* and *Ivanhoe*, Dozer could build S.F.B.'s for fifteen hundred people instead of the eight hundred forty currently groundside. Boredom had been no problem that first week, when everybody who could handle a laser, a cartridge of bonder/sealer, or a multi-tool had turned to breaking down the pods and reassembling them in their new and allegedly more glorious bodies.

After lunch Parkes and Tyndall walked down the hill behind the mess building to the inner edge of the perimeter strip. The two-hundred-meter strip looked no different from the rest of the rather soggy landscape inside or outside it, which was exactly the idea. An invisible defense could be just as deadly as one that stuck out like the Amazon's nose, and was a lot harder for a would-be attacker to study.

Every square meter of the strip was monitored by sensors both inside the strip and outside it, covered by at least two machine-guns, and within range of the duty launchers at the end of the landing field. Not to mention the armed vertis (one airborne, one on alert), the balloon-mounted sensors, the lasers and R.P. dispensers, and the ground patrols outside the perimeter, ready for any attack that didn't involve an attempt to enter the camp.

A P.F. Main Base was never attacked except by enemies who were very sneaky, very strong, or very stupid. Parkes wondered what category Rancher terrorists or the Game Master's people would fall into, assuming that either of them wasn't a figment of Intelligence's frequently overheated imagination.

And speaking of patrols—there was one coming in now, stopping for both electronic and visual identification. Not only stopping, but spreading out so that whoever was on the visual monitor could see each face. A point to the monitor watch; electronic signatures could be faked a lot more easily than faces.

The patrol came on through the perimeter to the foot of the hill. As they started to climb, Parkes realized that the patrol leader was Forbes-Brandon. She was bringing up the rear, and it looked as if she'd hurt her left ankle. She wasn't limping; instead, she was trying so hard not to limp that it must have been causing her more pain than a limp would have.

Parkes walked down to meet the patrol and fell in behind Forbes-Brandon. From close up he could see her trying not to flinch each time the weight came on her left ankle.

"Lieutenant, do you want me to call a medic?"

"What for?"

"Your ankle."

"Oh, that. It feels more like a pulled muscle than anything really serious. I'll be all right once I'm off my feet."

"Better soak the foot in hot water, if you don't mind my suggesting it."

"Thank you." She took another step, and this time he heard her breath hiss between her teeth. For a moment she stood swaying slightly, unable either to move or meet Parkes's eyes. Parkes gave a quick hand signal to Tyndall, who slipped into the patrol's line and quietly herded them up the hill, leaving Parkes and the lieutenant alone.

"If it's hurting that much, you might tear something trying to walk any farther."

"Maybe," she said. Her tone implied that she might prefer to break an ankle rather than accept his help. For a moment Parkes was inclined to let her do just that. The next moment he had one of those impulses that he'd learned it was best to follow.

"Lieutenant, I'm a pretty fair hand with massage. If there's nothing too badly wrong with the ankle, maybe I can help enough to let you walk in."

The Amazon looked around. Parkes could see her calculating the relative merits of accepting his help in private and rejecting it at the risk of having to be publicly carried to the medics. Then she sat down and started taking off her left boot. It came off easily, which encouraged Parkes to believe that maybe it really was just a pulled muscle. The foot and ankle exposed were as shapely as Parkes had expected, but small, almost dainty in proportion to the Amazon's height. He bent over and began working cautiously up from the sole of the foot toward the ankle.

"You don't have to be so delicate," the lieutenant snapped. "I'm not fragile."

"No, Lieutenant." She was fragile in proportion to what she put her body through. Parkes wondered how many sprains, minor fractures, and other injuries her medical record would show. With those long, light bones he could understand why she must have looked gawky, almost gaunt, before she filled out.

Suddenly Parkes felt that he knew Katherine Forbes-Brandon a lot better. He'd been exactly the same physical type in his teens and

100

early twenties, with tougher bones but all arms and legs no matter how much he ate or how much running and unarmed-combat he did. It didn't matter that most of what lay over his bones was muscle and sinew, and that anyone who thought he was a skinny weakling was in for a very nasty surprise. There was still too much bone and not enough over it. He hadn't stopped driving himself to compensate for that until he was damned near as old as the lieutenant was now either.

Something of what he felt must have passed through his fingers. He heard Forbes-Brandon laughing: "Sergeant Major, you must have had a very good massage teacher. I somehow don't think she limited herself to ankles though."

"She was a bath girl at the Daimyo Hotel on Yamato, and no, she didn't."

"Well, you were a good pupil." She pulled off her other boot and rolled both legs of her trousers halfway up her calves. "Don't expect anything more to come off, or you'll really be putting your foot in it."

For one terrifying moment Parkes saw stamped on his death certificate, "Died of Lieutenant Katherine Forbes-Brandon's first pun." Then he managed to limit himself to a strangled chuckle and went back to work on the ankles and beyond them to the calves, which were quite up to the standard of the rest.

An order was an order, so he dug in hard but the stifled grunts of pain quickly gave way to small, contented sighs. At last Forbes-Brandon lay back, lifted both legs, and flexed her feet and ankles.

"I'm tempted to put that bath girl in for a Civilian Assistance Commendation." She started pulling on her boots. "Thank you, Sergeant Major."

"You're welcome, Lieutenant." Parkes kept the grin off his face until Forbes-Brandon had bounced to her feet and hurried off uphill. He was still grinning when Tyndall rejoined him.

"I took them straight to the Mess Hall. They'd covered thirty kilometers since breakfast, with no lunch except C-bars. The Amazon—well, if you don't mind my saying so, she's got a lot to learn about troop leading."

"Oh, yes," said Parkes. "But I think she's beginning to learn it."

* * *

"What about the arsenal of the Mobile Guards?" said the man known in Havre des Dames as *L'Hibou*—the Owl.

"What about it?" said the Team Leader. "Is there something about it that you know and I do not? The information will of course be paid for."

"Of course," said the Owl. "But it was not information that I was thinking of. I was thinking of—let us say, changing the ownership of some of the weapons in that arsenal."

"Indeed," said the Team Leader. "That is a thought worth discussing." *If only to find what price the Owl expects me to pay for his alliance.* "Although I am not sure that either the quantity or the quality of what is in that arsenal is such that it would be worth the price we might have to pay for changing its ownership. One might, in fact, say the price you would have to pay."

"Oh. Is our alliance one of expedience that you plan to abandon when you can throw us aside like an empty magazine?"

"All alliances involve expediency on both sides, and this one more than most. I cannot imagine that you are an empty-headed idealist any more than I."

"Indeed, if you imagined that you should become a novelist instead of a professional—man of violence. However, I do not think you have entirely answered my question."

"Very well. I simply remind you that I may *wish* to go on operating in the Havre des Dames area and other places within reach of the Mobile Guards. I do not *have* to do so.

"You, on the other hand, depend on this area for your profits, and on men who might be fish out of water anywhere else. If the Mobile Guards lose a major portion of their arsenal, they will blame you, they will hunt you, and they will give you the choice between ceasing operations and being destroyed, or at least crippled."

"You have more faith in the Mobile Guards than anyone could who knew them well, my friend. Also less faith in the ability of my men to hide."

"My faith in the Mobile Guards is no greater than yours. But are you sure that they are the only opponents you would face? The

Peace Force is an opponent of quite another order from the Guards, as I am sure you know as well as I."

"True. Yet would the Union permit them to be tied down in local security operations?"

"If that was necessary to secure the continued cooperation of the Nouvelle Bretagne government for their presence on Bayard at all—yes, it very well might."

"Perhaps. But even if the Group was turned into a garrison for Havre des Dames, would that not serve your purposes, regardless of what happened to my men?"

"It would not serve my purposes to have allies destroyed. Does a man burn down his own house in order to keep warm on the first cold night of winter?"

"One supposes a wise man would not. I have seen no reason to suppose you are not wise."

"I hope that is not intended to flatter me."

"It is not. I do not imagine that you will respond to anything except a clear statement of what I would ask in return for leaving the Mobile Guards alone."

"If you are in a position to make such a clear statement, I will listen to it with interest. Perhaps even with pleasure."

"If I were not in a position to make such a statement, I would have so little control over my men that the last hour's talk would have been entirely futile. Since that is not so—" The Team Leader nodded, encouraging the Owl to continue.

The Owl's price in weapons, ammunition, electronics, and unlicensed drugs was considerable, but not beyond the Team Leader's ability to meet. It also suggested that the Owl had a fair amount of control over his men as long as he was able to pay them reasonably well in whatever they valued. That was a good thing to have confirmed, since the Team Leader had been quite sincere in stating that he did not wish potentially useful allies destroyed when nothing could be gained by it. It was also useful to have some confirmation of the sources who'd told him about the position of the Owl in Havre des Dames's criminal underground.

Not that he planned to make the Owl his sole ally in Havre des Dames. He was also using local people to exploit the source he was developing in Group Fourteen itself, although that would be a slow, painstaking matter. The Team Leader still could not make Havre des Dames his base of operations without leaving his newly organized Rancher units dangerously independent of his control and perhaps dangerously willing to show off their new skills and weaponry.

He would have to be exquisitely careful about hiding his in-Group source from the Owl. That might be expensive; it would certainly be essential. To give the Owl access to information from inside Group Fourteen would promote him to an independent warlord rather than a valued ally. That would not be desirable even if it was the Team Leader's purpose to unleash full-scale civil war on the Storm Coast of Bayard, which would be exceeding his orders by a dangerously large margin. This time the Game Master was fighting the Union for points, not for blood—or at least not for very much blood.

"You can expect the first half of your shipments within seven days," said the Team Leader, pulling out a cigar and offering it to the Owl.

"The PFers will be coming to town on liberty before then," said the Owl dubiously. "Are you sure we want them looking over our shoulders?"

"I am sure that you can arrange for those places you need to use for receiving your shipments to be Restricted," said the Team Leader. "Or we can delay the shipments for an additional week, until you've seen where the P.F. men prefer to go."

The Owl shrugged, with a sour look on his face. He'd been given a choice between not being able to pay his men quickly and using up a good many of the favors the bar owners and restaurateurs of Havre des Dames owed him.

"I think we can arrange everything to permit the shipments next week," said the Owl. He lit the cigar and began puffing away on it as if he was determined to fumigate the cellar. Fortunately the negotiations were nearly over, so the Team Leader was able to escape into fresh air before his lungs started protesting against the fumes of the crude Bayard tobacco.

The operations in Havre des Dames were well begun. But well begun was *not* half done, and as for what might come of needing an ally like the Owl—once more the Team Leader allowed himself to dream briefly of what he might have been able to accomplish by now if he'd been able to bring two hundred and fifty men to Bayard, instead of thirty.

CHAPTER 11

The big blond man at the corner table had obviously drunk more than even he could carry. He'd started off muttering in Scandic, low enough that Parkes, Dozer, and Shapely could get on with the business of wetting down Tyndall's new stripe. Now he was talking out loud in Anglic, in spite of his smaller dark-haired companion's efforts to calm him down.

He was also attracting the attention of a good many of the other customers in the Mouton d'Argent. The watchful eye of the three Port Guardians didn't surprise Parkes, but he'd also noticed a table of four men who looked like off-shift dock workers watching the drunk even more intently. It was those four men who really started to spoil Parkes's mood for a quiet celebration and made him nudge Dozer under the table.

"Call a rally?" she whispered after taking in the three tables.

"This might be none of our business. If that big Viking walks out before he blows his top, nothing may happen anyway. Be ready to move though." The other three nodded.

The blond man took long enough over his next drink to let all four PFers shift their chairs to allow for quick stands. None of them was carrying a gun, but anyone who expected that would make them easy meat would have plenty of time in the hospital to ponder their mistake.

The blond man finished his drink and signaled the waitress for another. She came, but the blond man's companion shook his head at her. She hesitated a moment too long, and the drunk snatched the glass off her tray. She tried to grab it back at the same time as the dark-haired man tried to grab his companion's hand. Drunken strength was too much for the two of them put together; the waitress toppled over onto the table with a crash, scattering empty glasses onto the floor. Her scream sounded more angry than hurt.

The three Port Guardians jumped to their feet and started for the two men. The blond man stood up, saw them coming at him, bellowed a curse, and launched a roundhouse punch at the leading policeman. His friend grabbed his arm, turning the punch into a glancing blow. The dark-haired man's free hand darted toward the inside of his coat, then hesitated and withdrew.

The movement hadn't escaped the attention of the four workmen. While the policemen's attention was on the blond, they quietly moved around behind the dark-haired man. Suddenly two of them were grabbing him from behind and starting to turn him around. A knife gleamed in the hand of the third man. At that point Parkes jumped up on his own table and shouted, "Rally!"

The shout stopped the movement of everybody except the Peace Forcers and the waitress, who was getting out of harm's way as fast as she could. Tyndall jumped up and headed for the door to spread the rally call, while Shapely picked up a chair and held it out in front of him and Dozer pulled on her gloves.

The blond man wasn't too drunk to see the knife threatening his friend. He gripped the near edge of his table with both hands and heaved. It went up and over with a crash, sweeping three of the four workmen off their feet. The fourth backed away, drawing a pistol as he did. The blond man promptly dove behind the table, which proved heavy enough to stop the three shots the workman fired.

When Parkes saw that the Guardians were backing toward the door without paying any attention to attempted murder, he crossed them off the good-guys roster. He came down off the table as the pistol swung toward him, rolled as it went off, and came up with his head under the man's chin and both fists driving hard into his midriff. The man seemed to fold up into about one-third his original size, and Shapely kicked the fallen pistol out of his reach without taking his eyes off the retreating policemen. Shapely's look when he was fighting mad wasn't one to encourage loitering; the policemen were out the door before Shapely bent to pick up the pistol.

Meanwhile Dozer and the blond man were hauling the table off the other three workmen and their victim. One of the workmen showed a little fight, until Dozer taught him the wisdom of nonresistance with three quick jabs to the jaw. There was hardly any fat on Dozer, and for business occasions like this she wore sap gloves.

By this time the bar owner was standing behind the bar holding a riot gun cradled in both arms without apparently knowing which way to point it. Parkes was about to go over to the bar and suggest that he put the gun away before it started a new riot by going off accidentally, when Tyndall ran back in.

"I called the 'rally' and we're getting some people from Transportation, I think. It looks like there's trouble all over town though. Not aimed at us, but—"

With a *whooomph* and a blast of heat the stairway at the rear of the room erupted in flames.

The blast shattered bottles and sprayed embers all over the room. More flames gushed up behind the bar as the spilled liquor caught fire. The owner broke all records for bar-jumping while holding a riot gun, sailing over the bar and nearly knocking Dozer and Parkes flat on the floor. Parkes beat out the smoldering patches on the owner's clothes and took the opportunity to relieve him of the riot gun.

Meanwhile the four brawling workmen and the few remaining customers who hadn't evacuated when the brawl began had taken to their heels. Parkes looked around for a fire extinguisher, then looked more closely at the fire. It already completely filled the stairs and the space behind the bar, where exploding bottles now sounded like a mortar barrage. It was also spreading rapidly toward the rear of the building. Fighting this fire wouldn't be a job for amateurs.

He gripped the owner's arm to urge him toward the door, but the man shook him off with a scream. *"Gabrielle! La pauvre petite, elle est—"* followed by a torrent of Francone. Parkes understood only about one word in three, which was enough to let him know that someone named Gabrielle was trapped in the owner's bedroom on the second floor.

Parkes knew enough about the owner to have grave doubts that

Gabrielle was a human female, but she certainly seemed to be someone he was concerned about. "Now—*comment on ascend*—?" he began.

Apparently there were rear windows to the bedroom where Gabrielle was trapped, opening on an alley behind the bar. Parkes thought briefly of the possibility of an ambush, then decided that the owner wasn't a good enough actor to be faking his panic.

By the time they were all outside, the fire was through the roof. The bar's walls were slabs of plascrete, but everything inside seemed to be wood or at least burnable. Whoever she was, Gabrielle wasn't going to last until the firemen or even more PFers arrived.

"Follow me!"

Parkes posted Tyndall with the riot gun to guard everybody's back and welcome new arrivals, then led Shapely and Dozer into the alley. Smoke was already streaming out of the windows the owner pointed out, but not so thickly there couldn't be any hope for Gabrielle.

"Pyramid!"

Shapely and Dozer stood side by side and made a stirrup of their hands, lifting Parkes onto their shoulders. Tyndall would have been an easier lift, but she was twelve centimeters shorter than Parkes. Even Parkes had to stretch to reach the windowsill, but it was rough enough to give him a good grip once he'd reached it. Swinging himself up and through the window, he found himself in an austerely furnished bedroom that might have belonged to a monk with no interest in any other earthly creature.

The heat and smoke were building so that Parkes would have given a good deal for his mask and battle dress. Tying his handkerchief over his nose, he began to search the room. Nothing and nobody in the closet, on any of the visible shelves, under the bed, under the desk, or in any of its drawers—this might not be an ambush, but what about a wild-goose chase?

Nothing on or under the dresser. He started opening each drawer, aware that the door to the hall was all that stood between him and a medium-sized inferno. When that door gave...

He finished the dresser, ran to the bathroom door, opened it a crack, and instead of a blast of hot air heard frantic mewing. Opening the door wider, he saw a half-grown black cat with a white patch on her chest perched on top of the medicine cabinet over the sink and looking thoroughly unhappy.

Parkes laughed and reached for the cat, who promptly spat and raked his hand. Parkes gritted his teeth and pulled the cat down with one hand on the scruff of her neck and the other under her hind legs, ignoring her struggles, mewings, and frequently successful attempts to claw and bite.

He'd just left the bathroom when the door to the hall burst into flames. Knowing that he had only moments before the bedroom turned into a furnace, he dashed for the window, stuffed Gabrielle inside his shirt to the accompaniment of more clawings and protests, put both hands on the sill, and swung himself out and down. He landed in a puddle of mixed garbage and mud just as the bedroom door gave way and the window above spewed flames.

Parkes stood up, brushing much off his uniform with one hand while he opened the top of his shirt with the other. Gabrielle promptly tried to bite his hand, then calmed down as he began to scratch her ears and under her chin. By the time Parkes reached the street, Gabrielle had her head tucked up under his chin and was purring contentedly.

On the street Parkes saw that reinforcements had arrived—Lieutenant Forbes-Brandon, Corporal Dietsch, and a pfc from Transportation.

The Amazon looked him up and down. "I didn't know you were cat people, Sergeant Major."

"I—when I was a boy, my sister and I fed strays out behind our barn."

No need to tell her that our stepmother drowned them and sometimes their kittens whenever she found them.

At this point the bar owner provided a useful diversion by running up to Parkes and embracing him in frantic gratitude. This drew a howl of protest from Gabrielle as she was squashed between the two men, but she promptly calmed down as the owner took her on his shoulder and began murmuring endearments into one silky black ear.

Freed of cat duty, Parkes began to look around for the two men who'd been at the center of all the evening's troubles. They were both going to have to answer a lot of questions officially, but Parkes had no faith that the official questions would cover everything that he and Group Fourteen would need to know about tonight's events.

The blond man's drunkenness had finally turned into an asset. He'd collapsed halfway down the block, and since he weighed about half again as much as his companion, the dark-haired man hadn't been able to do much more than make him as comfortable as possible. He was sitting with a pistol in his lap and a wary expression on his face when Parkes and Forbes-Brandon walked up.

"I'm Sergeant Major Parkes and this is Lieutenant Forbes-Brandon, of Peace Force Company Group Fourteen. I think you know something about what's happening tonight. Perhaps you'd care to tell us."

"And why should I tell you anything?"

The Amazon looked ready to lean on him with rank, but Parkes spoke first. "Because we can be witnesses that you were attacked deliberately and that the Port Guardians neglected their duty in letting this happen. I think the Guardians aren't exactly your friends, are they?"

For a moment the dark man's face showed an intense struggle between suspicion of any stranger and the need to trust somebody. Then he shrugged.

"I am Paul Rebenc, helmsman of the *Celestine Auphan*. My friend is her boatswain, Nils Bergstrom. You have perhaps heard of our ship?"

Parkes and Forbes-Brandon exchanged looks, then both nodded. "The Ranchers sank her three months ago, didn't they?"

"Yes, and my friends and I are trying to salvage her. But those bastards want to keep her on the bottom, and now they have friends in Havre des Dames. Friends who may be your enemies too."

"They might find that an expensive mistake."

"Perhaps. But if you do not know who they are, all the expense will not be theirs."

"Maybe not. So suppose you tell us what you know that you think we don't?"

"Suppose you sent Peace Force people to the Customs Quay to guard—a certain barge. When you have done that, it will be worth my telling you more of what I know."

For the first time in his life Parkes wished he had an officer's freedom to decide a matter like this. His gut reaction was to believe

111

Rebenc and send at least a squad. Those Port Guardians giving the hired guns a clear shot at Rebenc and Bergstrom stank of somebody fairly high up playing dirty games.

That "somebody fairly high up" might also withdraw cooperation from the Peace Forces if they barged into his little games on no more evidence than the gut reactions of a Sergeant Major and the bargaining skill of a beached sailor. Then tonight's violence might be only the first and far from the worst.

This wasn't the first time that Parkes had faced a situation requiring this kind of decision. All the other times he'd been glad to pass the job of the final decision on to an officer. Now he would rather have made it himself. Was this just because he hadn't seen how well the Amazon would handle herself in a tight spot?

Parkes tried not to fidget as the Amazon stared off into space for so long that he half expected to see the eastern sky turning gray. Finally she nodded.

"We've had reports of incidents—fires, minor riots, burglaries, sabotage—everywhere *except* the port area. The Peace Force people are now about the only uncommitted security forces in Havre des Dames except for the Port Guardians. They don't seem to be your friends, and I'll assume that's not your fault.

"Tyndall!"

"Yes, Lieutenant?"

"Scramble to Captain Dallin—"

"She was out looking for a sushi bar. That's why the other three Transportation people who showed up didn't stay. They wanted to find her and make sure she was safe."

"Damn! Then we'll have to organize the barge guard ourselves. Scramble to all P.F. people—draw weapons, then form into groups of not less than six and close on the Customs Quay. Be alert for ambushes, but don't fire without an identified hostile target.

"For Dallin—as soon as she thinks the vertis and the armory at the airport are secure, I suggest she put one verti on firefly patrol over the port area. She might want to put a squad aboard it if there's one available."

She turned to Rebenc. "Now—who are your friends, who might be in danger from whoever's playing games tonight?"

Rebenc frowned. Parkes wanted to shake him. "Come on, man. We're putting our asses on the line to protect your—barge. You can trust us! Or do you *want* your friends kidnapped?"

Rebenc swallowed. Maybe that possibility hadn't occurred to him. He was a tough sailor and a determined man, but both soldiers and criminals had a different kind of toughness and determination.

"Joseph Vasi, Juliana Geesink, Roman Talgas. And there's Katie Halloran in the nursing ward of the hospital."

"Add a message to all Peace Force personnel. If you meet any of these people"—she rattled off the names—"take them into protective custody. No interrogation, just don't let anybody except Peace Force people near them. Invoke Article Ninety-two if you have to."

Article Ninety-two gave Peace Force personnel superior jurisdiction over planetary forces in any case where there was a reasonable suspicion that Union security was involved. Invoking it on unreasonable suspicion could mean a court-martial.

For the first time. Parkes felt he had hard data on how Katherine Forbes-Brandon would shape up as a field leader. Right now the evidence seemed very-much in her favor.

"All right, Monsieur Rebenc," said Forbes-Brandon with the ghost of a smile. "I hope you belong to some religion that obliges you to pay debts and show gratitude, because otherwise we're all in trouble."

Rebenc looked as if he would have fallen on his knees and kissed the lieutenant's feet if he could have moved at all. Instead, he stood open-mouthed as she turned away to order Shapely to commandeer a vehicle and the transportation corporal to stay behind and report on the incident to the firemen when they arrived.

Tyndall was staring nearly as blankly as Rebenc. Parkes elbowed her gently in the ribs. "Come on, Sergeant. I told you she'd turn into a reasonably good officer sooner or later. It just seems to be happening faster than I expected."

CHAPTER 12

The Team Leader would have preferred to be carrying more than one rocket launcher with five rounds, but he and his squad were already so close to the Customs Quay that it seemed unlikely they would fail to reach a good firing position. Then even one or two rounds would be enough to defeat those stubborn fools who were determined to raise the *Celestine Auphan*.

The alley came to an end in a narrow street. Across that street lay a low warehouse, and beyond the warehouse the Team Leader saw the boom of the barge's crane. They could have fired one round then, but that would be enough to alert even the Port Guardians and might not do fatal damage. A quick dash across the street and around the warehouse would put them in a position to make every round count.

The Team Leader checked the portable I.F.F. that would fool the Guardians' surveillance sensors. If they hadn't been drawn off to reinforce the Mobile Guards, the firemen, and the rest of the local security forces handling emergencies everywhere except along the waterfront, they would probably have gone to ground in their fortified headquarters about two hundred meters south of the Customs Quay. Either way, the electronic deception should buy the few extra minutes the Team Leader needed.

He turned to look at his squad, their black clothing and masks making them nearly invisible in the darkness. Only eyes gleaming through narrow holes showed that there were human beings inside those black suits, to hold the rocket launcher, the extra rounds, the rifles, grenades, and first-aid packs.

"Now!"

They dashed across the street and into the driveway beside the warehouse. They crouched behind the loading dock, four facing the street with rifles aimed as the fifth man wound demolition cord around the posts of the gate that was the last physical barrier to the Quay.

Chffftttt!

The demo cord made a sound like a giant spitting, a few sparks, and even less smoke. The gate post wavered, then toppled, pulling the gate with it. The clatter of several hundred kilos of wood and wire falling was much louder than the explosion. Before its echoes died, the Team Leader was sprinting down the last fifty meters of the driveway.

The launcher man was the second one onto the Quay behind the Team Leader. The man with the four spare rounds was the third. The launcher man knelt, flipped his sight up, let it transmit the target picture of the crane to the rocket, and pressed the trigger.

As he did, searing blue-white light suddenly flooded the whole Quay. The launcher man flinched, jerking the launcher off-target as the rocket popped out. It soared off down the Quay in the general direction of the barge, its own tail flame nearly invisible in the glare from the flare burning on top of the crane. The Team Leader hoped the rocket wasn't so off course that its guidance mechanism couldn't recapture the target picture. At least the Team's training was holding. The second rocket was in the launcher before the first one was halfway to its target. As the launcher man gave the second rocket its sight picture, a roaring voice thundered up and down the Quay.

"Throw down your weapons! You are surrounded! Throw down your weapons!"

The launcher man said something obscene, and fired. The rocket leaped toward a pile of shrouded machinery, and two rifles opened fire from the crane cabin, a third from the bow of the barge. As the rocket burrowed into the pile of machinery with a gout of flame and flying debris, the launcher man was slammed back into the Team Leader, half his head blown away by a burst.

The Team Leader snatched up the fallen weapon, but as he did, another of the squad went down. Whether or not they were surrounded, they were certainly facing a firefight against ridiculous odds if they stayed where they were. The Team Leader loaded the rocket launcher, set the rocket's fuse as a booby trap, then dropped it on the Quay and pointed toward the driveway. If it was blocked at the other end, they would have to cover a hundred meters along the Quay with minimal cover.

The loader knelt to return the fire from the barge as the Team Leader and the other rifleman darted into the driveway. The loader had just risen to his feet to follow when one of the riflemen on the barge fired a grenade into the mouth of the driveway. The explosion set off the loader's two remaining rockets plus the booby-trapped round in the abandoned launcher. The combined explosion hurled the Team Leader and his remaining companion back down the driveway as if they'd been tossed by a bull. Only the irregular fragmentation pattern and their armored vests kept them from being shredded like their three comrades on the Quay.

As he limped off down the driveway, supported by the rifleman, the Team Leader could at least take consolation in the smoke rising from behind the warehouse. The two rockets fired had done some damage. He could also take another kind of consolation from the fact that the Peace Forcers—he refused to believe that anybody else on Bayard could wield that much firepower that effectively—would not only have no prisoners to interrogate, they would barely have any bodies to examine!

Major Vela turned on the scramblers and everybody except Parkes sat down at the table improvised from structural panels laid across drying racks. As junior man present, he was coffee detail—if you could call the local brew coffee. At least it was hot, it contained caffeine, and the two liters in this pot had been tested for poison.

As Parkes served the coffee he counted the night's incidents shown on the paper wall map of Havre des Dames. Fourteen assorted brawls, sabotage, arson, vehicle accidents, and snipings had kept the Mobile Guards and the Havre des Dames police and firemen not only on the move but well clear of the port area. Nobody had been killed and only three buildings had actually been destroyed, but if the plan

116

had been to give somebody a clear shot at *les copains'* barge, it had been entirely successful.

Or rather, it would have been entirely successful except for the luck of having Rebenc drinking at the Mouton d'Argent and having Lieutenant Forbes-Brandon know her business.

One more incident was recorded on the map as a red pair of crossed rifles. Half a kilometer from the waterfront and just inside the city limits there'd been a short but nasty firefight. From the amount of blood there'd certainly been casualties, but there'd been no bodies, no witnesses who claimed to know anything about the fight (it was an industrial area, mostly deserted at night), and no word from any city official, civilian or security. Parkes agreed with Vela's remark about "thieves falling out, obviously," but he would have liked to know which thieves and why they'd fallen out.

When everybody had choked down the first cup of coffee, MacLean called the improvised council of war to order. "We're keeping two platoons in the Havre des Dames area until further notice, one in reserve at the airport and the other in squad-size teams on roving patrol. We're also keeping a verti at the airport on pad alert, with a gun pod and tanglefoot rockets.

"As for the politics, Captain Cooper, Mediator Goff, and I will be meeting tomorrow with Dr. Lewis, two people from the Embassy including the military attaché, and about a half-battery of fairly big guns from the Nouvelle Bretagne government. Everyone here may be called on to help brief the visiting firemen, so I suggest you all put your heads down when this meeting is over.

"What I want to do now is prepare a list of suggestions to present to the meeting, for the more effective execution of our mission. I haven't the foggiest notion of what political constraints we'll be facing, and neither does the Mediator. The N.B. government would certainly like to wash its hands of any responsibility for investigating last night's events, and I very much doubt we have any way to pressure them into doing otherwise. At least not now.

"As far as suggestions are concerned, I think the sky is the limit. I particularly want to hear from Captain Dallin, Lieutenant Forbes-Brandon, and our Sergeant Majors."

Parkes saw Dallin visibly relax. She'd clearly been uneasy

about what she saw as a failure to get her vertis in the air in time to prevent the survivors of the attack on the barge from getting away or detecting the mysterious firefight in time to at least make it less mysterious. Now MacLean had just passed what amounted to a public vote of confidence in her judgment.

"With all due respect, Colonel," said Goff, "I'd suggest that we not only collect proposals but start implementing as many of them as we can without waiting for the meeting. It will be a lot harder for the political types to tell us to stop something we're already doing than to tell us not to do something we've only suggested."

"I didn't know Mediators were supposed to lead mutinies along with their other duties," said Major Vela, not quite under his breath.

"Major—" began MacLean, but Goff shook his head. "No, the Major may be right. We'll certainly have to choose carefully, things that will rally all the people who are hoping we'll prevent a repetition of last night or something even—"

"The *Celestine Auphan!*" exclaimed Forbes-Brandon. Heads swiveled, Parkes's included. He'd never heard so much emotion in her voice.

"What about her?" said Goff.

"Let's help her crew salvage her. That will give the Fishermen the offshore fish-processing plant they badly need, so they should support the idea. If the Fishermen are behind us, the N.B. government won't dare actually publicly order us to stop. We'll have to move fast to get the barge out of the Port Guardians' hands today and inventory the equipment that survived the rocket attack, but—"

From the way the words tumbled out of the Amazon's mouth, she was obviously thinking faster than she could talk, and she'd only just started thinking about this at all. Somehow she was still carrying conviction, and that conviction seemed to be winning over the doubters.

Parkes himself had never been one. The Port Guardians were a menace only as long as *les copains* and their salvage gear were in Havre des Dames. It shouldn't be hard to persuade the Prefect to let them go rather than answer some pointed questions about why his men had deliberately neglected their duty. With the Guardians out of action, it should also be fairly easy to find some fishermen willing to tow the barge south to Les Fourchettes.

That didn't solve the problem of replacing the equipment destroyed in the rocket attack, particularly one of the big air compressors the salvagers would need to pump out the *Celestine*. There were no pontoons or cranes large enough for the job on the Storm Coast and very few on Bayard, and blowing the water out with solid fuel rockets was effective only if you were going to cut the ship up (or scrap after she was salvaged).

Even there, however, Peace Force aid could make a big difference—specifically, the difference of one Rufus Goff. The *Ark Royal*'s Chief had never actually put together a Yariv Drive out of holoprojector parts and used ration cartons, but some of the things Parkes knew he'd done had been close to it. Goff would be sure to get his groundside duty and his commendation, and all in the process of doing something useful.

Except—Parkes remembered Rebenc's face and that old-young woman—Juliana Geesink—as they'd told him of what they'd done to get as far as they had toward salvaging their ship. They'd even worked side by side with the Port Guardians, "testing and repairing as necessary" the "defective" equipment, which was why Rebenc and Bergstrom had been at the Mouton d' Argent last night. Bergstrom desperately needed to get the taste of working with the Prefect's scum out of his mouth, and didn't much care how.

These people had too much pride to want their beloved ship handed back to them on a Peace Force-issue platter. What they needed was somebody to guard their backs while they did most of the work themselves...

Forbes-Brandon was finishing her presentation and heads were beginning to turn toward Parkes as the other expert on *les copains*. He had the chill feeling in his stomach that he was about to flush away forever his chances of working with the Amazon, but...

"I think we should make seeing that *Celestine Auphan* is salvaged our main project, and start implementing it at once," said Parkes in reply to MacLean's nod. "But I don't think we should just step in and do the job for the crew."

As he explained his alternative tactics Parkes was aware that his presentation was even less organized than the Amazon's. He still didn't want to drag out *les copains'* love for their ship and their pride in being able to salvage her and expose them naked for all to see.

"So if we simply guard the crew and help them obtain replacement equipment as necessary, they'll be in a much better position after we leave," Parkes concluded. "They won't look so much like Peace Force charity cases.

"Also, I don't think whoever was responsible for last night's fireworks has shot off their last round. If we're on guard without being too obvious about it, the next time these people take a shot at *Celestine Auphan* they'll find themselves having to come through us."

Major Vela's grin told Parkes he'd won his first ally. The Mediator was frowning.

"We're supposed to stand between the Fishermen and the Ranchers, not suck the Ranchers into a fight."

"The Ranchers don't need any sucking," said Vela. "You can't keep peace between two factions when one of them is willing to fight until they're forced to change their minds. A good bloody nose the next time the Ranchers try for the *Celestine* might help them along."

At this point the discussion turned to geography and logistics, and Captain Dallin took the floor. Parkes was grateful not only for what turned out to be a new ally but for someone who kept him from having to meet the Amazon's eye.

"It'll help if we can establish an auxiliary base here, at Baie des Puces," Dallin said, tapping the map with her cigarette holder. "I know, that weakens South Base. But so far the two factions of Ranchers haven't shown any signs of wanting to do anything we'd have to notice. Besides, we need another air base that's clear of the Massif DeGaulle's weather, and port facilities for an offshore patrol to prevent any more torpedo attacks..."

The arguments went back and forth, and Parkes began to breathe easier as he realized that his approach was likely to be chosen, without any need to mention the pride of *les copains*. There were the objections to static defense, though surprisingly not from Major Vela but from Captain Hansen. There was the undeniable problem of what would happen if the opposition simply went to ground until Group Fourteen had shipped out—and universal agreement that this was something they'd have to leave to luck.

Finally there was Colonel MacLean's question—and Parkes had never heard his voice more level than when he asked, "You realize, Sergeant Major, that we could wind up essentially using your friends from the *Celestine Auphan* as bait for our fish. Have you discussed this with them? And if you haven't, do you think they'll cooperate? They'll certainly have to be told."

"The voice-stress analyses show they're telling the—" began Vela.

MacLean made an impolite suggestion for a non-regulation method of disposing of voice-stress analyses and looked at Parkes again.

"They have a score to settle with the opposition," Parkes said finally. "If we're offering them a chance to settle it as well as bring up their ship—I think they'll buy in."

After that Parkes didn't remember much until the meeting had broken up and they were filing out into the dawn of what promised to be a beautiful day. Parkes was scanning the harbor for suitable tugs for the barge when he heard footsteps behind him. He turned to face the Amazon.

"Sergeant Major, I think I owe you something for your— alternative strategy for dealing with the *Celestine Auphan*."

"Lieutenant, I'm sorry if I ruined—"

"That's not what I meant. You didn't ruin anything. You saved their pride, and I should have thought of that. I didn't, and you saved me from—"

Parkes wasn't sure he wanted to know what he'd saved the lieutenant from. In any case, he was too relieved to learn that she wasn't angry to care. He smiled. "No problem, Lieutenant. Now, I think there's a workboat tied up to the ferry pier that would make—"

"*I* think we're going to have breakfast before we do anything else," said the lieutenant. "Dig out Do—Sergeant Major di Leone—and we can all go to the Sept Cygnes. The owner's a dear friend of the owner of the Mouton d'Argent, so I think Peace Force people should be safe enough there. I *cannot* face rations on top of the local coffee!"

CHAPTER 13

The Team Leader fed power to all four wheels of the truck, waited until he felt the front end begin to dip, then hurled himself through the open door. He landed rolling, stopped himself by digging fingers and toes into the turf, and rose on hands and knees as the truck went over the edge of the bluff. It bounced once with a satisfactory crunch on a rocky outcrop, then flipped end over end and plunged tailgate-first into the lake. Spray from the splash nearly reached the Team Leader and Kassim. In a few moments nothing visible remained of the truck and its late owners except a spreading pattern of ripples.

The Team Leader permitted himself a sigh as he turned to Hiko and held out his hand for the camouflage coveralls. His own black clothing was on one of the bodies at the bottom of the lake, to further confuse the Peace Forcers or anyone else who might find the truck about the identity of the bodies.

Dry clothes, hot tea, and a mild painkiller quickly put the Team Leader in a more settled frame of mind. His ribs and knee wouldn't do worse than keep him out of unarmed combat for a week or two, but meanwhile they were just sore enough to be a distraction.

He still couldn't feel entirely at peace with the world, not after taking five men into Havre des Dames and coming out with two, without succeeding in destroying the salvage equipment. Still worse, a team to cover his retreat was supposed to have been provided by the same gang leader who'd put him onto his source of intelligence in Group Fourteen. That team had vanished in what must have been a lively little fight, but who or what had fought them was a mystery. The Peace Force radio broadcasts certainly hadn't claimed them. The Owl was a good possibility, but an accusation without evidence would merely turn him from a possible into a certain enemy.

Hiko poured out more tea and bowed. "Your return will bring us strength and joy, Leader." At the look in Hiko's eyes, the Team Leader nodded to Kassim, who stepped to one side until he was in a good lookout position.

"Are we having trouble with the Rancher recruits, Hiko?"

"Not yet. Nestor brought the new weapons."

"I hope they haven't shot off all their ammunition trying to improve him."

"On the contrary. They talk of saving it for raiding."

"Raiding? Against whom?"

"Some would like to drive the smaller fishing settlements into the sea. Most seem to prefer the idea of raiding the neutral Ranchers, or 'the renegades' as they call them."

"What does Nestor say to this?"

"He has neither made any suggestions himself nor opposed any made by others."

The Team Leader didn't waste time cursing. It wasn't surprising that his Rancher recruits wanted to strike first at those they regarded as traitors. The friend who betrayed you was always easier to hate than the open enemy you took for granted. It would still be a course of action more than likely to bring the Peace Force south in strength. Against a Peace Force company with full air and space support, the Rancher militia would quickly learn how little they knew about war, without living to apply the lessons elsewhere.

Still—did he have any choice? He was coming back from Havre des Dames without three of his men and with no decisive victory to compensate for their loss. His mole in Group Fourteen might become less cooperative if he thought the Game Team was no longer a force to be reckoned with. Even if he continued to cooperate, he'd have to send out his intelligence even more cautiously, and that meant even more slowly. The Team Leader was needed more than ever in the south to restrain the militia, and the tighter security in Havre des Dames would have made his returning there unacceptably dangerous even if he hadn't been needed elsewhere.

At least in the south the Team and the militia could gather their own intelligence (with a little help from Nestor), pick their time and place to strike, and finish their work before Group Fourteen even knew that anything was going on. In fact, if a few of the renegade Ranchers simply disappeared without a trace, it might increase the support from the C.G.P.O. for those who'd made them disappear.

Enough to offset the Peace Force? Probably not, at least at the military level, but that wasn't the only level at which this battle was being fought. If the C.G.P.O. influence brought to bear on the N.B. government increased the political constraints on Group Fourteen...

Definitely, raiding the renegades offered a significant number of opportunities, starting with giving the recruits a few easy and satisfactory victories. The Team Leader would have to command the attacks in order to retain his authority over the militia, but he wouldn't be the first officer forced to, adopt a less than optimum tactical solution to solve non-tactical problems.

"Hiko, how far is your plane?"

"Seven hours' fast walking. Probably twice that if you wish to save your strength."

It probably wouldn't be a good idea to have to be carried off the plane, but every extra hour spent this close to Havre des Dames meant more danger of the Peace Force picking up his trail. As for bringing the plane closer—why not send Group Fourteen's C.O. an engraved invitation, complete with directions to the militia camp?

"We'd better move fast."

Hiko nodded, and Kassim took the point while Hiko's companion, Shiro, fell in at the rear...

Paul Rebenc finished checking the lashings on the crane boom and decided that none of them had loosened enough to worry about. He and Bergstrom had done a thorough job before the barge left harbor, but Bergstrom was afraid the first couple of hours under tow might have jerked something loose.

Now that *les copains* had more hope and at least for the moment fewer active enemies, Bergstrom had almost sobered up and taken back most of the leadership that Rebenc had never really wanted anyway. Of course there was a price for the new situation, being bait for the Peace Force's enemies on Bayard, but that was a price *les copains* were willing to pay. They and the Peace Force had the same enemies, and the Peace Force knew its business. As for that most difficult of enemies, the one prepared to die as long as he killed you first, Katie Halloran had summed that up when they all went to say good-bye to her before starting the tow South.

"I don't have the feeling that we're dealing with people who'll go that far. They want cheap victories, and they don't want to pay in blood. Even if I'm wrong, we'll be no worse off than we were."

Rebenc started to jump down from the crane boom, then looked forward. The tow lines to the fishing boat and the workboat ahead were dipping in a steady rhythm, and the waves were beginning to show white crests. He decided not to risk coming down as the deck came up. That could mean a broken ankle. *Les copains* couldn't afford any more casualties, even with Rufus Garron aboard.

Ark Royal's "Chief of the Ship" had joined *les copains* aboard the barge last night, with one small bag of personal gear and four medium-sized crates of tools and equipment. These included not only every imaginable sort of powered hand tool, but a complete miniature lathe. He'd improvised a machine shop in the forward end of the barge's hold, and after that he'd spread out a sleeping bag, curled up, and gone to sleep.

As Rebenc made his way along the crane boom back to the control cabin, he saw that Garron had come out on deck. Stripped to the waist in spite of the breeze, he looked like a great black tree growing from the deck, with his green trousers taking the place of moss or lichen.

Rebenc also saw Geesink staring out the cabin window at Garron, even more intently than she had when he arrived. Rebenc remembered her unsuccessful efforts to bring him coffee and sandwiches while he was setting up his machine shop.

Garron was certainly a fine-looking man. One did not need Roman Talgas's habits to notice that. One also did not have to be jealous of Ju's interest in him. It was a law among the men of *les copains* that Katie and Ju were everybody's sisters, although with Ju that was not easy for any of them except Roman.

Perhaps, though, that was a law of the old *copains*? Surely something new was going to come out of this experience, which would need new laws?

Perhaps, but that was not a good reason to risk offending not only Ju but a man whose help might make the difference between success and failure. There was *no* good reason for that, and besides, Garron was almost old enough to be Ju's father...

Rebenc found himself sweating in spite of the breeze and stepped behind the crane cabin until he was sure he had his face under control. Looking aft, he could see the chartered fishing boat that formed half the newly organized Peace Force Maritime Squadron (Bayard) rolling along in the barge's wake. *Ramilles* carried six experienced small-boat handlers, their personal weapons and gear, two machine-guns, and devices to decoy torpedoes, detect mines and swimmers, and confuse the target-seekers of missiles.

She also carried a dish antenna that let her communicate with *Ark Royal* and her arsenal of orbital weapons. If half of what the Peace Forcers said about those weapons was true, Rebenc could almost feel sorry for anyone facing them.

The whine of propellers swelled to port. One of Group Fourteen's vertiplanes banked so low that a wingtip was barely fifty meters above the barge. Rebenc could make out the auburn hair of the woman in the pilot's seat, and the long-range tanks and rocket pods mounted under the wings. Rebenc didn't even want to guess what might be in those pods, but he noticed that most of the paint under the left wing was discolored and part of it seemed freshly applied.

That must be the verti that had been hit by a sniper's explosive round two days ago. Fortunately the pilot, Captain Dallin, had dropped the burning fuel tank before any major damage could be done. The sniping and another verti's making a forced landing with a sabotaged fuel line reminded everyone that their enemies were only defeated, not destroyed.

Rebenc knew that some of the relief he and the others felt at being out to sea rose from simply being once more where you could see your enemies coming. The only people left in Havre des Dames, with its dark back alleys and hidden knives, were the ones trained and equipped to deal with that sort of trouble.

"*Halte là!*"

Hiko's accent could never have been mistaken for Bayard Francone, but reinforcing the words with his raised rifle made the message clear enough. The two adolescent boys—no, one was a girl—reined in and raised their hands.

"Who are you?" said the boy.

"That's not your concern," said the Team Leader, stepping out onto the trail. "You're our prisoners, whoever we are. Don't ask stupid questions and you'll be well treated."

The Team Leader saw the look passing between the two and had both his mouth and his holster open in the next moment. The moment after that he wished he'd been faster. The boy dug in his heels, and his horse lunged at Hiko. Hiko jumped aside, caught his toe in a root, and would have fallen if he hadn't crashed into a tree.

The Team Leader had just enough time to get off one shot before he also had to jump clear. He aimed at the boy, assuming that his solid pistol rounds couldn't stop the horse, and saw the boy reel in the saddle. From the ground the Team Leader squeezed off two more shots, saw the boy tumble from the saddle as his horse galloped off, and saw two of the Rancher militia bring it down with body shots.

Meanwhile the Team Leader heard three more rifle shots and stood up to see the girl trying to pull a pinned leg out from under her fallen horse. He nodded his thanks to Hiko.

The boy was dead, shot twice in the head and once in the chest. The girl had a broken ankle and a wrenched knee. She also had the look of raw fear on her face, one that the Team Leader admitted was quite justified by the looks on the faces of the militiamen gathering around her.

Casually he showed them the muzzle of his pistol, while Hiko switched his selector to automatic and shifted position so that he could cover the whole group.

"She's a prisoner. She's more use to us in good health. We want to influence the renegades' behavior, not make them our blood enemies."

The ugly lust was replaced on most faces by a look that said just as plainly, "The renegades are already our blood enemies. The only behavior we want to influence them to is begging our mercy on their knees." In the face of the two Game Teamers in sight and the others back somewhere in the woods, no one cared to say it out loud. After a moment one of the men knelt beside the girl and began cutting away the pants on her injured leg while another unhooked his first-aid kit.

"Pity about the horses," said the Team Leader. He wasn't going to strain his authority by having the militiamen carry a corpse five kilometers to the nearest marsh, even if it might be desirable to have the boy vanish apparently into thin air. It would be hard enough to make them carry the girl the twenty kilometers to the plane.

Hiko shrugged. "I thought it best to delay any warning's reaching the farm."

The Team Leader nodded and reached for his radio. Hiko had politely reminded him that the farm might already have been warned if the shots had been heard by anyone with a radio link to it. It was time to act accordingly. The Team Leader sent the rocket squad its coded orders for five incendiary rounds on the farm's buildings and a quick retreat afterward.

He heard the five explosions less than a minute later. Chkalov, the rocket squad leader, knew his business. He also had the advantage of having four Team Members, only eight militiamen to be nursed through their first taste of combat, and no danger of having to guard prisoners. The Team Leader acknowledged hearing the explosions, then turned off his radio and knelt beside the girl.

Shock, painkillers, and fear seemed to have frozen her face into a pale mask. "As I was saying before your brother foolishly got himself killed, you're our prisoner. You'll be well treated as long as you behave yourself and don't try to escape. We'll leave your brother here so that he can be found and given a decent burial. Do you understand?"

The mask broke, but the girl looked as if she couldn't decide whether to cry or to spit in his face. Finally she compromised on a jerky nod.

"Good." He stood up. "Hiko, take the point. The rest of you, take turns on the litter. We've done as much damage as we can safely do today, and enough so that the renegades won't forget it."

CHAPTER 14

"Ready to run, Sergeant?"

"How far?"

"Ten kilometers, out and back."

"I don't think this road goes that far."

"Then we'll head cross-country to make our distance."

Sergeant Tyndall's eyebrows rose. "That'll kill the whole morning."

"We have the morning to kill."

"If you say so, Sergeant Major."

Parkes would be damned if he'd admit that he really didn't want to go back to work until he could get the sight of Katie Halloran out of his mind. Maybe tiring himself out with a good run would help. It wasn't that she was badly disfigured—you couldn't tell under the masking. It wasn't that she was depressed either—she was so damned confident that the *Celestine Auphan* would be salvaged by the time she was back on her feet that you didn't dare twitch a muscle that might have implied doubt.

It wasn't even that she wasn't cooperating with Parkes's and Tyndall's inspection of the nursing ward for possible security precautions, in case she needed to be put under guard. "Certainly there may be some men who are big enough fools to want to come at me through the good Sisters," she'd said. "So I'll do as you want. Then they can live just long enough to know what fools they are."

If Parkes or the rest of the Group had anything to say about it, any prisoners taken in a raid on the hospital were going to live a while longer than that—until they'd been interrogated by agents of the Nouvelle Bretagne government. That might get the government off its butt long enough to at least investigate the possibility of high-powered Rancher support for the troublemakers. An investigation in turn might be enough to teach the Ranchers that they couldn't simply lead the government by the nose every time they wanted to kill Fishermen.

And pigs may fly. Parkes decided to put Katie Halloran and her mysteriously depressing good cheer out of his mind and concentrate on covering distance.

He and Tyndall were in the middle of their warming-up exercises when they saw the Amazon walking down the steps from the hospital. She waved.

"If you're running, can I join you?"

"We're doing ten kilometers," said Tyndall.

"My ground event at the Academy was the ten kilometer," said Forbes-Brandon.

Parkes knew that he really wasn't in a mood to be polite to anyone except Tyndall. He could hardly admit that, however, and he couldn't flatly turn the Amazon away without cracking the almost amicable truce between them, which went back to breakfast the morning after the Night of the Troubles. Being able to relax around each other was agreeable for both, and it helped the Group too.

Meanwhile, Forbes-Brandon was taking off her jacket and tying it by the sleeves around her neck, opening the top of her shirt, and adjusting her boots. By the time Parkes and Tyndall returned to their exercises, she was ready to join them.

When they finally started off, she seemed to flow from standing to moving in one smooth sequence of movements. After half a kilometer Parkes was willing to admit that she'd certainly been a distance runner rather than a sprinter. After a kilometer and a half he began to believe in the ten kilometers, because she was definitely keeping up without working too hard. Of course, those long, elegant legs had to help, and he was holding down his own pace for Tyndall, but still, the Amazon was carrying a good five kilos more than either of them...

Just over two kilometers down the road ran past the mouth of a

131

draw where the woods on top of the bluffs spilled down toward the shore. They were halfway across the draw when Parkes heard the unforgotten and unforgettable sound of an explosive bullet tearing human flesh. At the same time the cheek and arm toward Sergeant Tyndall were spattered and stung.

Parkes shifted direction in mid-stride toward the edge of the road and shouted, "Down, Lieutenant! Sniper!" His only answer was another shot hitting the road, and the sound of bushes and grass crushed under someone landing on them.

Parkes rolled down into the ditch until he hit standing water. Then he crawled along the ditch with only the top of his head above the water, until he reached a bush thick enough to let him raise his head.

The movement drew a third shot, just close enough for fragments to clip leaves off the bush. Parkes stayed still, and a fourth shot went harmlessly into the hedge behind him. When he finally risked a move his first discovery was that he'd jammed the antenna of his radio by falling on it. While trying to free it he looked out at Pat Tyndall.

The sergeant lay sprawled on her back, one shoulder completely destroyed and the arm blown off by the exploding bullet. Parkes swallowed bile. No matter how many times you saw it, it was still hard to remember how much blood a human body held.

At least it had to have been quick. The explosion must have driven fragments into her heart if the blast itself hadn't done the job. Pat would have been dead before she hit the road.

Across the road the Amazon's bedraggled blond head showed from behind a clump of tall grass. The cheek turned toward Parkes was a raw, bloody abrasion from scraping the road, but she was already talking into her radio. Parkes would have kissed her if they'd been on the same side of the road. That would certainly get them out of here faster than waiting for passing traffic to frighten away the sniper or a search party to arrive after their E.T.A. at the hospital passed. (Not to mention the charming prospect of the sniper coming down to finish his job, matching his rifle against their sidearms.)

Parkes gave up the struggle with his radio and moved into a position that let him draw and inspect his pistol without disturbing the bush. At least the pistol tested operational on all counts, which would have helped more if he'd loaded the magazine with explosive rounds instead of solids, with a spare of flechettes for riot work. Solids could be too easily deflected by brush, and flechettes were virtually useless against any sort of cover.

"Parkes!"

"Yes, Lieutenant?"

"I've raised a fishing boat who's relaying to the Alert verti at the airport. I told them to put a squad aboard and drop it at the head of the draw. Are you and your pistol all right?"

"Yes. What about you?"

"My cheek's going to need a bit of patching, but otherwise everything's on-line. Can you give me covering fire while I climb up the draw and try to scare our friend up there into moving? I don't think he'll be able to see me, and he'll be easier for the squad or the verti to hit if he's on the move."

That was sound tactical thinking, provided that you ignored a few awkward facts like their solid shells, and the range advantage of a rifle over a pistol. Parkes pointed these out, half-expecting the lieutenant to damn him for something unmentionable and start climbing the draw herself. He recognized the note in her voice; right now she was too angry to be frightened, but she knew she had to *do* something to keep the fear from getting at her. He'd been there himself.

Come to think of it, Fruit Merchant, you aren't far from there right now. A man couldn't go two New Frontier years without being shot at and then have a terrorist sniper belonging to the Wise One knew what faction pick off a friend at his side without jangling the nerves just a bit.

"So your advice is don't just do something, stand there?" said Forbes-Brandon.

"Right."

That was all the talking either of them seemed to feel like doing. They settled down, with Parkes watching the draw and the lieutenant watching the road and the edge of the sea cliff behind Parkes. He doubted that there was a second man involved, or none of them would have made it to cover, and hoped that he could at least spot the sniper moving into a new position for a clear shot Forbes-Brandon. She would need only a few seconds' warning to reach enough cover to spoil his shot.

Once they heard a plane droning by, but it seemed to be a commercial fixed-wing passing high up. A party of cyclists came trundling down the road from the direction of the countryside, but needed no warning. The lead riders saw Tyndall's body lying in the road and the whole party turned before it reached the draw, then fled at a speed that would have done credit to a hovertank under full throttle. Parkes hoped the P.F. squad would arrive before the Mobile Guards that the cyclists would undoubtedly call the moment they reached a telephone. In a situation like this he would be as afraid of the Mobile Guards as of the sniper.

After what seemed like enough time for a complete cycle of the universe but which actually turned out to be less than ten minutes, Parkes heard the fluttering whine of a verti in a rapid descent. Then grenades went off like a string of firecrackers. White smoke poured up from the head of the draw, screening the squad as it deplaned on the L.Z.. The verti swung out of sight to the left, then reappeared a couple of kilometers up the road, diving toward the sea.

It disappeared below the top of the cliff, but Parkes heard it approaching fast. When it reappeared it was almost directly above him, and he had to clap his hands over his ears as its gun pod sprayed the draw. Under cover of that fire Forbes-Brandon jumped up and sprinted across the road to plunge into the ditch beside Parkes. She'd just realized she'd got wet nearly through, when a rope dropped from the verti and Major Vela came down it, followed by his driver, Lance-Corporal Gough. Vela had his rifle and grenade-launcher, Gough a light machine-gun.

"I thought I would save time by debriefing you people while we waited for our friend," said Vela as soon as the verti was far away enough for him to be heard.

Not to mention getting a better chance at the bastard who killed one of his people, thought Parkes, but he only said, "Thank you, Major."

The story of the sniping didn't take long. Vela was going back over a few details when they heard a burst of firing from the draw, followed by a peremptory squealing from Gough's radio.

"They caught him," said Vela after listening briefly. "Wounded him, offered him a chance to surrender, but he winged Corporal Dietsch for a reply." He made a throat-cutting gesture and stood up as a second verti floated in from the sea to land on the road a hundred meters to the right.

Parkes and Forbes-Brandon also stood up. The sea breeze promptly cut through Parkes's soaked fatigues until he felt as if he was naked.

"I think we have one dry garment between us, and that's my jacket," said Forbes-Brandon. She held it out. "Or at least one non-soaked garment. I think there's room inside it for both of us, if you don't mind an officer's company..."

There was room inside or at least behind the lieutenant's jacket if it was spread out and they stood close. They'd just discovered that they could stand more comfortably with their arms around each other's waists, when the squad came out of the draw with the sniper's body and Corporal Dietsch on stretchers. Captain Laughton and two medics were already trotting up the road from the second verti.

The Surgeon wore athletic shoes and a bulky white sweater over her fatigues, but she didn't blink during her quick examination of the two bodies before she went to work on Dietsch. Parkes had seen more experienced Surgeons than Laughton flinch at less ugly corpses than Tyndall's.

Clearly there was more to Laughton than her blithe unconcern for military regulations. In fact the whole Group seemed to be shaping up better than Parkes would have expected. The final test of combat couldn't be far off, and it would come long before the bad actors had time to get into trouble for lack of anything better to do.

Pat Tyndall was the first member of Group Fourteen to die in combat. She wouldn't be the only one for long. The thought made Parkes shiver involuntarily, and that made him just as involuntarily tighten his grip around Forbes-Brandon's waist, so that he could feel the human warmth creeping through the wet uniform...

CHAPTER 15

Parkes came out of the hall from the wards into the reception room, waited for identification by the guard at the reception desk, then crossed the room to the outer door. He wanted a drink badly, but some fresh air was the best he could manage for now.

Outside at the top of the stairs Parkes automatically looked up to the guard post on top of the cliff. With all-around vision and first priority on the alert verti and its squad, the post could probably defend the hospital against a platoon-sized attack without the guards inside having to chamber a round. That wouldn't please Sergeant Brautigan, who was itching for a fight, but it would make the Hospital Supervisor a lot happier. Letting guards into the reception room was as far as Mother Marguerite would go, even if her hospital might suddenly have moved a lot closer to the firing line.

The guards waved back. With Major Vela dropping by twice a day and the C.O. himself an ever-possible visitor, they had to be on the alert even if they might agree with Parkes that they were guarding a barn that had never contained any horses in the first place.

They would also probably agree with Parkes that until somebody came up with a better idea of what Group Fourteen should do in and around Havre des Dames, guarding the hospital at least couldn't do any harm. It might even do some good if Katie Halloran had been on the target list of the terrorists.

Celestine Auphan's engineer had been properly sympathetic about Tyndall's death when Parkes visited her, but she'd seemed more interested in the progress of the cofferdam being built inside *Celestine*'s hold. Since the hole from the explosion was resting against the rocky bottom, it had to be patched from the inside, which involved a lot of dives and a lot of working mostly by touch in a dark hold.

"At least it's easier to build a patch that's held in place by pressure rather than pushed out by it," Halloran said cheerfully. "If it had been any other way, I doubt they'd be doing it without my help, as God is my witness."

At least Parkes now understood why visiting Halloran always left him unaccountably depressed. She reminded him far too much of his mother, cheerful in the face of the pain of her missing leg and the operation that had ended so disastrously. Cheerful in assuring a boy of ten that he and his little sister would always have her with them, to take care of them and keep Father from marrying that wretched Willow woman.

Cheerful in lying, too, or at least the boy saw it that way for years afterward. The man saw more clearly—but every so often the boy came alive again inside the man. Bifrost had done it, so had Fergie Macintosh's death, and now Pat Tyndall's being chopped down was doing it. He hadn't known her that well, just enough to remember her as a happy, hard-working career N.C.O. from a family with a long tradition of sending sons and daughters into uniform. They would welcome her ashes home with tears but also with a solemn pride.

She'd been a lot like Fergie Macintosh, come to think of it, and they'd both been like quite a few of the other people whose deaths had left Parkes taking a long look into the darkness. That was a fact, not an explanation, but no explanation ever came without facts.

Meanwhile, Parkes realized that if it hadn't been for the warmth and human contact of the Amazon yesterday, he'd be needing to drink away a really fine case of the shakes. A drink or several would still be fine, but he also realized that what he really wanted was to hold and be held by a warm, comfortable woman who would put her arms around the man until the little boy inside went away.

That thought took him onto the narrow stairway carved in the face of the cliff, leading up to the guard post at the top. As he started to climb, an air ambulance landed on the lawn by the bus stop and the attendants started unloading stretchers. Parkes stopped to watch until he was sure it was all civilians, then resumed his climb.

Behind the guard post was the landing zone for the vertis linking the hospital post to the airport. Once he'd reached the airport he could probably find some excuse to go into town. He'd need one, although Havre des Dames wasn't strictly off-limits yet—something about not embarrassing the local and national governments by implying they couldn't keep order. The C.O. and the Squadron commanders had still made it clear that anybody found swanning about in the city wasn't going to like what happened.

Parkes knew he might not find it as easy to come up with the excuses as Hatcher. The Gray Eminence had gone right on managing to spend most of his off-duty time in the city, although everybody wondered why: nobody believed he had enough vices to need that much time to cultivate them. Parkes was also sure that if he couldn't think of *something* convincing, he deserved to lose at least his torch.

But—would he find what he was looking for in a bought embrace? He'd have better luck propositioning the Amazon! Not to mention that a good many of the available women in Havre des Dames were licensed through the Owl, the criminal chief suspected of being behind the sniping of Pat Tyndall. A PFer's chances of being caught literally with his pants down with one of those women were just a little too good if you dreamed of dying in your own bed.

At least the sniper himself had been identified as one of the Owl's men. His weapon, however, was something else—an SG/Charlemagne 7mm with a 20-round magazine and a combined laser/telescopic sight that the sniper hadn't even tried to adjust. A weapon, in short, too good for the man carrying it, but identical to the ones carried by the highly professional squad that attacked the barge on the Night of the Troubles. Parkes would have given long odds that the squad was not the Owl's men.

Parkes increased his pace to a brisk trot. He wanted to check out the file on that mysterious fight on the Night of the Troubles, the one that left blood but no bodies, and the nearest place for that was at the airport. A hypothesis was suddenly forming in his mind, one that made sense to a field soldier with Parkes's experience of both battles and plots.

Suppose there were two groups working on the Night of the

Troubles, the Owl's men and—call them the Game Master's? Suppose that the mysterious fight was the Owl's men ambushing the Gameplayers, not only eliminating them but stealing some of their weapons. Then what could be easier for the Owl than staging an attack on the Peace Force that had the appearance of one by the Gameplayers, to sow confusion and maybe divert Peace Force attention away from him?

It made sense, but no more. It didn't explain why the Owl hadn't considered a more convincing deception. Did he simply underestimate the Peace Force? He wouldn't be the first to do so, or the last to find the mistake fatal, although it was a less common mistake now than fifty years ago. Also, why simply a sniping instead of a rocket attack on the airport—although come to think of it, there had been those two attacks on supply vertis...?

Parkes bumped into a man descending the stairway and had to grip the railing. "Excuse me—"

"Sergeant Major Parkes! Just the man I wanted to see."

It was the Mediator. Goff's voice had the tone of every senior Parkes had ever heard declaring him the ideal man for a really rancid job. He somehow doubted that the Mediator would be an exception, but he still had to listen.

"Can I speak with you unofficially?"

"How unofficially, Mediator?"

"Nobody but the C.O. hears about it. In fact, the C.O. sent me from the airport to look for you."

"He's at the airport?"

Goff nodded. "This stairway is a little public. Shall we go up or down?"

"Up, I think. We can find a nice dark patch of grass between the guard post and the L.Z. and talk."

The sensors of the guard post outranged any weapon closer than the Fourth Empire or the Gros Chaudron militia battalions. They could arrange not to be silhouetted for anyone lucky or smart enough to reach visual aiming range.

Goff and Parkes found their patch of soft grass near the anchor of the transparent balloon that lofted a set of sensors to eight hundred meters, greatly increasing their range. Of course the balloon itself was vulnerable, but any attack on it would be an even more blatant warning than any IR or radar signature. Parkes halfway hoped that the Owl *was* stupid enough to ignore that fact and try an attack on the hospital guard post. Then Group Fourteen could break him into little pieces, move out into the field and mop up the outlaw Ranchers, watch the *Celestine Auphan* come up, and finally get the Hades off this planet!

It occurred to Parkes that anything cooked up between a Group Mediator and a Group C.O. might be a long step in that direction, so he listened with attention as Goff recited facts they both knew about the sniping, the firing on the verti, and the forced landing caused by the sabotaged fuel line. Three incidents, and that only one had been lethal was no fault of the good intentions of the people behind them, whoever they were.

"I've been trying to puzzle out the Owl's motives myself," said Parkes, mostly to remind Goff that he had a voice too. The Mediator's academic background gave him a tendency to lecture even with a class of one. "I've been thinking that he and his allies may have had a falling out, and—"

Goff grinned. "The C.O. told me you'd have figured things out that far. Now, what we've figured out is that the Owl is trying to expose the mole the other party has in Group Fourteen."

Parkes didn't remember his jaw hitting the grass but doubted he could have opened his mouth so wide without its doing so. He got his mouth closed, resisted a temptation to dribble Goff three times around the balloon anchor, and jerked his head. "One of our people, the Gameplayers' mole?"

"Let's say—the Primary Opposition. Also, I used the wrong word, calling it a 'mole.' There'd have been no way to plant anyone in advance. This is someone who was recruited after we reached Bayard, may or may not have given anything to the Primary Opposition, but definitely gave the Secondary Opposition the pip. Now Secondary, or the Owl, is tapping the data-transmission channels and using what they pick up to stage incidents that are intended to provoke us into investigating and exposing the individual." Goff had the decency to sound slightly out of breath after that last sentence. It didn't last long, even though Parkes would have given a finger for a minute's silence, to get his thoughts in order and quiet the churning in his guts at the idea of a traitor in P.F. ranks. It wouldn't be the first time, but it was never something you thought could happen in your Group, not if you had any loyalty to it at all.

"The C.O. concluded that the two verti incidents depended on intelligence from somebody who knew the flight routes and schedules. The sniping depended on somebody who knew that you were going to be running down that road after visiting the hospital."

"Now—you don't have to answer this question. I can't order you to. Colonel MacLean can, but he thought it would save time—"

"Spare me the apologies." No point in prolonging the agony. "Who did I tell, and who might have overheard?"

"Yes. And at least two hours before the incident."

That let out the people at the guard post. It brought in quite a few at HQ, except that come to think of it, he hadn't said anything out loud. He'd left a written memo for—

Hatcher.

Sergeant Major Hatcher. The Group First. The Gray Eminence.

Parkes desperately tried to recall if anyone had gone into Hatcher's office cubicle at the airport before Hatcher himself returned as Parkes was going out. They'd passed as usual, with polite smiles but no words exchanged.

In fact, Parkes distinctly recalled that no one could have seen the memo before Hatcher—and the compulsively tidy Group First would certainly have tidied it into oblivion the moment he read it.

Now Parkes distinctly recalled other unwelcome things:

Hatcher's change of expression when the identity of the mission planet was announced.

Hatcher's remoteness, as if preoccupied, and his frequent absence during the Alert phase on New Frontier.

Hatcher's baggage being unloaded at Main Base, showing signs of tampering but Hatcher saying nothing.

Hatcher's frequent trips into Havre des Dames—always with some excellent reason, but adding up to quite a total-a total of opportunities to establish and maintain contact with anybody.

"Hatcher?" said Parkes. He forced himself to make the word a question even though he doubted it could be.

Goff nodded; "We were looking for someone with a prior

connection to Bayard. Of the four people who had one, Hatcher was the only one in a position to have all the intelligence."

"What was the prior connection?" The words came out easily now. Parkes felt purged, rather as if he'd just vomited an indigestible meal.

"Hatcher had broken service, a four-year gap between his third and fourth enlistments. Some of those years he spent as a mercenary on the Petit Continent, apparently in the Fourth Empire itself. I don't know if it was friends he wanted to help or enemies he wanted to settle with, but he had some business here and he wanted help badly enough to pay a price for it."

"Then—he could have been working for the Fourth Empire, or—"

Goff shook his head. "The Owl's is one organization you can be sure would never take pay from the Fourth Empire. He's the son of a Fourth Empire refugee and lost his mother to their Security."

"Oh." The small comfort of knowing that the Fourth Empire probably hadn't put its bloody fingers into the pie didn't outweigh the pain of knowing about Hatcher, but it helped somewhat.

"So—what does the C.O. want done, and who does he want to do it?"

"For now, Hatcher's been given plausible orders to return to Main Base. That should keep him from doing any more damage for a while. It should also keep his friends in the city from being able to get at him easily."

So Hatcher would be both watched and guarded by the five-hundred-odd PFers at Main Base. Parkes knew he would have to speak to Dozer about this as soon as possible if she hadn't already been told. Whatever was done to Hatcher, he and Dozer had to be part of it. That was another job that went with the six stripes and torch.

A soft cough behind them prevented an awkward silence. Parkes turned, to see a man in his early thirties in the clothing of a working rancher in time for a holiday. He was small and shaggy-haired and generally had the air of a sheep trying to pretend it was a sheepdog.

"Pardon me, messieurs, but you are of the Peace Force?"

The only thing that could be said for the man's Anglic was that it was better than Parkes's Francone, hypnosis or no. Goff replied in excellent Francone, but the man shook his head.

"Please, it is better that you both hear." Goff shrugged and looked at Parkes, who nodded.

"We're listening."

What they heard was a frightened man's account of why he was frightened. Yves Massu and his brother were ranchers in the St. Pierre district. Yesterday they had been attacked by terrorists, fanatics of the C.G.P.O., but much better armed and trained than he would have expected. They had destroyed four buildings on the ranch, killed two people, and badly burned three others. He'd accompanied the wounded here on the air ambulance.

They had also killed his nephew and kidnapped his niece, promising to release her unharmed if no one brought word of the attack to the government or the Peace Force.

"I think my brother believes this. I think my brother is crazier than the terrorists to believe it. The children, they can only be avenged now."

A civilian realist, thought Parkes. *Now let's see just how realistic.*

"Why should we operate in the area of these guerrillas? That might not fit our tactical objectives."

"I think you would not have made your camp in the south if you had no wish to fight such people. Also, it is the law for Peace Groups to do so.

"Furthermore, I can offer you something you want, something that will help the people of the *Celestine Auphan*."

This was the first time Parkes had actually seen Goff look startled. "What's that?"

"An air compressor. A big one."

First a knowledge of tactics, and now this.

"Where is it?"

"In the Massif De Gaulle, in a mine, that I will show you how to get to when the Peace Force agrees to avenge my brother's children. My brother and I are both directors of the corporation that owns the Faucon Noir, so we have the legal right to dispose of its property. I myself also have fifty armed men who will follow me to the mine to give security."

Parkes decided that suggesting they might not need his cooperation to learn that would be a time-wasting threat. This man had clearly done his homework. He signaled to Goff and they stepped around to the far side of the balloon anchor, out of Massu's hearing. Parkes unsnapped the flap of his holster and didn't take his eyes off the rancher.

"Is this guy worth taking seriously?" said Goff.

"Short of hypnosis—"

"That would take too long. Besides—security."

"Yeah." If the opportunity the man was offering was real at all, it was also one that could disappear very quickly at the slightest leak. "I think he's playing us straight. Unless *he's* a Fourth Empire agent, trying to lure the Peace Force into trouble..."

Goff waved the idea away. "Let's forget about seeing the Fourth Empire under every bed. I agree with you. I think he's making a real offer, and I think it's one worth accepting. The sight of Ranchers committing themselves to help Fishermen will be hard to overlook. If everyone sees us helping these Ranchers, it will also send the right kind of message to the C.G.P.O. fanatics who must be supplying the terrorists."

Parkes nodded. He would leave the political implications to Goff. Right now, he was thinking of the tactical implications of the man's offer of fifty men to go for the air compressor. Fifty men, and the Group probably had a way of letting the terrorists know that they were going. Now, if MacLean could just be persuaded to keep Hatcher at the airport...

"Mediator. Let's get our friend aboard a verti. I think it's time to talk to the C.O."

Goff looked over the edge of the cliff and saw that the air ambulance was still grounded by the road. "I'll declare that there's a medical emergency at the airport and we can borrow that one. A little more camouflage too. Nobody ever suspects anything with an air ambulance going somewhere at odd hours of the night."

Parkes shut his holster. Even if nothing else came of it, this episode had done at least one piece of good: he no longer worried about his depression at Pat Tyndall's death or needed a woman.

CHAPTER 16

The militia "lieutenant" drew a line on the map from the north bank of the Villeneuve River to the tip of a spur of the Massif De Gaulle. "That will be our approach march, eighteen kilometers through the forest. We will move in two columns, with the heavy weapons in the rear of the left column and the command team at the head of the right."

"Why don't the off-worlders on the left stay up front too?" came a harsh voice from the rear of the militia company. The Team Leader searched the company for the speaker, but it was impossible in the twilight to pick him out of eighty shadowy faces under green fatigue caps. Lucky for the speaker that the light was going, otherwise the Team Leader would have been somewhat inclined to have Hiko arrange an "accident" for him at the mine.

At least the question would be a good test of the lieutenant's leadership and tactical knowledge. Not just his knowledge of tactics, either, but his ability to explain them. The Team Leader turned his attention back to the man by the map, who was at least managing not to look nervous or surprised at the question.

"The heavy weapons squad can't afford to be caught at the head of the line if we run into an ambush in the forest. They have to be free to move until they have a clear field of fire for their weapons. Once we reach the mine, they will be as far forward as any of us, in case we need direct fire against any defenders of the mine."

A good answer. It seemed to satisfy the questioner too. The

briefing continued.

"Our march is timed to bring us to the mine at dawn. One platoon will set up ambushes covering all approaches; one will demolish the mine entrance and every accessible piece of machinery, and one will remain in reserve."

"Wouldn't a night attack be easier?" A different voice.

"No. Some of the defenders at the mine will probably know the ground better than we do. They might be able to hold us up long enough to call for reinforcements."

Another good answer. It did not mention what the lieutenant might in fact not know, that the militia were fit for a night march but not yet for a night battle. It also left out what he probably knew intellectually but hadn't accepted emotionally, that those reinforcements could include Peace Force rifle units.

"After we've finished with the mine we will return to our trucks with our casualties and prisoners. We will then either travel to Bivouac C by land or else withdraw to Landing Strip K and await air evacuation."

"Can't we do some raiding on the way home? It's mostly renegade territory up there. I'm thinking that a few burned farms would be a good scare for the bastards."

The second questioner again. Obviously a man with promise, once he learned to temper his enthusiasm with some knowledge of the limitations of his fellow militiamen.

"We don't know how much time and ammunition we'll expend at the mine. If we made any raids on the way back, we could find ourselves in a big fight, short of ammunition, and with our wounded to think about. We can't bring the trucks any closer to the mine without risking them being caught on open ground.

"Besides, let's eat our banquet one course at a time. We'll have the survivors of fifty-odd renegades as prisoners. That and the mine itself should be a big enough victory to keep the renegades looking over their shoulders while we pick the place to hit them next."

"Will any of the prisoners be women?" Somebody entirely new, with a tone of voice that made the Team Leader's hand jerk involuntarily toward his pistol.

"They will all be prisoners. They're worth a lot more alive and healthy back in our camps. If we do need to impress their friends, we can always dispose of one or two of them there, with the rest looking on, and send the film around. That will do more for our victory than just littering the ground around the mine with corpses."

Which might persuade the government to turn loose the Peace Force, or even bring a battalion of the Light Brigade from the east coast. That would end any possibility of the barely trained militia being useful to the Team Leader's plans, even though he might be able to take some advantage of the confusion that would follow their rounding up.

Indeed, it seemed only too likely that the battle at the Faucon Noir mine would be the first and last battle for his militiamen, and a battle they might not win. As the lieutenant proceeded to list the ammunition, rations, and other equipment each man would be carrying, the Team Leader wondered for the twentieth time if there'd been any alternative to this goddess-forsaken gamble.

For the twentieth time he concluded that there had been none. Once the militia learned that fifty renegades would be conducting a salvage operation at the mine, they were possessed with one and the same idea—go to the mine and smash the renegades. The Team Leader would have had about the same chance of stopping them and still keeping any authority over them as he would have had of pushing a starship into Yariv Space with his bare hands. He felt more and more like the man running along after the mob, shouting, "Wait for me, I'm your leader!" and he wondered if this would be common among the Game Team Leaders sent out-system.

Never mind future Team Leaders; consider his own situation in this particular battle. It was within the capabilities of the militia, if just barely. Some of their leaders might emerge as really good with the seasoning of a combat victory if they survived. The lieutenant commanding the Second Company was one of them; he'd started out as the man who stayed under cover and opened fire when the smoke bomb went off.

They would also be keeping the irreplaceable vehicles and aircraft out of places where they'd be easy targets for Peace Force air or space support. The Peace Forcers were like a very powerful boxer who had to land every punch squarely on his opponent's jaw or be penalized. They had to let fly at precisely delimited, unequivocally hostile targets or not let fly at all. They could not chew large chunks out of the landscape of an inhabited planet or shoot down any unidentified aircraft entering a prohibited area simply on the probability that this might take out an enemy.

Besides, even if the worst happened and nobody who left tonight for the Faucon Noir mine came back to this camp, did it matter? A Peace Force Company Group would have been deployed, kept busy, and suffer casualties. A planet's politics would have been disrupted, factional conflicts embittered, and the Game Master's plans (or those of his unknown and never-to-be-discussed financial backers) advanced rather substantially. Not as substantially as they would be if the mine mission succeeded, but certainly enough to make ninety lives a small matter.

Except that perhaps it was not such a small matter after all. These men would die as soldiers because the Team Leader had made them soldiers, using the knowledge of war given him by the goddess. In Kali's eyes he had assumed some responsibility for their fate. If that fate was to be slaughtered like sheep, what would her judgment be? The Team Leader did not know. He only knew that he could no longer be as indifferent to the possibility of disaster as he had been. One did not offend Kali lightly.

Juliana Geesink shrugged herself out of the last of her diving gear and began stripping off her wetsuit. Paul inspected the gear and hooked the air bottles to the small compressor to recharge, then picked up a towel and started giving all of Geesink's exposed skin a brisk rubdown.

"Oh, that feels good, Paul," she said as he ran the towel in between her pale toes. "The water temperature must have dropped five degrees since yesterday."

"Thank God you only had to make one dive, then," said Rebenc, and wished he'd bitten his tongue. She hated male protectiveness, and even worse, she'd had to make only one dive today because that was all they needed. *Les copains* had come about as far as they could without the second heavy compressor needed to blast the water out of the sealed, plugged, and coffer-dammed *Celestine Auphan* and bring her to the surface.

Geesink said nothing, only bowed her head so that Rebenc could dry her hair and rub the back of her neck. His hands rested lightly on her shoulders for a moment before he started toweling, and she didn't try to shrug them off.

"Paul, is there such a thing as too much pride?"

Rebenc's first thought was that she wanted his advice on whether to try seducing Rufus Garron. It wouldn't be the first time that she'd ask for fraternal advice on a love affair from the man's point of view, but it would be the first time giving the advice hurt.

"Well, I don't think Garron's like Roman, for a start, so—"

"Garron! He spends all of his time in that shop of his, most of the time with the door locked! I think he's faithfully married to that lathe of his! If he'd just father an air compressor on it—!"

That didn't sound like the fury or even the pride of a woman scorned. Rebenc still felt guilty at being so relieved. "He said it wouldn't be all that easy to produce a compressor powerful enough from the available components."

"Don't the Peace Forcers have some big ones aboard their ships?"

"Yes, but they're part of the ships' built-in equipment. I don't know if they could dismantle one, bring it down, and make it work on our barge even if they wanted to."

"Then what damned good is the Peace Force to us?"

Rebenc looked out to sea, where one of the Peace Force boats was throwing up a white bow wave about a kilometer beyond the farthest reef. "For one thing, they're keeping all the loose maniacs with guns running around from running toward us. Or bombs, to put in *Celestine* and blow her apart so God Himself couldn't salvage her! Nobody but the Fourth Empire's going to get past their patrols, and I don't think we're on their enemies list."

"Yet. And what if the boats have to withdraw, the way the vertis have done?"

"They've withdrawn them for a training exercise out of Camp Tyndall. That won't last forever."

"That's what they say. Maybe they're even telling the truth.

But I think there's something to that rumor about the terrorists upcountry being the same people who killed Sergeant Tyndall. *I* think the Peace Forcers are going off chasing those people, and God knows when they'll be back.

"Besides, they don't have to be gone long. Just enough for some swine to build a bomb and hire a commercial plane to fly over us and drop it. How do we salvage our salvage equipment if that happens, oh tactical genius and expert on the Peace Forcers?"

Rebenc said a few impolite things under his breath about women. To his own conscience or his confessor—and that reminded him that he hadn't been to confession or Mass since they left Port Tourville—he would have admitted that Ju was right about the one-plane, one-bomb problem. He would also have admitted that he was just as frightened and tired and frustrated as she was, besides having a few aches from his attack of the bends. The price of saving their pride by playing bait for the Peace Forcers' enemies was getting a trifle too high.

Instead, he snarled, "And what's wrong with their going after the terrorists? Those bastards killed one of their people."

"One out of nine hundred."

"One out of a *family* of nine hundred. Or maybe a clan. But haven't you seen how they all behave toward outsiders? Touch one and you have to fight all of them! What wouldn't you give up, if you had a chance at the people who sank *Celestine* and blinded Katie?"

Geesink sighed. "I suppose you have a point. Although I wonder if that big blond lieutenant is anybody's friend."

"Jealous, Ju?"

She grinned. "Maybe I would like a few of those extra centimeters. Just enough so that I could punch you out when you become too overbearing. The rest of the time I can stand having you around." She turned and kissed him lightly on the chin, the only part of his face she could reach without standing up.

"I'd better go get a dry towel," said Rebenc, retreating hastily. He really didn't want to follow up any of the lines of thought that were presenting themselves to him where anyone else could see.

No, there was one he wanted to discuss with the rest of *les copains*, and then with Garron, to get the Peace Force viewpoint. There were five or six heavy compressors in private hands on the Storm Coast, and probably many more on the east coast. If *les copains* could persuade the rest of the Fishermen to pool their money and buy one of those machines, could the Peace Force transport it and Garron repair and run it? That would not take too many Peace Force resources, and it would save time, which they now needed almost as badly as they needed the compressor.

The spring storms had passed while *Celestine* lay snug thirty meters down. Now they were in the lull of good weather between spring and summer; with maybe another half-month of good diving and working conditions available. After that, for months the weather would be as treacherous an opponent as any terrorist, and one that no Peace Forcer could do anything about.

The Peace Force retaliation for Sergeant Tyndall's death might keep the terrorists too busy to think about *Celestine* and her people. It could do nothing to keep a storm from blowing up when they were trying to tow the derelict ship out through Les Fourchettes and throwing her on the rocks, tearing her open or wracking her so badly that she'd never float again.

Rebenc made a low animal noise in his throat and felt a hand on his arm.

"Don't, Paul. We are going to see her rise again. We are going to see her rise again. We are going to see her rise again. What I tell you three times is true."

He turned and slipped Ju's arm through his, not daring or wanting to do more. They stood that way until they heard Vasi shouting from aft that dinner was ready.

"Another reason for finishing this job quickly," said Geesink.

"Yes?"

"I can't stand much more of Joseph's cooking."

"He tries."

"Yes. Very badly, at almost every meal."

Arm in arm, they walked aft.

CHAPTER 17

Small bells tinkled from the control panel of the verti. Warrant Officer Gallagher listened for a moment, eyes still aimed at the heads-up display, then slapped a switch. Another set of bells replied to the first one, then both tinkled into silence.

Parkes was already unstrapping himself from the co-pilot's seat. The tinkling bells were the challenge and reply for the naval liaison and assault party, waiting for their reinforcements in the form of "Captain" Yves Massu's improvised militia.

Or at least that was what the militiamen believed.

Parkes squeezed past the co-pilot returning to her seat and squatted beside Massu. The man was obviously fidgety and trying not to show it. He had one thumb hooked casually in his webbing while he fiddled with the cuff of his trousers with the other hand.

"You actually dropped the fuel and the assault people from your ship in orbit?" said Massu.

"What makes you think we couldn't do that?" said Parkes, more abruptly than he'd intended. Was Massu getting suspicious now? Couldn't he wait another ten minutes, when it wouldn't matter—and when Parkes would know if the naval liaison party that set up the fuel depot for the assault force from Camp Tyndall had landed without any casualties.

"It seems—well, a rather dangerous way of doing things."

"Nobody takes on this job without knowing it's dangerous."

"Nobody? Ever?" Parkes heard a note of mockery in Massu's

152

voice. Was the man going to try calming his nerves by getting on Parkes's?

If so, he never had a chance. The floor shook as Gallagher put the verti over from level into vertical flight. The noise of the turbines rose, the vibration made Parkes grip his rifle more tightly, then all conversation became impossible as the door gunner at his sight console popped all four doors. Parkes swallowed hard and went on swallowing to save his eardrums from pressure changes and noise as the verti slid down an invisible hillside in the sky to a bumpy but safe landing.

Parkes was the first out of the verti, even before the engines died. Ever after they did, it took a minute for his ears to recover. Fortunately he didn't need hearing to pick out the other four vertis parked around the L.Z., the hoses leading from two to the fuel pods, and the assault party's command group strolling toward him.

"Sergeant Major Parkes reporting with the militia reinforcements."

Major Vela nodded. He wore civilian clothes, work trousers and a bulky green sweater with his rank badges pinned on to the shoulders. Forbes-Brandon wore a similar sweater and a farm wife's woolen skirt with heavy stockings and boots. The rest of the command group was similarly dressed.

The last verti landed and started disgorging its militiamen. Captain Massu hurried up and saluted. Vela's mouth opened to bawl him out for saluting in the field, then shut again as he saw Massu staring around him at the apparent civilians.

"What the devil—?"

"The devil has nothing to do with it, I think," said Vela. "Your pardon, Captain Massu, but I'm afraid we had to work a little deception on you. We have reason to believe that the government agency which had to approve the salvage from the Faucon Noir mine has been infiltrated by Rancher spies. The risk of flying your men into an ambush seemed excessive. "So your militiamen are going to stay here, along with twelve of our people to provide communications and extra firepower in case the hostile Ranchers do mount an attack against this L.Z."

Not that this was very likely, in the amount of time the militiamen would be here. The L.Z. was at least thirty kilometers from the nearest Rancher town. Getting your allies killed unnecessarily was still never wise.

"Our assault team of one rifle platoon, one launcher squad, the naval liaison people, and our salvage crew will fly to the Faucon Noir and execute the planned salvage. We would like the three miners from your militia to accompany us. We can't order them, and we do have mining and pump experts ourselves. The work will go faster if your people are with us, however."

Massu was giving a remarkably good imitation of a man trying not to grind his teeth or stamp his feet with rage. Finally he said, "It is an insult to my men that we are not to be allowed a post of danger—"

"You have a post with some danger right here. We may need this L.Z. badly if we have to leave the mine in a hurry, for evacuating our wounded or flying in reinforcements. Only your men can properly defend it if the Ranchers attack."

Massu looked a trifle mollified. "Well, then it is acceptable if the miners go with you if they wish. I cannot order *them*. On one condition though. That I also go with you."

Vela shook his head. "I don't doubt your courage or your honor, Captain. Only consider who is to lead your men here if you go with us? Do you have several reliable subordinates in case some become casualties? Or will your men obey the orders of Sergeant Voorhis, in charge at the L.Z.?"

Massu's face showed a battle between pride in his men and common sense. Common sense won. He shook his head. "You are right. But at least a token—three or four of my best men, to fly to the mine? Is that within reason?"

"Sonny!"

"Yes?" came Captain Dallin's voice from the cockpit of the nearest verti.

"Do we have the extra lift for about a half-ton of militiamen?"

"That's cutting it pretty fine, but if it's important to them—"

"It is."

"Then tell them to hop aboard Dog Able Six and Fox Eagle Two."

"Thank you, Major," said Massu. He turned away and started shouting to his men to gather around. Parkes hoped he would cut the

154

speeches short. Seven of Group Fourteen's ten medium vertis were here on one L.Z. in technically hostile territory. That was a target that could tempt the opposition to commit air or missile resources if they had any. Parkes wouldn't care to bet the future air mobility of Fourteen on Bayard that they didn't.

Massu's speech and choosing volunteers to go to the mine lasted long enough for Parkes to wander over toward the Amazon. Forbes-Brandon looked tired, which was no surprise considering that she'd been pulled out of bed for the highly improvised council of war that launched Operation Flagwaver. (A lousy name, Parkes thought, but then they'd all been saving their energy and imagination for tactical details. This operation wasn't going to be in the history books unless it failed and in that case most of the council of war wouldn't be around to hear the complaints.)

Once she'd finished her part in the council, Forbes-Brandon had spent the next twenty-nine hours successively shuttling up to orbit, picking up a naval liaison team from the *Ark Royal*, shuttling down to a drop at L.Z. Cucumber (not a good name either, but at least it was shaped like one), guiding the fuel and supply drop and setting up the pods, and guarding her back until the vertis with the assault party showed up from Camp Tyndall.

If she'd had more than two or three hours' sleep in all that time, it would be a miracle.

"Why don't you sit down, Lieutenant?"

"Oh, I can manage for as long as I need to. There won't be that much to be done at the mine unless we need another supply drop or get hit. I don't want to leave Sub-lieutenant Holland in charge of the final loading." She frowned. "Or maybe I shouldn't have told you that."

"Lieutenant, I never forget anything anybody tells me about somebody I'm serving with. I never pass it on, either, unless there's a real need for somebody to know."

"Thank you, Sergeant Major." She sat down on a stump and stretched out her legs. Parkes couldn't help noticing the extreme elegance of those legs, even in their long wool stockings and boots. He also couldn't help noticing that the usually square shoulders sagged with fatigue.

"Holland's a lot like me when I was his age," she added. "Very enthusiastic, very confident, knows a lot but thinks he knows everything. There's only one difference, and that's—" Parkes didn't hear what the difference was, because Major Vela's voice suddenly blared through a bullhorn: "All Peace Force personnel board your aircraft and prepare to lift out. All militia personnel clear the L.Z. and take your assigned positions in the defense perimeter."

He repeated the message twice, but by the time he'd finished the second time everybody Parkes could see was on the move—the PFers only looking confused, the militiamen blundering about and bumping into each other with Massu trying to straighten them out with shouted orders that only made matters worse. Parkes hoped they'd all be clear before the vertis started engines, because they couldn't afford to have a verti out of action with a propeller bent by chopping up a militiaman. The militiamen were a lot more expendable than the vertis, allies or not.

By the time Parkes climbed into Major Vela's verti behind Forbes-Brandon, the militiamen were mostly out ofhann's way. Parkes still thanked the Wise One and all the gods of war that the militiamen weren't flying to the Faucon Noir, They had enthusiasm, but not much else to let them stand off a determined terrorist attack. Fifty-five armed Peace Forcers, substituted for the militiamen under circumstances that shouldn't let—the leak (let's not say Hatcher out here; it might be bad luck) warn the terrorists, should be able to handle anything the terrorists could throw at them.

They could also call on air and orbital fire support, and if necessary reinforcements. Four of the vertis would be flying straight back out after landing the assault team, then returning to Main Base Camp and waiting there until the air compressor had been dismantled into components small enough to lift. In an emergency they could lift reinforcements either to L.Z. Cucumber or all the way to the mine.

Parkes settled onto his bench and hooked his rifle in place beside him. Captain Dallin was cursing a couple of slowpokes as they scrambled in with a clatter and thump of equipment and boots on the floor.

No, Operation Flagwaver had a sound plan and good top leadership. There weren't even too many weak spots Parkes knew of at the lower levels, although one of them could turn out to be in a bad place. Sergeant Kiley of the rifle platoon would be taking over if Lieutenant Gleason got hit, and he was really too excitable to handle that kind of a situation. He tended to concentrate on what he could see in front of him and ignore what might be sneaking up behind. If there'd been any choice, Parkes would rather have used a different platoon, but they had to use what was available at Camp Tyndall or else risk tipping their hand to the leak by suspicious troop movements in advance of the jump-off.

As the engines started, Parkes made a mental note that he'd better be ready to take over the platoon himself if Gleason's luck ran out. He was also conscious of an unexpected weight on his left shoulder. He cautiously turned his head and saw that Lieutenant Forbes-Brandon had fallen asleep with her head resting on his shoulder.

Parkes smiled. Sure that no one could see him in the darkened interior of the verti, he put his arm around the lieutenant to brace her as the floor tilted under them and the verti lifted out.

CHAPTER 18

The trees were giving way to bushes, but many high and thick enough to provide both cover and concealment. The Team Leader held up a hand and behind him the militia column came to a ragged halt. In the silent upland dawn he heard the wheezing breath of some men for whom a twenty-kilometer hike with full pack and weapons was more than just healthy exercise. The average level of physical fitness among the militiamen was extraordinarily high, but no "average" ever excluded a few laggards.

A kilometer ahead the bushes gave way to bare rocky ground and stubbly blue-green grass. Neither the map nor the local informants had lied; the mine entrance was two hundred meters short of that point. The militia would have concealment and even some cover right up to the final rush on the mine.

The Team Leader scanned the area around the mine entrance with his binoculars. The two renegade posts the scouts had reported an hour ago were still there. Neither had been reinforced. One machine-gun commanded the ravine that approached the entrance from the right. About a squad of riflemen was posted to cover the approach over open ground from the left. Neither group looked particularly alert. The Team Leader wondered if they had acquired some electronic sensors or were relying on quick reinforcement by their comrades. The Team Leader trusted to his jammers to deal with the first, and the heavy weapons to interfere with the second for long enough.

It was a pity that he couldn't just stand off and bombard the mine entrance rather than subject enthusiastic but untested troops to what could still be a nasty little firefight. Unfortunately there was still too much equipment the renegades could salvage if he did that. Men laying demolition charges were the only way to take the Faucon Noir permanently off the list of anyone's available resources.

The Team Leader punched in the "Execute" signal for dividing each column into the covering and assault teams. The squirted signal lasted less than half a second; Hiko's acknowledgment from the left column was even shorter. It would have been better to bring one column around from the rear of the mine, but coordinating the two columns would have increased the load of detectable signaling. Beyond a certain point the Peace Forcers couldn't miss a stream of mysterious signals or resist trying to solve the mystery by dropping in uninvited. His source of intelligence couldn't give a goddess-forsaken minute's warning of such a visit either!

Dividing the Team Leader's column took the better part of five minutes and made enough noise to wake a drunken bonze. It took another minute before Hiko announced that his column had also divided. The Team Leader led his assault team forward, trying to keep well to the right and clear of the supporters' line of fire. The support team would be at fairly long range for their grenade launchers, and their temporary abundance of ammunition might tempt them to wild shooting.

The Team Leader and the lieutenant went to ground ten meters ahead of their men and studied the ravine and its defenders. Their civilian clothes were unmistakably ragged, and one woman's boots looked as if they hadn't been shined in a year.

"I think I should take one squad right up over the lip of the ravine," said the lieutenant. "We can grenade anyone in it, then drop down and take the M.G. in the rear."

In a properly organized army that wouldn't have been a lieutenant's job, but then, the militiamen didn't qualify on either count. They were an improvised force where the kind of personal leadership the lieutenant wanted to show counted for more than rank or T.O.

"Very well. Stay to the left of the red-streaked boulder, at least ten meters to the left. I'll send a message back to the fire support to have them keep their grenades to the right of it. When the messenger returns, you can jump off."

The Team Leader needed both fingers and toes to count his battles and skirmishes, but that didn't make the messenger's round trip pass any faster. He was vaguely surprised that his watch wasn't showing at least 1100 when the messenger returned. The Team Leader clapped the lieutenant on the shoulder and sent the "Execute" to both Hiko and the heavy weapons team in the forest.

Three rockets howled out of the trees and scrawled smoke trails across the sky. They were aimed at the crest of the hill above the mine, to air-burst there and discourage any reinforcements camped in the open.

Instead, one rocket burst at the height of its trajectory. Another tipped over and went straight down, its smoke trail ending in a harmless puff of dust on the near side of the hill. Only one rocket flew straight, so that smoke and flying rocks blossomed beyond the crest.

The Team Leader frowned. That looked remarkably like jamming and anti-missile lasers at work, except that the renegades— no, he would *not* use the phrase "couldn't possibly have such equipment."

At least the heavy weapons people knew what to do about what they thought they saw. Three more rockets followed the first salvo at a minimum interval, to take advantage of the effect of the smoke on any lasers. At the same time the lieutenant and his squad plunged forward, the Team Leader led his men out to the right at a trot, and the fire support opened up, spraying the edge of the ravine and the area around the M.G. with grenades.

This time two of the rockets burst in the air. The Team Leader saw the glowing line of a laser beam darting up at one of them. The third rocket went home and the laser beam died abruptly, but he knew that where there were lasers there would also be other weapons his militiamen would find it hard to handle.

The M.G. at the mouth of the ravine opened up as the Team Leader signaled to his men to lie down and provide covering fire for the lieutenant. Then he punched the code and "Execute" for an order to the heavy weapons that translated: "Shoot three more rockets at the mine and then run as fast as you can." For now he would assume that they were facing Peace Forcers, who would sooner go into action with spears and swords than without air support on call.

The heavy weapons being temporarily out of the fight didn't mean the militiamen had to run too. They were too close to their opponents for heavy weapons to be easily turned loose on them. In a close-range firefight many things could go wrong for even the best-trained people, and if only a few of them went wrong the demo team could still have their few minutes in the mine.

The lieutenant vanished over the lip of the ravine and the M.G. fell silent. About time too; three of the men with the Team Leader were already down in spite of their armored vests. He signaled the others to their feet, and they rushed the mouth of the ravine just as the increasing volume of fire to the left hinted that Hiko's column was also heavily engaged.

All five of the M.G. squad were down and two had lost enough clothing to expose Peace Force body armor underneath. The Team Leader made a mental note to keep his men from stripping the bodies. Peace Force weapons and gear were superb but too hard to disguise.

The firing from the left was even louder, although all small arms. The Team Leader realized that he'd rushed the mouth of the ravine without signaling to his own support to cease fire, and that it was Kali's own gift that he and his men weren't dead. More precisely, it was the gift of the support leader's unexpectedly clear eye and cool head. There was another man to be commended and promoted if he lived through today.

The Peace Forcers were now bringing their reserves up over the crest, slower than the Team Leader had expected. Their formation was also a trifle ragged. Very likely the two rockets had done damage even Peace Forcers couldn't shrug off.

"Take cover! Engage targets of opportunity! Single shot!"

The Team Leader ignored his own first order long enough to shoot the apparent Peace Force leader, then found a rock almost large enough to hide him, and slipped a new magazine into his rifle. While he was doing that the firing rose both around him and from up the hill. In the general uproar it was hard to tell, but most of his people seemed to be using single shots. This phase of the fight was going to be a gigantic sniping competition for at least a few minutes, and his men's marksmanship should be given every chance to do as much damage as

161

possible.

Farther down the ravine the lieutenant and his survivors were also under cover and shooting, but mostly on full automatic. That was a fine way to ruin aim and waste ammunition. At least the combined militia force in the ravine seemed to be tying down most of the Peace Force reserves. That should keep them off Hiko's column. They could go on doing this unless the Peace Forcers decided that the M.G. team was dead and they could afford to grenade all the way up and down the ravine, wiping it clean of life...

The Team Leader had been lying nearly on his back. Now he saw a verti float across his field of vision, silhouetted against a patchwork of scruffy clouds and blue sky. He saw four fat containers detach themselves from it in puffs of smoke and hurtle out of his field of vision. He didn't need to see or hear anything more, but with nowhere to go he still listened, hands now locked around his rifle as if it were a Peace Forcer's neck.

The explosions came on schedule, three of them almost simultaneously a long way off, then a fourth much closer. The last one sent a wave of debris flying over the ravine and dislodged fist-sized rocks from the sides. One of them cracked the Team Leader in the ankle. He put the pain into a comer of his mind and picked off a Peace Forcer whose cover had been stripped away by the blast of the F.A.E. bomb.

The heavy weapons were gone; three Peace Force F.A.E. bombs would have been dropped to produce overlapping blast patterns, and the overpressures would have been endurable anywhere the squad could have reached. The fourth explosion would most likely have been a command-detonated bomb hitting Hiko's fire support. A gamble, using F.A.E. this close to your own position, but the Peace Force C.O. obviously had a cool head and the verti pilot a good eye.

The Team Leader knew that he had a debt to pay in the name of Kali to Nestor, who had refused light AA missiles to the militiamen. Even a few of them would have imposed a little discretion on the Peace Forcers in the use of their hard-to-replace vertis. More explosive small-arms' rounds would have been a tolerable second-best. Neither had come, in spite of several requests. Clearly the C.G.P.O. wanted to make sure their pawns stayed pawns.

The Team Leader signaled to the lieutenant to prepare for a rush up the ravine. The only chance of winning now was to combine the survivors of both columns, rush the mine, and hold the entrance while any surviving demolition men did their best. If the militiamen could do that much, they would still have an honored place among the servants of Kali, and the Team Leader would not deny to the goddess herself that he'd been proud to serve with them.

The lieutenant rose to his feet just in time to be smashed back to the ground by a burst of fire in his back. The Team Leader whirled, shot the "dead" Peace Forcer who'd miraculously come back to life on the M.G. and nearly died himself in the next moment as a P.F. squad appeared at the mine end of the ravine. The lieutenant's squad broke and ran, sweeping up the Team Leader's men with them, and the whole militia force went stampeding out of the ravine.

The Team Leader had the slight consolation of being the last man out. His fire support opened up again, and the grenades bursting in and over the ravine kept the Peace Forcers from too close a pursuit. That lasted until the P.F. brought a second M.G. into action up the hill. The supporting fire was dying away as the Team Leader led his surviving men back to their starting point.

A glance at his watch and a longer look around told him that it had taken less than ten minutes for him to lose nearly two-thirds of his men. He had five survivors of the attack on the ravine. Hiko had ten survivors from his whole column. There were also eleven thoroughly shaken survivors of the Team Leader's fire support, who'd lost five men to the second M.G. in one minute, including their leader. Neither they nor any of the other militiamen wanted to do anything but head for the forest.

Add to these losses in front of the mine the six Team members and ten militiamen with the heavy weapons, and the Team Leader had to admit that he no longer commanded a combat-effective force. He still forced them to wait long enough for a count of their remaining ammunition, while he commended both the lieutenant and the fire-support leader to the special favor of Kali. Then he put Hiko on the point and himself at the rear and the militiamen crept down the hill, running where they had cover and crawling where they didn't.

It was nearly noon when the Team Leader ordered a break for

cigarettes, water, and first-aid for minor wounds. He leaned back against a tree, let Hiko apply ointment and a bandage to his sore ankle, and ignored the man's polite efforts to save his Leader's face by exaggerating the extent of his own column's defeat. For Hiko this was a ritual; and he would be worth listening to only when he'd completed the ritual and was ready to give an accurate report. Also, the firefight in the ravine had left the Team Leader what he hoped was temporarily half deaf.

At least the Peace Force wasn't following up their victory with a vigorous pursuit. This wasn't completely a surprise, because the Peace Forcers might be only a platoon plus a fire-support observer. If so, they'd probably been hit hard enough to be reluctant to dash into the forest after an enemy who knew how to shoot and might still be able to lay ambushes.

Or did they have some easier plan in mind for finishing off the militia, such as laying an ambush with air-lifted troops around the vehicles? They would certainly know the location of the vehicles after they finished interrogating prisoners.

The Team Leader made another mental note: signal the leader of the vehicle drivers and security squad to move the whole convoy to an alternate rendezvous about ten kilometers west of the now-compromised one. The new rendezvous would let the Second Company's survivors merge with civilian traffic after a comparatively short cross-country trip.

Kali, grant that is enough to save the vehicles. A two-hundred-kilometer hike to safety would finish off the survivors as thoroughly as the Peace Force could, besides leaving the surviving Game Team men without leadership for several possibly critical days. What the surviving militia officers in the First Company would think, say, or do after word of this defeat spread was not pleasant to contemplate.

Right now the Team Leader wasn't even sure if he and Hiko should stay together during the march out to guard each other's backs or stay apart to make a more difficult target.

Just before sunset Parkes came over the crest of the hill to the

164

already-shadowed rear slope where the two tents of the aid station were set up. From behind him came the whine of a verti taking off with another load of compressor components.

The job of disassembling and shipping out the compressor was going fast. Major Kuzik knew just about everything anyone could know about machinery for moving air and water, and in spite of limping from a rock splinter in one knee he'd saved the salvage crew several hours' work already. A few components would need repair or replacement before the compressor was ready to start pumping air into the *Celestine Auphan*, but nothing that Rufus Goff couldn't fix. The Faucon Noir's upper gallery, where the compressor had been, was exposed to the dry upland air, and rust and corrosion had made surprisingly little headway.

From the aid station Parkes could hear Dr. Laughton dictating a list of supplies and equipment she'd need to make the last six wounded (three of them prisoners) fit to be evacuated. The wounded were in good hands, even if those hands were a bit shaky in their grip of military detail.

He was more concerned about 2 Platoon, temporarily his command. Lieutenant Gleason was among the evacuated wounded, and Sergeant Kiley was dead. Kiley had done just what Parkes had expected him to do, losing the tactical picture and getting tied up with the firefight in the ravine. Parkes had to lead the reserve up himself, and by the time they had finished with the ravine it was too late to cut off the retreat of the other enemy column.

They might be back, too, and before that happened Parkes wanted another platoon on the position. He was prepared to go on leading 2 Platoon as long as they were at the Faucon Noir. In fact, he could do more to shape them up than some lieutenant who hadn't been through today's fight. He still didn't want to trust the defense of Fourteen's position at the Faucon Noir to a platoon down to two-thirds strength, minus its C.O., and mishandled by its late platoon sergeant.

Parkes saw the stooped figure sitting by one of the stretchers holding the dead, and turned toward it. He was nearly on top of it before it straightened up, suddenly growing too tall to be Major Vela.

"Oh, good evening, Sergeant Major."

"Good evening, Lieutenant."

Forbes-Brandon looked old enough to be her own mother, but her face was more set than ever. As she stood up, Parkes noted that in profile her face was practically all nose and jaw, and that she was still in her civilian clothes. Now they looked as if they'd been stolen from a street derelict.

Parkes looked down at the stretcher. The tag on it read "Holland, Keith. Sub-lieutenant, P.C.N.F., K2-41755212-14G." He'd been one of the first to die, when the rocket landed among the naval liaison party and took out half its strength.

Forbes-Brandon didn't seem interested in talking, although her eyes were dry and her hands clasped firmly in her lap. He was about to turn away when she began to talk in a low, expressionless voice, her eyes on Holland's poncho-shrouded body.

"It shouldn't have been you, Keith. It shouldn't ever be anyone like you. You were looking forward to your first leave. You weren't going to have to sneak home to see your nurse and the grooms. You were *enjoying* yourself, damn you!"

Even the last words came out totally without expression. Parkes held his breath, hoping that if he did the lieutenant wouldn't notice him and he could sneak away. Meanwhile, the cause of his depression over Pat Tyndall's death was falling into place in his mind with an almost audible click.

It was another side of the guilt he'd never been able to shake, over abandoning his father to help Louise escape their stepmother. It didn't curdle his stomach, so he hadn't recognized it until now. He owed Forbes-Brandon a good deal, for knowing that she had something like the same problem had taught him about himself.

He still didn't want to intrude on her any more than he welcomed spectators when he was wrestling with his own nightmares. Also, it was just possible that if he didn't get away from her he would take her in his arms, sharing grief and exchanging comfort in a way that went back much further than armies.

He was turning to go when a pebble moved under his boot. The faint rasp brought the lieutenant's head around sharply.

"Who—oh, good evening, Sergeant Major. Can I help you?"

Parkes swallowed. "I was looking for Major Vela." This was at least part of the truth. He wanted to discuss the question of a medal for

Private Ortiz, who'd played dead at the M.G. in the ravine, then came back to life briefly to help wipe out the enemy there.

"You must have come over the eastern trail. He just went back to the mine by the western one."

"Thank you, Lieutenant." The Amazon was already looking back down at Holland as Parkes turned away.

As he climbed back up the ridge, Parkes wondered if he also now had the reason why he'd always refused a commission. He didn't think he had the right to enjoy himself as a soldier, at least not in the ways that went with bars or leaves instead of stripes.

Parkes's instincts and experience told him that no really worthwhile insight ever came this quickly, particularly when you were drained and wobbling on your feet after a battle. It was still something to think about, so that he would have integrated it into his reasoning before the next time he was offered a commission—

With a shock, as if he'd tripped, Parkes realized that he hadn't finished the thought. "...So that he could refuse plausibly." The virtues of refusing a commission no longer seemed absolutely self-evident, and that was going to take almost as much mental readjustment as a Forty-six relationship with the Amazon!

Parkes decided to put aside any more of that kind of heavy thinking until he was out of a combat area. Then he could also decide if he should talk to anyone about Forbes-Brandon's blank face and dead voice. Parkes had known a good many people who made the mistake of trying to pull that kind of mask firmly over their wrestling with some kind of private hell. The lucky ones had the sense to resign or the luck to get medical discharges. Of the four unlucky ones Parkes had known, one was in a mental hospital, one an alcoholic the Wise One only knew where if he was still alive, one had OD'ed on Extasine, and the last had gone berserk and shot five people before she was gunned down.

He was approaching the crest of the ridge now and slowed down to avoid surprising the sentry post there.

"Halt! Who is there?"

"Sergeant Major Parkes. And find some cover. You're still silhouetted against the sunset." He heard feet scuffling as the sentry shifted position. "That's better."

"Pass, Sergeant Major."

As Parkes started down the forward slope of the hill, someone turned on a blacklight projector over the entrance to the mine. He pulled his IR goggles down over his eyes and walked the rest of the way as fast as if he'd been in daylight.

CHAPTER 19

"Hullo, Dozer," said Parkes as he climbed down from the verti at the Havre des Dames airport.

Di Leone nodded silently. She was wearing fatigues with an armored vest instead of a jacket over her shirt, a sidearm, and her sap gloves. "The C.O. sent me."

Parkes stepped away from the verti and lowered his voice. "Hatcher?"

"Yes. Want to come?"

"No."

"Erase and correct. *Will* you come?"

"Of course." Parkes pulled out his own sidearm, chambered a round, and left the holster open. "Lead on."

Hatcher's office in the airport HQ of Group Fourteen was the last room in a converted warehouse, with its back to a steep, wooded hill that dropped away toward the perimeter fence around the airport. The door was in sight of the HQ sentry, who according to Dozer had his orders about keeping an eye on Hatcher. "For his protection from terrorists," was the cover story.

"Any word from Sergeant Major Hatcher?" asked Dozer.

"No, ma'am. He must have gone to sleep on the cot in there. I didn't want to wake him, 'cause he looked like he needed the sleep. Being on the terries hit list must be getting to him."

"Who wouldn't lose sleep over not knowing if you're about to join Pat Tyndall?" said Parkes. "He'll want a report on the fight at Faucon Noir, though, and that means coffee. I'll relieve you while you get some. If they have any donuts, get enough for all four of us."

"Can do, Sergeant Major."

Having disposed of the sentry, the two Sergeant Majors went to work on the locked door, with Dozer wielding the laser and Parkes shielding her from casual passers-by. The door and its lock were flimsy enough to yield within a minute, even on low power.

Hatcher must have started his last and longest sleep during the night, before the rainstorm about 0300. There was a large puddle of red-tinged water on the concrete floor, and the window was open.

Hatcher himself was sitting in his office chair, a comparatively small, neat entry hole under his jaw and a large, messy exit hole in the back of his head. The silencer-equipped pistol lay beside the chair.

Since di Leone was wearing the gloves, Parkes let her pick up the gun, unscrew the silencer, and hand it to him. He held it in his handkerchief and looked from Hatcher to Dozer.

"He may have been responsible for Pat Tyndall's death."

"He probably was. Plus whatever else he had cooking. I still won't piss on his grave. If you don't want to play along—"

"Dozer, if you think—"

They both broke off as the sentry returned with a pot of coffee and a sack of cups and doughnuts. He looked around the door and swore.

"The bastards! They made their hit after all, didn't they?"

"Looks that way," said Dozer. "You'd better alert the security squad and send for the senior Med Corpsman."

"Yes, ma'am."

As soon as the sentry was out of sight, Dozer removed a folded sheet of paper from Hatcher's breast pocket and stuffed it into her holster. "We owe somebody for this, even if he did it himself," she said quietly.

"Dozer, the senior Med Corpsman's probably going to be the Surgeon herself. She was on my verti with the wounded who are going to the hospital."

"Damn! What do we do if she decides to be honest?"

"We pray she doesn't."

Dozer seemed to take that advice literally. At least her lips started moving and her fingers twitched as if she wished they held rosary beads. Parkes went to the window and looked up at the sky, trying to find the right words for asking the Wise One to judge Hatcher fairly. Fatigue, hunger, and Hatcher's fate were making him a bit muzzy-headed.

The security squad gave him something to do when they showed up five minutes later with enough ammunition to fight all the terrorists left on Bayard by themselves. He sent them down the slope to check for traces of the assassin "...although since he must have come during that rainstorm Dozer says you had last night, it probably washed them away."

"I'd bet on it," said Hagood, sporting new lance-corporal's stripes. "It was a real goose-drowner. He may have dropped something, though."

They were well down the slope and safely out of hearing when the sentry returned with the Surgeon. She splashed through the red puddle, looked down at Hatcher's body, then out the window, then intently at the two Sergeant Majors. Parkes tried not to look back, but if a meteorite had smashed through the roof at that moment and spattered the Surgeon all over the hillside, Parkes would have found it hard to mourn.

The Surgeon bent, pulled her belt comp out of her bag, and punched in a code Parkes couldn't make out without craning his neck. He forced himself to stand still as the silence stretched on. Then: "I'll certify the death as a combat fatality from terrorist activity," said Laughton briskly. "One of those pigs must have thought he was avenging his friends at the Black Falcon." The comp went *squeeeen* and spit out a red death certificate. Parkes managed not to sigh with relief.

"If we're going to keep the aid station here at the airport, I'll need more security for it," she went on. "Can you assign a squad under a suitable leader for the job?"

Parkes grinned. "You've already got a good leader in Corporal Dietsch if he's ambulatory yet."

"It was just a deep graze, the leg wound. I've already had to threaten him with charges to keep him in bed. I can mark him for Light Duty."

"Fine. I'll see about having the rest of his squad sent over, and they can be his legs."

Dozer had been pulling the case off the pillow on the cot. Now she laid it over Hatcher's face and straightened up. "Captain, is there anything else—?"

"There's an aid team and an ambulance on the way. If you can break the news to Colonel MacLean, I'd appreciate it. He and Hatcher were once in the same unit together, weren't they?"

"I believe so. We'll take care of it, ma'am."

Parkes didn't need Dozer's waldo-claw grip on his elbow to urge him toward the door.

The story in Hatcher's letter was simple and grisly.

He'd fathered a daughter on the Petit Continent during his service there as a mercenary. Before joining Group Fourteen, he'd learned that the daughter was about to be forced into prostitution.

To save her, as soon as he knew the Group was going to Bayard he embezzled twenty thousand New Frontier dollars in Group funds and used it to buy eight kg of illegal-strength Extasine. He'd reckoned correctly that he could sell it for ten times that much on Bayard.

The man who bought the Extasine, however, also sent his name to the Leader of the Game Team on Bayard. The Leader threatened him with exposure and the death of his daughter if he didn't provide intelligence on Group activities. Then came the Night of the Troubles, and the Owl learned of his identity by torturing it out of one of the Extasine-buyer's men. Those men were also being armed by the Team Leader, which explained how a professional soldier's weapon wound up in the hands of one of the Owl's thugs.

For a while Hatcher was providing intelligence to both sets of the Group's opponents. Then the Owl decided that he'd outlived his usefulness and set out to blow him, culminating in Pat Tyndall's murder.

After that I knew I couldn't go to Jacqueline with Tyndall's blood on my hands. I knew that you were planning some kind of trick at the Faucon Noir mine, but kept my mouth shut about my suspicions. I'm glad to know that it worked well enough to be part of the vengeance for Pat Tyndall. I'm now going to take care of another part of it myself.

Half of the money for the Extasine has been returned to the Group funds, which will repay what I embezzled and provide something left over for the Group Welfare Fund. The other half has been left with the owner of Le Repos on the Rue Clemenceau. Please see that he transmits it in some acceptable form to my daughter and her mother.

I am sorry for all the trouble this has caused a new Group at this stage of its career. I hope Fourteen will go on to make a name for itself anyway.

> *Yours respectfully,*
> *G. Hatcher*
> *Group Sergeant Major*
> *Company Group Fourteen*
> *Peace Force*

"I wonder if his daughter really was in danger," said Dozer.

"From what I know about the Petit Continent, he couldn't take the chance. That place seems to be the armpit of the human-inhabited Galaxy.

"Maybe there's a Peace Force job, going in and cleaning it out."

"It would take a division just to clean up the city-states," said Parkes. "For the Fourth Empire we'd need a general mobilization. Maybe that's what our friend the Game Team Leader and his Master would like to push us toward, come to—"

The thunder of solid-fuel rockets drowned him out. A Group Fourteen verti was rolling down the main runway, streaming white smoke from R.A.T.O. units racked under the rear wing, all four engines straining. After what seemed like an endless takeoff run, it finally lurched into the air, wobbled over the end of the runway, and steadied into a slow climb as it passed over the perimeter fence.

One by one, three more vertis followed the first, also making horizontal takeoffs to save fuel but without needing R.A.T.O.'s. The air compressor was on its way south to be reassembled, loaded aboard *les copains'* barge, and start pumping air into the *Celestine Auphan*.

If Hatcher's death bought *les copains* their ship, as well as a good start for Group Fourteen, then indeed he'd died to as much purpose as most. His name could go on the Roll of Honor along with Pat Tyndall's and the six dead from the Faucon Noir fight.

Parkes's spirits didn't exactly rise like the vertis at the thought, but they twitched slightly.

"Anyway, that's politics," said Parkes. "Right now I suggest we turn the note over to the C.O. on a 'Your Eyes Only' basis. If he doesn't have the political contacts to check on Jacqueline himself, he can pass the word to Goff."

"You think the Mediator will keep his mouth shut?"

"He's a civilian, not a fool."

Dozer's shrug suggested this might prove a distinction without a difference. "All right. But you and I are going to visit Le Repos. The owner can choose. He can give us Hatcher's money to hold while the C.O. investigates, with a small commission for his pains. Or he can lose all the money, a few teeth, and maybe his business as well."

"If he's not one of the Owl's people, let's not be too rough on him. I hear that the Owl's—competition—has turned in quite a few of his people to the police and the Mobile Guards. Most of the rest have hauled out of Havre des Dames for parts unknown. If he's one of the competition, he may be thinking nice thoughts about the Peace Force for getting rid of the Owl."

"Yeah, and you may Forty-six the Amazon one fine—whoops, sorry about that. My mother always told me never to give men advice on their love lives. The good ones don't need it and it's wasted on the rest."

"Dozer, suppose we hit our friend at Le Repos for a free breakfast and call it quits. I just realized I haven't eaten since yesterday morning."

"Oh, was that your stomach rumbling? I thought it was another verti taking off on R.A.T.O.'s . By all means let's see if Le Repos can make pizza."

Parkes knew he was hungry when his stomach didn't shudder at the thought of pizza for breakfast.

CHAPTER 20

The Team Leader's first thought when he saw Nestor lead the Owl out from behind a tree was to wonder if he'd been betrayed. He didn't reach for his gun; Nestor was much too cautious to plan any treachery if he didn't have the Leader, Hiko, and Chkalov covered by at least a squad's worth of weaponry.

His second thought was to wonder if it wasn't perhaps the Owl who was the victim. The gang chief looked as if he hadn't slept for a week, then been dragged feet first and facedown through the forest to this meeting.

Although perhaps no treachery was required to give the Owl that look. In his overweening pride he thought he could strike at the Peace Force itself in order to strike at the Team Leader. Now he was paying the price. It was no secret that a fair number of his men had simply been killed by other gangs and their bodies dumped into the Gros Chaudron. More had been arrested, and those left alive and free were fugitives or in hiding.

If the Owl wanted to do anything for those men, he would have to dance to Nestor's tune—and perhaps the Team Leader could add a few notes of his own. If the Owl abandoned those men, he would be a fugitive himself for as long as he lived, which wouldn't be long unless someone found it worthwhile to buy him a passage off-planet—

"Gentlemen," said Nestor. "I believe it is time to discuss our business. Would you care for a drink?"

The Team Leader refused the brandy, but the Owl drank

thirstily. When he'd corked the bottle, Nestor pulled out a map, unfolded it on the grass, and weighted the corners with the bottle, the corkscrew, and his belt comp. It was a map of the area from Havre des Dames south to Les Fourchettes. Peace Force operations and bases and renegade militia units were shown in red, the Team Leader's militia in blue. At Les Fourchettes itself was another red mark—the *Celestine Auphan.*

"Gentlemen, I think we have another chance to resolve the matter of the *Celestine Auphan* satisfactorily if we are all able to cooperate. If not, those who fail to cooperate will bear the responsibility for a regrettable and unnecessary failure."

The polite tone didn't deceive the Team Leader. One of his last bits of intelligence from the late Sergeant Major Hatcher was a clue to Nestor's status, if not his identity. He was a high-ranking official of the C.G.P.O., the leader of a faction willing to go to any lengths short of civil war to damage the Fishermen. If the *Celestine Auphan* was salvaged, "a regrettable and unnecessary failure" would be hanging around his neck too. Somehow the Team Leader doubted that Nestor's enemies would be much more forgiving in that case than the Owl's, although they would perhaps take away only his power instead of his life.

"I will have to know something more about your plans before I can promise anything," said the Owl. The Team Leader knew perfectly well that he was bluffing, but it was not disagreeable to see even an enemy with the courage to go down fighting. He nodded his agreement.

"At the moment I am the only one here who has a force of armed men loyal to him available," he added. *For at least one more battle.* "I assume that the outcome of cooperation would be more men, or at least more weapons and ammunition for mine. Remember, from here on any attempt at the *Celestine Auphan* must go through the Peace Force. My militiamen gave a good account of themselves—"

"You will sound like a wiser man if you do not refer to certain recently organized militia companies as *your* men," said Nestor.

This time the Team Leader did have to suppress an urge to draw his gun. "I do not think you are the best judge of my wisdom, unless you think you can convince the militia units in question to follow you. Even after their recent casualties there are a hundred and twenty of them, armed with weapons that you provided. They are unlikely to be persuaded to follow anyone else quickly enough to be useful in the situation we face. If you continue to try assuming authority without responsibility, or at least without your fair share of the risks, it is a waste of time to talk about cooperation."

Nestor's look made a cobra seem benign. The Owl seemed startled at finding the Team Leader not allied with Nestor against him. The Team Leader threw the gang chief a polite smile. He didn't trust the man enough for a formal alliance, but they might be able to work along parallel lines long enough to keep Nestor in line and the last chance of victory from slipping away.

A red-faced Nestor finally grunted. "You do not need to fear that I am asking you to go where I will not. My plan for dealing with the *Celestine Auphan* involves providing forty men under my own leadership, plus any reasonable amount of weapons, ammunition, and specialized equipment. If you two gentlemen between you can provide two hundred men and certain—special skills—I believe we will have every chance of success."

The discussion turned rather more smoothly to tactical planning. The Team Leader wasn't particularly surprised to discover that Nestor had an unduly high opinion of his own military expertise. He'd seldom known a politician who didn't. However, Nestor was at least willing to listen to objections, even though the Team Leader had to raise so many that it was nearly noon by the time they'd hammered out a plan.

They each ate the food they'd brought, sitting with their guards well apart and alert. However, after lunch the Team Leader found himself seeking the shelter of a bush next door to one the Owl was using for the same purpose.

"Do you think your men would mind accepting a few of my militia as guides?" he asked the gang chief.

The Owl's startled look made him resemble his namesake even more than usual. "Can we trust your men not to lead ours into ambushes?"

The Team Leader doubted that a good many of the militia-men could recognize an ambush soon enough to plan anything of the kind.

Instead, he replied, "Can my men trust yours not to shoot them in the back or disobey orders?"

"We are fighting a common battle."

"Yes, but your men are not used to fighting in the open country. How much do they know about cover and concealment, march discipline, camouflage, purifying water, and so on?" The Owl's face gave him the answer.

"I thought so. I also imagine you would rather your men were taught by my Ranchers, who are less likely to memorize names and faces and hand them on to Nestor or the Mobile Guards."

The Owl's look of relief was unmistakable. "I was wondering how to get around that problem. The price of our aid is passage to the Petit Continent or else new identities. I could not help wondering how to make sure that we left as few tracks as possible."

The Team Leader suspected that the Owl's own plans didn't go beyond taking the men with new identities and building up a new gang somewhere else. It wasn't his job to help the authorities of Bayard with their law-enforcement problems. It was his job to make his allies in the coming battle as combat-effective as possible. Regardless of who won, this battle would be even bloodier than the fight at the Faucon Noir; the best that could be expected was to see the blood shed for victory.

The Team Leader didn't much care whether one of Nestor's men had overheard his conversation with the Owl. He was very careful that no one, not even Chkalov, overheard his words to Hiko as they walked away from the clearing after the conference.

"Hiko, if you are alive after this battle and I am not—"

"I know my duty, Leader."

"I'm not sure you do. It is your duty to survive, lead any other Teammen who do so, and take them and yourself back to Earth. The Game Master needs a full report on the first out-system operations, which he will not receive if you give too much thought to your honor."

"There is no such thing as giving too much thought to one's honor."

"Not even when I order you?" The Team Leader didn't want to put his wishes into the form of an order; it would be obeyed but it would also darken what might be the last days of his comradeship with

179

Hiko.

"Would it be acceptable, if the report reaches the Master, whether I do or not?"

"Yes, as long as— No, you use your own judgment as to whom you can trust. You'd probably do well to pick several people, in case the Peace Force involves Article Ninety-two and starts searching outbound ships."

"Thank you, Leader."

The Team Leader watched Hiko walk away, even more straight-backed than usual. It was more than likely that these were indeed the last few days of comradeship with Hiko. It was long odds against both of them surviving such a battle as this one promised to be. They would not even be fighting together, because the Team's specialized skills meant breaking the surviving twenty-one men into four widely separated squads.

Of course, one of those squads held in its rubber-gloved hands the last remaining chance they had for an easy victory...

"The wind's kicking up. I'd better go below and see how Joseph is coming with dinner," said Geesink. She pointed to the Peace Force boat offshore. She was rolling heavily and the lightning-bolt-and-olive-branch banner stood out stiffly.

Rebenc nodded. These past few days he'd found that his throat was so dry it sometimes hurt to talk. At least he'd had to give up smoking, but he hoped he wasn't coming down with Storm Fever. It didn't kill you, it just made you wish you were dead—and now it would make him miss *Celestine Auphan*'s coming up and leave *les copains* shorthanded when she did.

Tomorrow they would be towed into the Peace Force Maritime Base at Baie des Puces, Geesink would fire up the crane, and the big compressor would be swung down into the barge's hold. By nightfall they would be back over the *Celestine*; next morning they would fire up both compressors, and then it would be just pump and pray.

It was almost over. *Please, God, make it be almost over.*

As Geesink disappeared aft, Garron and Bergstrom climbed out of the hold, brushing sawdust off themselves. Rebenc peered down into the shadows. It looked as if they'd finished the platform for the compressor.

"That's about all the lumber we've got," said Garron. "I hope you people have some more for replacing patches on the ship."

Bergstrom shrugged. "That little pile aft to port is all that's left."

Garron frowned. "That may not be enough if we lose too many of the patches. Oh, well, you can always leave the superstructure open to the sea if you have to."

"Look, spaceman, why don't you go fight the Ranchers and let us salvage our ship?" said Bergstrom. For the first time Rebenc noticed the reek of brandy on his breath. He'd been drinking on duty, either to celebrate their coming victory or to forget all the things that might still spoil it.

He'd also forgotten that Garron was even bigger than he was, and probably in better shape in spite of being twenty years older. Garron could probably strew Bergstrom all over the deck without working up a sweat, and right now he looked as if the thought had at least entered his mind.

Rebenc stepped between the two big men. "Look, Nils, that's ungrateful. The Chief has done so much for us that I, too, sometimes forget he's not a sailor.

"The problem is that an open superstructure would mean tons of free water high in the ship. She won't be too stable when she comes up even if she's mostly dry. If she came up with her superstructure flooded into any kind of wind, she could capsize before the superstructure drained. Even if she didn't sink again, we could never tow her out upside down.

Garron sighed. "Oh, Lord, get me out into vacuum again. I'll never understand things like gravity and water and weather." Then he grinned. "I still think you'd better be ready to lose a few patches from underwater explosions, and that's if you're lucky."

He pointed aft. Rebenc saw a second Peace Force boat cruising past the Tete de Chévre rock. "We're laying down a network of underwater detectors, acoustic and IR. We expect our friends to try for *Celestine* at least once more. They'd be incredibly stupid to overlook sending divers with demo charges. We're going to be ready for them with the detection network, homers with shock and poison warheads, and our own divers. Some of the charges may still go off close enough to rattle things."

"When do you expect the attack?" said Rebenc after waiting long enough to be sure Bergstrom was too stunned to say anything.

"Not before tomorrow."

"Oh, good. Two or three fishing boats are coming down. I think they're mostly coming to play tourist," Rebenc added bitterly. "But they can bring more lumber, cement, and bonder/sealer."

"I'll leave that up to you," said Garron. "Nils is right. She's your ship, and you shouldn't have to trip over Peace Forcers while you're trying to salvage her."

"Thank you." *Or at least she was our ship, and will be again if those bastards ever let us bring her up.*

It was almost over, but "almost" wasn't enough. Suddenly Rebenc felt chilly both outside and inside in spite of the sun, and thought of a cup of coffee well laced with brandy before dinner.

CHAPTER 21

"PAUL! PAUL, WAKE UP!"

Rebenc heard Geesink's voice clearly enough, but he knew it had to be a dream, along with the lights and the distant thumps and rumbles. He was reliving in a dream that Peace Force film *les copains* had seen last night after they secured the barge, the one about the Bifrost campaign.

Then he realized that if he could analyze whether something was a dream, he was probably awake. He rolled over, and the cot promptly collapsed with a crash. He tried to kick his feet clear of the blankets, then saw Geesink standing over him.

She was fully dressed, and although it had been a mild night since the wind dropped, she was shivering. "Paul, listen! I heard an explosion out to sea. Then I saw lights moving. Now—"

Rebenc sat up and nodded. "I can hear." What he heard was sirens, shouts, and the whine of a verti taking off. "Something's happened." The profundity of that remark impressed him for a moment.

Roman Talgas joined them, wearing nothing but a sheet draped around him like a toga but holding out Rebenc's gun. As Vasi joined them, to report that he couldn't wake Bergstrom, the door flew open and Sergeant Major Parkes came in.

He was in full field gear and looked ready to eat terrorists for breakfast if you gave him a little salt and pepper to put on them. The presence of someone in the business of shooting back when shot at was remarkably soothing. Geesink stopped shaking, Talgas went back to get his clothes, and Rebenc found that he could listen to Parkes without wanting to scream, "What about our ship?"

"The opposition is making its move," the Sergeant Major said. "So far the only ground action is a diversion out beyond Mount Victorine, but we've had to commit a verti there for observation and target-marking. Also, the offshore patrol has detected something. They've launched four homers and heard one explosion so far. Don't worry, it was at least five hundred meters from your ship."

"Thank God!" said Rebenc.

"Or whoever," said Parkes. "Of course, this certainly isn't everything our friends have in their magazine. It's too dark to start loading the compressor, and it might be safer for you on land anyway for a while. But I'd like you people out of these quarters. They're too isolated and too close to the edge of the perimeter."

"That can't make much difference, can it?" said Talgas. "They won't get even this far."

Parkes frowned, obviously trying to decide how much truth *les copains* could stand and if he could take the time to calm them down if he guessed wrong. "Go ahead," said Geesink. "We're all grown-ups here."

"How far they get depends on their weapons, firepower, and willingness to get killed. If they push a berserker charge through our defenses, the next wave would have a free ride for a while."

"How long?"

"Damned if I know," said Parkes. "The problem is, we're going to be thinner on the ground than we ought to be for a while. We took one platoon to Faucon Noir and got it chewed up, then replaced it with another that just came back from the mine and is still at Main Base. So we've got two platoons and a company headquarters, plus base personnel. Call it a hundred people all together, and the opposition may have twice that many."

Rebenc started to curse, then stopped himself. The Peace Forcers were soldiers, not miracle workers. They would do their best and many of them might die doing it, but still—

"What about your ship's weapons?"

Parkes shrugged. "Depends on whether the fighting gets really close in or not. If they get a party down here in the middle of everything, we have to do most of the job ourselves. Even the vertis would have to be careful. The *Ark* can't let fly at all until she's got a clear target at least a kilometer from any friendlies."

"Some armies follow different rules, I've heard," said Vasi.

"Some armies can afford to use up their own people with shorts and overs," said Parkes. He looked as if he'd smelled something rotten. "The Peace Force can't. Or at least the rules are that we can't, which amounts to the same thing.

"Anyway, I'm just telling you the worst that could happen, not what will happen. We're bringing down a whole company from Main Base and Camp Tyndall, and then we can use two platoons as mobile columns outside the perimeter. They should be able to find and fix most of our friends far enough from the camp to let the *Ark Royal* or the battle stations lend a hand. I just wanted you people to know why we've had to wake you up."

"Bergstrom won't wake up," said Vasi.

"Drunk?"

"I suppose so."

"If he isn't up in ten minutes, I'll have a medic around with a stim shot."

"No, Sergeant Major. Not one of those. It makes him crazy."

"An allergic reaction? All right, get him up your own way, but make it fast. I may not be able to spare people to carry him if he can't walk." He reached into his belt and pulled out a pistol. "Which one of you wants this."

"Give it to Ju," said Talgas. "Paul already has one, I've got the riot gun, and Joseph has his knives." Ju took the gun, inspected the magazine and safety, then nodded and thrust it into her belt.

"All right, people. Signal in ten minutes, and I'll have an escort for you." Then he vanished as abruptly as if he'd fallen through a trapdoor.

Paul found himself gripping Geesink's hand tightly, ignoring the not quite suppressed smiles of the others. If an attack did come in while they were loading the compressor, she would be in the crane cabin, the most exposed place on the barge. She couldn't leave the crane controls either, not without risking the compressor that Peace

Forcers had died to bring them.

It was a question Paul Rebenc had never expected to face: Was the *Celestine Auphan* worth Juliana Geesink's life? At least it was also a question that he could now answer easily, even if this might not be the time to tell her.

The Team Leader looked at his watch.

"It's 0700. We have to assume that the divers either failed, or succeeded but won't be returning to report their success. May the goddess receive them with honor." He made the sign of dedication to Kali.

The other five men with him repeated the sign. None of them were truly devout, but none doubted that in their profession they were all in Kali's hands, along with those they sent to her. The Game Master was said to tolerate total unbelievers in certain positions around him, a rumor which the Team Leader hoped was false.

"We have to execute the direct assault." He pulled out the map and the others gathered around. "We will move along the shore to one kilometer west of the barge. At the same time a second squad will be dropped during the drone attack and advance under cover of the attempted penetration by the First Militia Company. We will move straight on the barge, using the cover of the forest to come within firing range. The second squad will move to cut off reinforcements to the barge.

"If the barge is at the pier, we should be able to reach it with rocket fire from the mainland bank of the creek. If the barge has been moved, we will have to cross the creek and use our rockets or demolition charges."

He did not add that if they had to cross on to the peninsula beyond the creek, the odds were very much against any of them getting away.

Chkalov raised his hand. "I wonder, Leader, if the *Celestine Auphan* is really a worthwhile target anymore. If the two squads infiltrated together, we could do much more for the First Company and a good deal of damage to the Peace Force as well."

The Team Leader suppressed an angry retort that he knew

would come only from resentment at Chkalov's voicing his own doubts. This was disobedience, but not the sort that entitled him to shoot the man on the spot. It did suggest a certain moral weakness that might let him become willing to be taken prisoner, and that would have to be prevented at all costs.

"Since the major Peace Force units will have been drawn toward the direction from which we entered, we will leave the target area to the north and join the squad under Hiko. Are there any other questions?"

There were none. The Team Leader hoped it was not just because no one wanted to be glared at like Chkalov. He knew that he was at the very limit of his effectiveness and leadership even over his own Team.

He still trusted them, and to a large extent even trusted his allies. He trusted even more in the amount of damage his squad could do with a launcher and four rockets apiece. They were light rockets, but half of them were incendiary and the H.E. ones could also be programmed as IR homing missiles for AA work. Nestor had proven almost as good as his word; the firepower he had placed in the hands of this morning's attackees would provide a disagreeable surprise to the Peace Force and their friends.

Just as Rebenc finished the last sausage, a colossal explosion made his plate jump off the table. The explosion rumbled on and on, finally dying away into faint thumps and bangs. By then everyone aboard the barge was on their feet, from Geesink in the crane cabin to the Peace Force machine-gunners at the bow.

Rufus Garron scrambled out of the hold, where he and Bergstrom had been checking the lashings of the compressors, and ran aft. Talgas ran forward to join the Peace Forcers behind their sandbags and armorcloth.

The sky was clear. It was also empty, except for a huge cloud of gray-white smoke that seemed to perch on the treetops to the east. It looked so nearly mushroom-shaped that Rebenc had a moment of sick fear that the enemy had thrown an A-bomb into the battle.

In that case they were all dead; it was just a question of how long it would take them to die. Although if the enemy had nuclear weapons, why hadn't they been used on the barge or on the *Celestine* herself?

As Garron reached the crane cabin, the Peace Force radio installed there made noises as if it had eaten too many beans for breakfast. Garron put on the headset and listened, his face setting into a frown. By the time he punched in a reply and hung up the headset, Rebenc was able to ask for the news in a voice that sounded almost calm.

"They're making their big push. That explosion was a drone aircraft loaded with H.E. and flown against our perimeter. It dropped off a stick of paras, then crashed. The paras got in, and now there's about a reinforced platoon at least coming through the gap in the perimeter. They have light AA missiles, so we have to be careful with the vertis."

Rebenc was now beyond fear. Surprisingly, he also found he was beyond cursing. "So what do we do? Can we have a tow out to the ship?"

Garron shook his head, then unslung his rifle and started checking its magazine. "You'd be a sitting target for rockets or air attack out on the reef, and we can't spare both boats to guard you. *Ramilles* is coming in to tow you around to the west side of the peninsula, where you'll be covered from the most likely direction of attack. The sentry post at the head of the peninsula is going to be reinforced and moved down to keep the opposition from getting on to the crest where they can hit or at least observe you.

"*Revenge* is going to stay over *Celestine* and act as the O.P. for air and orbital fire support. We've picked up four bodies and enough bits and pieces to account for a fifth, with no damage to your ship. We think that accounts for all the frogmen, but we'd rather not be proved wrong at your expense."

"Very well." The Peace Forcers were obviously going to fight this battle their own way. Rebenc couldn't blame them for that. He couldn't even blame them for wanting to concentrate on hitting the enemy—they not only had a debt to pay, but "a strong offense is the best defense" might really be true.

It still didn't make it easier to play bait. Rebenc looked down at his belt, half-expecting to see a hook thrust into his belly.

"Look," said Geesink, pointing toward the mainland bank of the creek. "The reinforcements for the peninsula must have arrived—"

Garron turned to look where she was pointing, then raised his rifle with one hand and grabbed Rebenc with the other. Rebenc flew through the open door of the crane cabin, nearly knocking Geesink out of her seat and painfully bruising himself on the control console. As he picked himself up he heard Garron shouting into the radio: "Hostile infiltration team on mainland side of creek mouth, position 987345. At least squad strength, carrying rocket launchers."

—Then the rattle of Garron's rifle.

Rebenc knew that it was stupid, but found that he couldn't stay down. He pulled himself up until his eyes were at a level with the bottom of the window. As he did, the rocket launchers opened fire.

Two rockets soared out across the water in tandem, heading for *Ramilles*. Some error in its guidance or jamming by the boat sent the first racing off to the right, a shrinking orange flame until it suddenly vanished in a column of spray. The second rocket ripped into *Ramilles*. Rebenc saw two explosions—the warhead, and then a much larger one that must have been fuel or ammunition. Except for her satellite antenna leaning drunkenly to one side, *Ramilles* completely vanished in a spreading cloud of smoke.

Two more rockets flew at the Peace Force machine-gunners just as they opened fire. One smashed into the side of the barge, hurling chunks of ferro-cement halfway to the crane. The second flew higher and would have plowed straight into the M.G. post if it hadn't hit a stanchion. The blast still hurled a Peace Force gunner and his weapon over the side. Rebenc said a prayer for him, and also for Roman Talgas, who wasn't wearing one of the armored vests that the Peace Force had loaned the rest of *les copains*.

One man on the shore was down now, from the machine-gun, and Garron's rifle staggered a second as he launched his rocket. It flew high over the crane cabin, but a second was close behind, coming low. Rebenc saw nothing but a swelling orange flame and Garron kneeling, shooting steadily but not hitting anything—until suddenly there was only Garron blocking his view.

A moment later the rocket struck, and a hundred and ten kilos of armored Rufus Garron was enough to set off the warhead. The crane cabin's windows vanished, Rebenc flew across the cabin and this time did knock Geesink out of her seat, and the pain in his ears made him want to scream.

Then he saw what was splattered all over the cabin and did scream-once. He cut himself off before he lost control completely by ramming his fist into his mouth and biting down on it hard. That hurt even more than his ears, but it took his mind off the fact that he couldn't move without touching a surface covered with what a moment before had been a living man...

"Ju! Start the crane motor! If you can snag the hook in a tree on the shore, maybe you can warp us around to where we'll be harder to hit."

Geesink's hands were already flying over the controls. As he crawled for the door, Rebenc felt the cabin beginning to swing. He wanted to see if Garron's rifle was still usable, because right now it was the only weapon that could reach those rocket-slinging bastards on shore and he wanted to die shooting back at them, just as Ju wanted to die doing something—

Two more rockets had hit one of the hatches, but well clear of the compressor. The heavy timbers had also absorbed a good deal of the explosion. There was still more smoke coming out of the hatch than the explosion alone could have left. This time Rebenc said his prayers for Nils and Joseph, and also for reliable fire extinguishers.

No more rockets were coming in. Rebenc supposed that the enemy had decided nobody could shoot back at them for a few minutes and that they could afford to close in and finish the job properly. They were wading the creek now, up to their waists except for one short man who was up to his chest—

Spray and smoke erupted around them as machine-gun bullets lashed the water. The first burst was a little short, hiding them from Rebenc. The spray turned red as the second burst found its mark, followed by several more.

Rebenc didn't care if there was someone still waiting on shore to shoot him the moment he stood up. He had to see where this miracle had come from. The machine-gun post on the barge was still empty, but on the bow of *Ramilles* somebody was standing with a machine-gun. Two or three somebodies, actually, although Rebenc couldn't count precisely with the smoke still pouring out of the boat. *Ramilles* was also low in the water, and the machine-gunner and his comrades were going to be swimming before long.

That didn't really matter. They had performed one miracle, and Rufus Garron had performed another. That was enough for one day, not to mention being more than *les copains* deserved.

God, help us to someday become worthy of that kind of courage and that sacrifice.

The Team Leader saw Chkalov's head fly apart from the explosive bullets at the same moment that he felt a savage punch in his arm and another in his thigh.

Now Chkalov will die in the favor of the goddess.

He tried to make the sign of dedication, but something had immobilized his arm. He couldn't stand either. The weight of his weapons and pack was dragging him under.

The next burst was a blessing for the Team Leader. It killed him before he had time to realize that he was dying or for even a single thought about the failure of his Team.

The observation verti carrying Parkes and three other reinforcements for the peninsula sentries had to make a short detour, to cautiously confirm a ground sighting of the first infiltration squad. It confirmed the sighting and drew a lavish display of poorly aimed small-arms fire but none of the AA rockets that had already destroyed one verti and grounded a second. The volume of fire suggested that the squad had been joined by some of the attacking militiamen, with lots of ammunition but not much fire discipline.

The lieutenant piloting the verti laid down flares, then sent coordinates to the *Revenge* to be relayed to orbit. Only a minute later the lasers were slashing down. The smoke rising from where they struck meant that the enemy was getting at least a fright and a bad case of the hotfoot. Low-altitude cluster bombs would probably have punched through the foliage more effectively, but the response time for any orbital missiles was too slow against targets this close to friendly forces. The enemy could also move or dig in while the bombs were on the way.

"That's Station Two," said the pilot. "But she's in direct line-of-sight to *Ark*, so the main computer has control."

Parkes didn't like to think that he'd so plainly shown he needed that reassurance, even if it was true. Fire support from orbit against an enemy actually inside a Peace Force position was usually a violation of both doctrine and common sense. The Navy boys didn't always have common sense when it came to trusting their computers and orbital firepower, and it was the ground pounders who paid the heaviest price for any mistakes.

This was one of those cases where doctrine had to be stretched, however. Four platoons were on hand, but two were fully engaged, one was being held in reserve, and the last had just deplaned on its L.Z. The assault landings in the rear of the enemy attacks were nearly an hour away, and even then the platoons would have a longer cross-country hike than the planners had anticipated. Those AA missiles couldn't give the militia a real victory, but they could make things very expensive for the Peace Force if they brought down a troop laden verti.

So right now the defenders of the Baie des Puces base were at full stretch. If cutting the margins fine on orbital fire support meant economy of force or even enemy casualties, it was the least of several evils.

At this point when he was debating a tactical problem with himself, Parkes usually went on to thank the Wise One that the final decision wasn't his. This time the gratitude wouldn't come.

It still hadn't come when the verti crossed the coast, dropped to sea level, and came back just above the wave tops. Parkes managed not to look away from the burning hulk of *Ramilles*. He still saw no clues to the question that had been plaguing him since the report of the boat's destruction came through.

Lieutenant Forbes-Brandon had been aboard *Ramilles* when the balloon went up, inspecting some malfunctioning radio gear. *Revenge* hadn't reported any survivors from *Ramilles*, but if there were any, they'd probably swum either for shore or for one of the above-water reefs.

Had the Amazon survived? And if nobody knew, how soon could he lead a search party for *Ramilles* survivors without people raising eyebrows?

Rebenc was listening to the unwounded Peace Force machine-gunner cursing at the silent radio when the verti flew in from the sea and landed on the gravel beach of the peninsula side of the creek. Sergeant Major Parkes led three other heavily armed Peace Forcers off, then it rose and flew out to sea again.

"Probably looking for survivors from *Ramilles*," said Geesink. They both looked aft, to where Lieutenant Forbes-Brandon sat on a bollard, bareheaded, barefooted, and busily oiling the parts of the machine-gun she'd brought in tied to two life jackets. The other three survivors of *Ramilles* were seated around her, two of them bandaging the third one's arm and smearing ointment on his face. All of them avoided meeting the lieutenant's eyes, and Rebenc didn't blame them. He'd done the same ever since he had the job of telling her of Rufus Garron's death.

"Welcome aboard, Sergeant Major," said Geesink as Parkes led his men up to the gangplank. "We're still alive, thanks to your Lieutenant Forbes-Brandon."

Parkes looked, took a step forward, then pulled himself to a stop so abruptly that he swayed. He looked them up and down.

"I think you people have been to the wars," he said finally. "Are you all right?"

"Garron's dead."

"How—?"

"He took a rocket—"

"Never mind. Garron's dead. The rest of you?"

"Ju and I are fine," said Rebenc. "Nils and Joseph may have smoke inhalation. Two rockets started a fire in the hold and they had to stay down there putting it out with no breathing gear. Roman is cut and bruised all over and his ears hurt, but he's tending the wounded machine-gunner."

"All right. We'll have medics around here inside of an hour, I suspect. If all of you are fit, there's no reason you can't be out on the wreck tonight and hitting the air on schedule tomorrow."

"Is it really over now?" said Rebenc.

"Except for rounding up the stragglers, yes." That didn't quite ring true, but Rebenc knew that it was as much as he was going to be told. "Now, what happened to Garron?"

Rebenc and Geesink told the story of Garron's death, followed by Forbes-Brandon's opening fire with the last machine-gun from the wreck of *Ramilles*. "She says she would have opened fire sooner, but she had to find a magazine of explosive bullets in case they were wearing armor. Also, she hoped to explode their rockets as well as killing them."

"Bloodthirsty, isn't she?" said Parkes.

Rebenc wasn't sure whether to laugh or not. "Then she and the other fit survivors put life jackets on the wounded and the machine-gun and swam in. We were closer than *Revenge*."

Parkes was measuring the distance to the wreck as Rebenc spoke. As Rebenc finished he whistled. "That was damned good shooting."

"Good enough to save us, certainly," said Rebenc, "and—where are you going, Sergeant Major? I think she wants to be alone."

"Mind your own business."

Rebenc and Geesink watched Parkes stride aft and knew to the step the moment he saw the look in the lieutenant's eyes. He stopped as if he'd run into an invisible wall, then drew himself to attention.

"Sergeant Major Parkes reporting with reinforcements for barge security, Lieutenant. What are your orders?"

"I'd like some dry clothes and somebody to finish over-hauling this waterlogged machine-gun. I'd also like somebody to call that verti back and have it fly me out to *Revenge* once I've changed. No, I don't need the medics. At least not badly enough to wait around for them now."

"Yes, ma'am."

Geesink went to show the lieutenant where she could change her clothes, while Rebenc forced himself to start cleaning up what was left of Rufus Garron. After a few minutes he realized that the Sergeant Major was working beside him, without commenting on the number of times he had to run to the side to vomit.

But then, the Sergeant Major was looking a little green in the face himself, and sometimes he, too, disappeared for a few minutes.

Only half an hour after he knew that the Team Leader had to be dead, Hiko found himself in a position to safely kill Nestor and his bodyguards. He'd expected it would take much longer. Now he and the four survivors of the Team had an unexpected head start on all pursuers.

As they trotted north through the forest, Hiko was mentally composing his report to the Game Master. There was no doubt that future out-system Game Teams needed either more men and modern equipment or better intelligence about local conditions. Preferably both, since it was no use to know whom to bargain with if you lacked the strength to make the bargain worthwhile.

He would not call the mission to Bayard a complete failure, however. It was not, and even if it had been, Hiko suspected that there were some truths the Game Master might not care to hear unless they were spoken very quietly in carefully chosen words. That thought bordered on disloyalty, but Hiko knew that it also bordered on wisdom.

At least the Team Leader had been avenged. But he had deserved more than vengeance. He had deserved victory, and some of the people who had denied it to him were forever beyond Hiko's reach unless he was willing to die himself. A year ago he would have considered that a perfectly reasonable price. Now the Team Leader had made him less willing to accept simple answers.

They passed a clearing hit by rockets, with two militiamen and one of the Owl's gang lying on the scorched and churned-up ground. They must have been killed by blast and fragments; the bodies were unburned and relatively intact. They also must have died quickly.

Behind him Hiko could hear more rockets and cluster bombs exploding in the distance, and sometimes in the intervals the rumble of superheated air as lasers played on targets a safe distance from Peace Force positions. Men who'd followed him were dying under a bombardment to which they could make no reply. Hiko knew that he owed them more than he would ever be able to pay.

He still owed the Team Leader and the Game Master more. He

had to do his duty to them first, then see about what he owed the militiamen—which was another reason for staying alive, because dead men pay no debts.

CHAPTER 22

Parkes looked up from the screen clamped to the bollard in front of him where Paul Rebenc seemed about ready to wear a hole in the barge's deck. He didn't bother suggesting that the man should sit down before he wore himself out. The whining roar of the two compressors would have drowned him out, and Rebenc wouldn't have listened even if he'd heard.

Better finish this transfer list and find Ju Geesink. Maybe she can calm him down.

Parkes returned to the business of evaluating the various people proposed for transfer from Support Squadron to Field Squadron's slightly frayed-around-the-edges platoons. Under Hatcher, he and Dozer would have worked out most of the details over some drinks and presented the First with a fait accompli. Now Hatcher was dead, Parkes was Acting Group First, and Voorhis was Acting Field First. If Parkes didn't want Voorhis's nose so out of joint that he might make it hard for Parkes to take hold as permanent Group First, Parkes couldn't rely too heavily on working informally with Dozer.

At least they'd issued him a micro and authorized him to take it out to the barge while waiting for *Celestine Auphan* to come up. He and Amazon were the Peace Force representatives there "because you got us involved with that ship in the first place," as Vela put it.

That was just as well, because Parkes would have broken out of close arrest to be there when the ship rose. He suspected that Forbes-Brandon felt the same way, although she hadn't said much about that or anything else since Garron's death.

She was now sitting on the platform of the crane, long legs dangling, bare head wrapped in a scarf thrown back against the side of the cabin. She looked about seventeen from this distance, where you couldn't see the eyes. Losing both Keith Holland and Rufus Garron had been a vicious one-two punch, but she was still locking herself away from anybody who might help her.

Maybe she doesn't think there's anybody who can? Probably. I once walked alone like that. Then she'd better get drunk, or laid, or bite somebody's head off, or even run herself to exhaustion so she can sleep! At this point Parkes would have cheerfully guarded the Amazon's back through a whole marathon course, or even been brought up on charges if that would relieve her feelings.

Bergstrom came around the cabin, looked down at the Amazon, and said something to her. Her reply made him open his mouth wide, then walk off without saying anything more.

The boatswain had been like a hill grumbler just waked from hibernation since Rebenc not only openly took over the leadership of *les copains* but made his first order locking up all the liquor until *Celestine* was salvaged. At least he wouldn't have to worry about Bergstrom and Vasi quarreling anymore. The two had made their peace while getting the lung flush that cleared out the smoke they'd inhaled fighting the fire in the hold.

Parkes turned back to the screen and completely lost track of the time before he finished the transfer evaluations. When he finally closed down the machine and stood up, the sun was touching the ridge of Isle d'Ouragon to the west. To the south a sullen mass of clouds was building up.

Rebenc came forward, puffing on a cigarette. "I hope those clouds don't mean a storm. If it really blows up before we have her ready for towing, she might be better off still on the bottom."

Parkes now knew just enough about ships to understand that handling a badly damaged and precariously patched derelict at night in a gale would be hairy indeed. With patches torn off, the *Celestine* might sink again, or even break loose from both the barge and her anchors and be thrown on the rocks, to suffer irreparable damage.

"What about that tug coming from Rougier et Filles?"

"She was supposed to be here at noon. She not only isn't here yet, she hasn't even signaled!"

"We could probably send out a verti to search—"

"It would probably find her at the company dock!" said Rebenc. He threw his cigarette to the deck and ground it out viciously. "They will come too late, if they come at all, and more good people will die or be hurt!"

"The fishing boats—"

Rebenc simply looked out beyond the reefs to the raft of five—no, six, somebody new had joined up—fishing boats, anchored under the watchful eye of *Revenge*. Then he spat over the side.

"Paul—"

Rebenc pulled out another cigarette, then suddenly crumbled it up, threw it over the side, and shrugged. "I am sorry. Not only do I rage at you, but I probably do the Fishermen an injustice. I know they wished us well but were too afraid of all our enemies to do anything. Yet how good is a good man who only sits while others work and die?"

"'The road to hell—'"

"'Is paved with good intentions.' Yes. Well, perhaps now that our enemies have been smashed, we can rely on more help." Rebenc looked away and said in a voice that seemed to expect disappointment, "They really are smashed this time?"

"Yes." For once Parkes was telling the truth. "The Rancher terrorists are dead, prisoners, or lying very low. So are the bullyboys the C.G.P.O. sent along with the weapons from National Militia arsenals.

"The Owl is dead. So are half his men. Most of the rest are in jail, on charges that are likely to keep them there for a while. There are still gangs in Havre des Dames, but they'll be busy fighting each other to divide up the pie they've inherited from the Owl. The Owl's fate should also make them think twice about hiring out to politicians."

Rebenc seemed satisfied with that much, so there was no need to break security and tell him about "Nestor" or the Port Prefect. Nestor, found dead on the battlefield and probably shot by one of his men, had turned out to be Raymond Le Telier, Deputy Treasurer of the C.G.P.O. That should embarrass enough of the party higher-ups badly enough to force a thorough house-cleaning and a squeaky-clean posture on supporting Rancher terrorism for quite a while.

By the time the C.G.P.O. was ready to try again, any Ranchers who came down past the Massif De Gaulle with guns in their hands would likely return feet first if at all, which should keep them from coming in the first place. Yves Massu hadn't led his men in battle, but he'd brought about vengeance for his nephew and the rescue of his niece. He was something of a local hero, and volunteers had swollen his fifty militiamen to nearly two hundred. They were applying for the status of a recognized unit in the National Militia, and the Peace Force was supporting that application.

As for the Port Prefect, at least two dozen assorted witnesses had implicated him in nearly as many serious crimes. Most of them seemed to be telling mostly the truth, even if they were also trying to get their own sentences lightened in the process. With any luck the least the Prefect could expect was dismissal in disgrace and the reform or disbanding of that bunch of third rate disgraces to even their shabby uniforms called the Port Guardians.

"Have you talked Paul into a good mood, Sergeant Major?" said Geesink. "Or can I call you John?"

"John will do."

"I hope it hasn't been too big a job, making Paul happy again."

"I suspect he would rather go through that—Bifrost—campaign again," said Rebenc. "I am sorry. It is just that we're so close, but I keep wondering what will go wrong *now*. What's that?" he added, pointing to a package Geesink had under her arm.

"Something I found going through Garron's effects," she said. "I thought the lieutenant would want to do that, but she told me to go ahead. Anyway, now we know what he was making all those days he locked himself in his shop."

In the package was a thirty-centimeter model of the *Celestine Auphan*, painstakingly put together out of metal scraps and minutely detailed. Parkes noted that the satellite antenna was on the mast and the main deck was clear of fish-processing gear.

"That's the way she used to be, isn't it?"

"Yes. He left a note with it. It's for Katie Halloran, so she can look at it after she gets her sight back, or—or—"

"Or touch it if she stays blind," Parkes finished for her.

Geesink nodded. Rebenc had just put an arm around her, when Roman Taigas popped out of the hold.

"She has neutral buoyancy! She should break free of the bottom and start up any minute!"

Parkes stepped back. The next few minutes would be critical. The bottom was rocky, so there should be no suction requiring extra buoyancy to break the ship loose as there would be with a muddy bottom. The ship had anchors fore and aft, the tide was flowing so as to take her away from both the barge and the nearest rocks, and the current here was negligible. The *Celestine Auphan* would still be four thousand tons of inert metal in an element—the sea—which humanity had learned to understand but never to really dominate.

"Right," said Rebenc. "Roman, get back to the monitors. Tell Nils to keep those compressors going if he has to seal the joints with his own guts. Joseph should get on the radio to the *Ramilles* and have her stand by to tow us clear. Ju, have both anchors ready to slip. John, can you help her?"

"Sure, if she tells me what to push and what to pull. Try recruiting the lieutenant too. I think she's done some yachting."

Rebenc hurried aft while Parkes and Geesink ran forward. In five minutes they had the bow anchor cable buoyed and ready to go overboard once a single shackle was knocked loose. Rebenc seemed to have the Amazon working too. Now there was nothing left to do but look over the side at the bubbles rising from thirty meters down.

From the number of bubbles, a lot of air was escaping from the ship. Was there more than there'd been a few minutes ago? Had a patch blown out as the *Celestine* started to move? If it had—

"Look!"

Parkes's eyes followed Geesink's pointing finger. The wreck buoy was moving, but was it just being tossed around by the bubbles or—?

No, it really was moving, fast enough to throw up spray. And the two hoses from the compressors were sliding across the deck, one of them coming up hard against a bollard. Pray that it didn't break and cut the air flow in half, besides lashing around and maybe killing somebody now of all possible times—

The *Celestine Auphan* rose into the sunset.

201

She was red with rust and slimy with weeds. Her mast was gone and most of the factory gear on her main deck was leaning at crazy angles, like a party of drunks going home in a storm. As she rose higher, her list increased, until several pieces of gear broke loose and slid over the side, taking most of what was left of the railing with it. Water poured out of the others, and as the top weight slowly decreased, so did the list.

Rebenc and Geesink had their arms around each other and probably wouldn't have seen anything but their ship and each other even if they hadn't both been crying. Out to sea, the *Revenge* was firing tracer into the sky, the fishing boats were sounding their horns, and a big catamaran tug was corning round Point Pommier. A signal lamp was winking from her bridge.

"Tug *Suzette Rougier* offering assistance to *Celestine Auphan*," said a voice behind Parkes. He turned, to see Bergstrom swaying there, a bottle of brandy in one hand and a hammer in the other. He must have broken open the liquor locker the moment *Celestine* was clear of the bottom. "Damned well time too."

"Better late than never," said Parkes, moving hastily out of Bergstrom's reach. The boatswain seemed too happy to care, and lifted the bottle to his lips.

Parkes picked up the model of the ship and headed aft to where the Amazon stood like the superlatively carved figure of a warrior maiden, holding her scarf in one hand. A rising breeze whipped her hair.

Two vertis whined overhead, one of them pulling up into a slow loop. Dallin, for certain. As Parkes laid the model on the deck beside the lieutenant, Peace Force signal rockets and flares started going off on the mainland, red, green, silver, blue, in a complete *feu de joie*.

Maybe it would help the Amazon to hand Rufus Garron's last piece of work over to Katie Halloran. Certainly something had to be done, or she would be Group Fourteen's last casualty of the Bayard campaign. Parkes realized that if this happened, much of his pleasure in Group Fourteen's first victory would evaporate.

This didn't make a great deal of sense, but now he didn't much care what made sense, and what didn't, as long as he was sure of it.

CHAPTER 23

From beside the main runway of the Havre des Dames airport, Parkes could look across the southern end of the Gros Chaudron to the lights of dockyard. The City Council and the Fishermen's Protective Association had come up with the funds to pay for night work on the *Celestine Auphan*, at least until she was seaworthy again.

Parkes could also look east and see two lights in the sky. One, shrinking rapidly, was the airplane headed for Rennes de Bayard, the capital of Nouvelle Bretagne. It carried a load that even Dozer di Leone had admitted must set some sort of record for being oddly assorted.

There was Arthur Goff, bound for the capital and three tedious if not thankless weeks tidying up the political loose ends of Group Fourteen's Bayard mission. He might not have to do much more than watch the government while it watched the C.G.P.O., but everybody in Union service on Bayard, civilian or military, agreed that the watching was necessary.

There was also the main reason why the C.G.P.O. was falling over itself to clean up its act. The body of Raymond LeTelier was on its way back to his family for a funeral that the government had made very clear was going to be a private one, not a party rally. Parkes didn't imagine there'd be much trouble with that; rumor had it that there'd been trouble finding a priest to say the funeral mass!

The Port Prefect was also on the plane, guarded by four plainclothesmen from Central Security. He would be standing trial on so many charges that it might be simpler and more merciful to execute him. By the time he got out of prison he would be too old to earn a living even if anyone would give him a job.

Finally there was Katie Halloran in a private cabin with a nursing Sister and guards from Group Fourteen. She was on her way to have her scars erased and her vision restored. She'd been clutching the model of *Celestine Auphan* when her litter was rolled onto the plane. Parkes hoped that when they strapped everything down for takeoff they'd tied it to her litter where she could still reach it.

The second light in the sky was blue-white, smaller, and moving so slowly that you had to watch for a while to realize that it was moving at all. *Ivanhoe* was on her way home, carrying most of the Standard Resupply Load that had arrived just after it was no longer needed. With the extra cargo aboard, *Ivanhoe* would have a slow return voyage and her crew a dull time of it. Parkes wondered if they would have exchanged the dullness for a share of the Bayard operation's casualties—sixteen dead and twenty-nine wounded from Group Fourteen, four dead and seven wounded from *Ark Royal*. Probably they would have.

That was too gloomy a thought for the modest amount he'd drunk so far tonight, Parkes realized. Maybe it was his own prospect of having to sit while others fought that was getting to him. It looked as if he was going to be confirmed as Group First, unless Force Command or the Brigade C.O. overrode MacLean, and since he was also in for a Letter of Commendation and a second bar to his Silver Star, they weren't likely to do that. This meant he'd soon be spending almost as much desk time as an officer—more, if Hatcher had let things slide in his last weeks—without an officer's privileges to go with it.

Parkes walked back down the runway to the cargo terminal, where he found Paul Rebenc and Juliana Geesink. They were standing in the shadows of the warehouse used by Group Fourteen, watching some of Major Massu's militiamen load crates aboard three civilian fixed-wing planes with hastily spray-painted National Militia insignia.

"Nothing to do on your ship?" he asked with a grin.

Rebenc grimaced. "I think it was easier to bring her up from the bottom than it will be to bring her out of the dockyard. I think they know what they are doing, but I wish I could be sure. And these people—" He pointed at the militiamen. "Can we trust them? Are they really a National Militia unit now?"

"Officially, they're Eighteenth Demi-Brigade of the Nouvelle Bretagne National Militia. What they really have is one battalion of two companies, each about the size of two reinforced platoons.

"If you don't trust them, what about raising the other battalion from the fishermen or the sailors and dockworkers? I'm sure Nils would volunteer in a minute. I never saw anybody who so badly wanted to leave his post and go shooting his enemies." He didn't add that almost anything would be better for Bergstrom than his two principal occupations at the moment, which were drinking and organizing a mob to run Warren's passage crew out of Havre des Dames.

"You're right about Nils," said Rebenc. "But that would mean breaking up *les copains*... No, you're right. We can't be what we were now that Ju and I are engaged and Nils is no longer the leader. If we tried to pretend otherwise, he and I would sooner or later have to fight for the leadership of something that doesn't exist anymore. Better he should be a militia officer, where nobody will fight him as long as he doesn't drink too much. But who will pay for the equipment for another battalion?"

"We're selling the government all the vehicles and portable equipment it would cost too much to ship back to New Frontier. They'll have enough left over to equip several battalions the size of Massu's left over anyway. Also, we're leaving the buildings and improvements at both Camp Tyndall and Camp Garron. Each battalion can have a separate camp and you won't be getting into brawls with each other.

"There would be a price for taking over one of the camps and a battalion's worth of equipment, of course. The camp and any equipment not used by the militia would have to be kept in condition for use by any future Peace Force units that came to Bayard. But that is something Paul could find out later if he wanted to seriously discuss organizing a Fishermen's National Militia Battalion."

"We'll think about it," said Ju. "Right now, Paul and I were going out to dinner in the city. Would you like to join us?"

"Thanks. I think I'll hop the next flight back to Main Base and turn in early."

"Then—no, I won't say good-bye. That hasn't the right meaning," said Rebenc. "*Au revoir*, my friend."

Rebenc and Parkes shook hands; Parkes kissed Ju and turned away as they headed for their car. He would not have minded company tonight, but not theirs. Not when dinner was obviously going to be followed by a short trip to the nearest bed and a long stay in it.

Parkes would have been happy with the prospect of ending his evening the same way. He also realized that would simply be putting off the need to do some serious thinking about why he no longer recoiled from the idea of taking a commission. *Had* he been punishing himself all these years for abandoning his father to save his sister from his stepmother? And was it time he stopped letting the guilty boy pull the strings of the grown man and decorated soldier?

Definitely serious thinking. He remembered the ancient Pershin idea about doing such thinking once while sober and once while drunk. Tomorrow would be soon enough to try it sober.

> When this bloody war is ooooover,
> Oooooh how happy I shall be...

The song floated down the street to Parkes as he strode determinedly toward the bus stop. He strode because he knew that if he relaxed, his pace would turn into a shuffle or even a stumble. The brandy had left him wide-awake enough to know the limits it had imposed on his muscles and nerves.

The singer sounded like a woman with a contralto voice that might not have been half-bad if she hadn't been considerably more than half-drunk. Parkes suspected it was a Peace Forcer; nobody on Bayard was likely to know that old song from the First Terran War.

He rounded the corner tightly, or at least thought it was tightly until he stumbled into the front steps of the first house on the far side of the street. He had to grip the railing to stay on his feet, and as he did so the singer broke off to lift a bottle to her lips. As she did, the streetlight shone on her face.

This time Parkes sat down abruptly. Lieutenant Forbes-Brandon was twined like a vine around the pillar of a tavern porch, holding a half-full bottle of brandy in her free hand. As Parkes watched, she swigged more. Some of the amber liquid trickled out of the corner of her mouth. It made a nice contrast with her rosy complexion.

Surprise had knocked him down. Duty brought him back to his feet. Walking an invisible chalk line on the pavement, Parkes reached the lieutenant just as she started to sing again.

I will kiss the Sergeant Maaaajor—

Suddenly the blue eyes were turned toward him—wide, staring, incredulous at first, then focusing. The Amazon giggled.

"Not tonight. Not tonight."

Then she hiccupped.

Parkes managed to make putting his arms around her one soldier supporting another rather than a man hugging a woman. Relief still warmed him. It would have made him drunk if the brandy hadn't done that already, so it made him sober instead.

The Amazon wasn't going to kill herself or anyone else, pretending that it didn't hurt to see friends die.

Parkes managed to untangle Forbes-Brandon from the pillar but couldn't get her to walk. They finally both slid down onto the steps, sitting side by side with their arms around each other. "When This Bloody War Is Over" had long run out, so they started on "Marching Through Georgia." By the time they were into "Meadowlands," Parkes began to find, his sudden sobriety oppressive. Since there was still that half-bottle of brandy left...

Half an hour later a Peace Force patrol called by the tavern owner found them. Forbes-Brandon was asleep, with her head on Parkes's shoulder, and the empty brandy bottle lay between his feet.

THE END

BE SURE TO PICK-UP THE NEXT NOVEL IN THIS SERIES:

PEACE COMPANY: THESE GREEN FOREIGN HILLS

ADDITIONAL BOOKS FROM
AUTHOR ROLAND J. GREEN

AVAILABLE IN PAPERBACK OR EBOOK

DON'T MISS ANY OF MICHAEL KASNER'S HARD HITTING MILITARY NOVEL SERIES

BLACK OPS

Formed by an elite cadre of government officials, the Black OPS team goes where the law can't - to seek retribution for acts of terror directed against Americans anywhere in the world.

3 BOOK SERIES

Armed with all the tactical advantages of modern technology, battle hard and ready when the free world is threatened - the Peacekeepers are the baddest grunts on the planet.

4 BOOK SERIES

CHOPPER COPS

America is being torn apart as criminal cartels terrorize our cities, dealing drugs and death wholesale. Local police are outgunned, so the President unleashes the U.S. TACTICAL POLICE FORCE. An elite army of super cops with ammo to burn, they swoop down on the hot spots in sleek high-tech attack choppers to win the dirty war and take back America!

4 BOOK SERIES

FROM CALIBER BOOKS

www.calibercomics.com

CALIBER
BOOKS

DON'T MISS ANY OF NEIL HUNTER'S NOVELS FROM CALIBER BOOKS

Reporter Les Mason is completing an expose on the Long Point Nuclear Plant. But before he can finish he dies an agonizing death. The doctors are baffled—and there are similar cases to follow...Chris Lane, his girlfriend, and organizer of the Long Point Protestors, discovers Mason's notes, and decides to find out for herself what the plant has to hide.

2 BOOK SERIES

In middle of the 21st century America – over-populated decaying cities are ruled by hi-tech gangs pushing every vice and wastelands are controlled by bands of mutants. Ordinary citizens are oppressed and face a hopeless future. But Marshal T.J. Cade is a new breed of law enforcer. Teamed with his cyborg partner, Janek, Cade takes on these criminals and works in the gray areas of the law to get the job done.

3 BOOK SERIES

The village of Shepthorne England wasn't being gripped, but strangled by a winter's blanket of heavy snow and Arctic temperatures. The trouble began innocently enough with a massive pile-up of autos on frozen roads leading to and from the village. Then, from the sky, a military transport plane with its top secret cargo of devastation crashed down towards the center of the village. Hell was just beginning to touch Shepthorne and its unsuspecting citizens...

CALIBER COMICS GOES TO WAR!
HISTORICAL AND MILITARY THEMED GRAPHIC NOVELS

WORLD WAR ONE: MO MAN'S LAND

ISBN: 9781635298123

A look at World War 1 from the French trenches as they faced the Imperial German Army.

CORTEZ AND THE FALL OF THE AZTECS

ISBN: 9781635299779

Cortez battles the Aztecs while in search of Inca gold.

TROY: AN EMPIRE UNDER SIEGE

ISBN: 9781635298635

Homer's famous The Iliad and the Trojan War is given a unique human perspective rather than from the God's.

WITNESS TO WAR

ISBN: 9781635299700

WW2's Battle of the Bulge is seen up close by an embedded female war reporter.

THE LINCOLN BRIGADE

ISBN: 9781635298222

American volunteers head to Spain in the 1930s to fight in their civil war against the fascist regime.

EL CID: THE CONQUEROR

ISBN: 9780982654996

Europe's greatest warrior attempts to unify Spain against invading foreign and domestic armies.

WINTER WAR

ISBN: 9780985749392

At the outbreak of WW2 Finland fights against an invading Soviet army.

ZULUNATION: END OF EMPIRE

ISBN: 9780941613415

The global British Empire and far-reaching influence is threatened by a Zulu uprising in southern Africa.

AIR WARRIORS: WORLD WAR ONE #V1 - V4   *Take to the skies of WW1 as various fighter aces tell their harrowing stories.*
ISBN: 9781635297973 (V1), 9781635297980 (V2), 9781635297997 (V3), 9781635298000 (V4)

CALIBER COMICS PRESENTS
The Complete
VIETNAM JOURNAL

8 Volumes Covering the Entire Initial Run of the
Critically Acclaimed Don Lomax Series

And Now Available
VIETNAM JOURNAL SERIES TWO
"INCURSION", "JOURNEY INTO HELL", "RIPCORD"

All new stories from Scott 'Journal' Neithammer
as he reports during the later stages of the
Vietnam War.

CALIBER COMICS   WWW.CALIBERCOMICS.COM

CALIBER COMICS GOES TO THE EDGE!
Science Fiction and Horror themed graphic novels

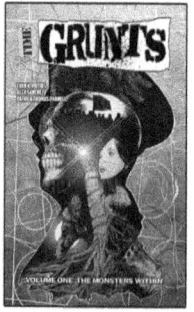

ALSO AVAILABLE FROM CALIBER COMICS

QUALITY GRAPHIC NOVELS TO ENTERTAIN

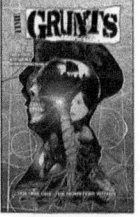

KAY STOPFORTH

Rite of Spring

For my mother, Alice Ward
1934 - 2022